Memories
of a
Lost Thesaurus

Katie Hall-May

Katie Hall-May

Printed by CreateSpace
Published by the Author in Hampshire, England

Publisher's Note: This is a work of fiction. Names, characters, places, and incidents are a product of the author's imagination. Locales and public names are sometimes used for atmospheric purposes. Any resemblance to actual people, living or dead, or to businesses, companies, events, institutions, or locales is completely coincidental.

Book Layout © 2018 BookDesignTemplates.com

Cover Design© 2018 Claire Rutter

Memories of a Lost Thesaurus Katie Hall-May. -- 1st ed.
ISBN-13:978-1981263202
ISBN-10:1981263209

Katie Hall-May

M

Thursday 22nd May
3 hours and 8 minutes to go

Unwell. That's the word they used. A little bland, really. When they could have had: *ailing, indisposed, poorly, peaked* or *sickly.* Or, for that matter: *unsound, unstable, cracked up, broken down* or *collapsed.* I have never been convinced that *unwell* is accurate, only nicely euphemistic. It's a hushed word. The sort of word you could use in polite surroundings.

It tells you absolutely nothing.

I would have said *peaked.* It describes it much better. I have *peaked* and am now gently descending. I have *piqued* and am too angry at life to continue. I have *peeked* at reality and found it wanting.

Hard to know, of course, exactly what classes as reality. Maybe the illness was some kind of mist, clouding my perception and altering the look of the world. Or perhaps the problem was in the way things were to start with, and now I have recovered and what is being described as an illness is simply a sharpening of understanding. A new clarity. Which is interesting, because of course *peaked* can also mean *pointed.* And *pointed* means *sharp.*

Prior to my peaking, I thought things were straight-forward. I could hold my blurring world together with alacrity, even enjoyment, and there was the thrill of the challenge, the allure of the impossible. The strange satisfaction of chairing a telephone conference whilst giving instructions to my secretary in improvised semaphore, drinking coffee, and emailing my wife.

And I am not sure when I started to see that the world was crumbling, that it was breaking its bones by travelling too fast. That the images, sounds, people, traffic, inventions were just the surviving particles of a civilisation dissolving in its own velocity. I can see it now, in small, horizontal lines through the blinds in the kitchen. In feverish fleeting flashes of colour, and odd little bursts of passing noise.

When my wife returns she will open the blinds. The room, for now, is very warm. I have sealed it with firmly closed doors and windows. Static, settled, nestling walls. It feels safer this way.

The problem with life is there is just too much of it. You identify one thing and it leads to another. Nothing is simply one thing only. Everything relates to everything else. It is like trying to read through a foreign thesaurus. You look up one word and you find another twenty. If you look up even one of those twenty, you are already forty meanings away from the first one.

And there's a good chance one of those brings you back to the start.

Cath

14 February
The Day of the Flood

This is Patrick's flat.

It has shiny tiles, shiny windows, and shiny chrome door handles. It has a lounge, presided over by a stern shiny kitchen, laminate flooring, two bedrooms and a cupboard. It has underfloor heating and bright, white walls. It has a shiny chrome fridge and a shiny chrome dishwasher. It has a wooden front door with a shiny chrome handle. Beneath the door there is a miniature river of brown water, steadily edging its way towards me.

This is Patrick's flat. There is a flood in it.

And I am paralysed with panic.

Patrick bought the flat early, on plan, but we moved in December, when the building was finished. It was his Christmas present to himself, he said, and I remember the pride on his face. It was his Christmas present to me too. He showed me the rental price for another flat in the building. He was charging me much less than he could.

"How's my lodger?" he would say, in those first few days. But his kiss was perfunctory, and his eyes on the chrome. Years ago, when he kissed me, I could feel an electricity building all the way through from my chest to my fingertips. More often than not we used to end up in bed.

We've been together nearly three years now. I suppose things change.

"Remember those days?" he said recently, as though reading my mind. And he smiled at me and I said yes, and then said that we must have matured now.

"Well, *I* have," he said, cheekily, with that grin on his face that first made me fall, heavily, in love with him. Like a stone off a cliff-top.

"Of course," I said, "you are a homeowner now."

And it pleased him so much and so predictably that I wanted to take him, and wrap him in blankets and protect him from the world that was going to disappoint him. From whatever they are, those broken ideals that can make him gasp and sob like a machine gun on a silencer, deep in the night, when he thinks I am sleeping.

Patrick's flat has a power shower and a heated towel rail. It has blinds which you close by hitting a button. It has bright chrome spotlights and a bright chrome soul.

It also has me. Perched on the edge of the sofa, knees drawn up to my chin, arms tightly round them, I am staring, fixedly, at the shallow pool of brownish water which is gradually inching its way through the hall and into the lounge towards me. I don't know how long I have been here like this. It would just all have been so much easier if it had been Patrick who was here when the flood started, instead of me, settling heavily into the ever increasing dip in the new sofa, failing, as ever, to take the right action. I adjust my position, shifting more to the edge, so that I am balancing half on and half off the sofa. Patrick gets worried about the sofa. I don't want my presence to leave a mark.

The sofa is Patrick's pride and joy. He bought it the Saturday after we moved in. We bought it together. It's white and gleaming, and very expensive. Fabric of course, nothing as vulgar as leather, though I nodded vaguely at this, thinking that leather might be easier to clean. I dread the day I will spill red wine on this sofa. The idea of it strikes something cold in my stomach and the impact reverberates through me briefly, so that I feel frozen. When I say that we bought it together I only mean that I was with him.

We noticed a depression after only a few weeks of buying it. Patrick pointed it out.

"Look at this!" he said one morning, when I appeared groggily in the lounge. It seemed that by sitting in the same place often, we had begun to create a slight depression in the seat, which did not spring back when we weren't in situ. He was nice enough to say 'we'.

"So maybe when we sit on it, we should sit somewhere else, so we don't make it any more uneven. Yes, Cath? When we sit on it, we'll sit in different places? Yes?"

"OK. Yes. Of course...um. Yes."

What Patrick and I both knew is that Patrick is tall and slim and I am shorter and rounder. Patrick is hard and streamlined where I am heavy, and soft. Touching me, Patrick says, is like stroking marshmallows. If there is a depression in the sofa it has probably been created by me.

Sitting in this position requires some concentration. I have to engage my core, as they say in all those dancing programs Patrick pretends not to watch. I have to lean slightly in towards the sofa to maintain balance, but not so much as to cause a further depression. I have to grip with my toes on the fabric. I think hard about my posture to embrace the distraction. The water has made it into the lounge now. It must have been halted, initially, by the threshold, but a little piece of wood isn't holding it back any more. There is a stealthy line of water in the grouting between the tiles in the open plan lounge and kitchen. It is creeping, in geometric squares, towards me.

When it first appeared I was working. I was settled into the sofa, enhancing the depression but not really caring, because I was genuinely focused on what I was doing. I had vaguely noticed certain things, like the sound of the rain and the fact that the day had grown suddenly, into evening, the way it does in England in February. I was hazily aware that it was dark in the flat, that I was working only by the blue grey light of my laptop, that I should get up, soon, and turn a light on. But I didn't really register what was happening outside and I didn't get up and flick the light switch. (Later I will tell that to Patrick as though it was deliberate. A sensible decision to protect his flat, not to turn on the electricity when we might have a flood problem.)

The fact is, my work is going well. Even, if I dare to say it, very well, at least for a humble post-doctoral fellowship. Without teaching hours, my research is flying. I sent a speculative letter to some publishers in early January. It turned out, through some wonderful quirk of fate, that somebody had dropped out of their planned collection celebrating the tortured American authors writing between the first and second world wars. Timing would be tight because they had been delayed once already and I would have to write something by the 31st March so they could bring the collection out on the 2nd July, the anniversary of Ernest Hemmingway's suicide. Could I, they asked, extend and rewrite my article more from a 'laypersons' point of view? I thrill with pleasure remembering that call, standing there, phone to ear, saying 'yes, absolutely' and 'yes, I understand' and 'yes, I will, I will definitely, thank you so much.'

I called my Mum and I did all the things people usually do, as Patrick said laughingly, when they've won the Nobel Prize or something. Not just been asked to write twenty pages on something they were already working on anyway. I barely heard him. I sat down and began work straight away.

Even so, just in case, just for now, I don't talk about it. I don't mention it to Patrick, I let him quietly forget. I don't even work on it much on the university servers. I've been working at home. It's my secret. My hope. It's a rare thing - a thing that is mine.

And so it wasn't until I paused, briefly, to stretch, that I saw it. A reflection of the streetlights in the car park outside glancing off something glinting in the hallway, by the door. A thin, patchy, puddle of muddy water.

In a flash the fluff that is my brain suddenly noted the rain, the river not so far from here, and the recent news reports of flooding. But those were far away, in other parts of the country. Not here, not us, not now.

And not, please Heaven, not in Patrick's new flat.

Alice

14th February
The Day of the Flood

"And you may have noticed, those of you who are still awake," a touching self-irony from a tired headmaster, "we have a new face here this morning."

A few heads turn in bored resignation, registering me as I sit at the side-lines. A gentle ripple across a sea of hairstyles, blonde and brown and, occasionally, green. The troublemakers, no doubt, who had been reprimanded, and a couple of accidents, a home dye kit gone wrong.

"This is Miss Crayer – she will be here today," he inclines his head modestly, "to ah...to work with the year twelves. I trust you will make her welcome."

There is a surge of whispering.

"It's the condom woman!"

"She's doing the tampon talk."

"She did us last year."

Periods.

Shagging.

Sex education.

They are never stupid. Year after year they are not stupid.

I grin covertly at the nearest whisperer, nod to the headmaster and say, very clearly, "Thank you. And you can call me Alice."

I do that every year too. And they always disapprove.

There are the usual staff-room introductions. Distracted and faintly embarrassed male teachers and the women, amused and conspiratorial, flashing me knowing glances. They sit themselves, quite often, beside me, to engage in girly conversation. Fleshy, nylon coloured legs, crossed at the knees and swelling at the ankles into tortured, leather ridden feet. This is of course a construction, a narrow minded fantasy. They are intelligent, self-possessed, interesting adults.

Why is it that school is still always so much like school? They lead me to the hall to await my first groupings, position me carefully and then leave with relief. The headmaster has provided me with some kind of lectern and an arc of uncomfortable grey plastic chairs. That concludes the first stage of the process. I am pleased that it's over. It is always a chore.

In the distance now I can hear my first clients, a muffle of giggling and the hiss of an adult. She will be a supply teacher possibly, or a first year student. I can hear nerves in her plosives, self-doubt in her 'shush'. Any moment her captives will burst through the doorway and fix me with shrewd, appraising eyes, assessing my outfit, my expression, my face. Sharp, defensive teenage minds gift wrapping me neatly and deciding their role. Captor or captive. Predator or prey.

I have swivelled the lectern so it faces my audience and as they begin to filter in, I perch on it, ignoring the doubtful gaze of the teacher. Sitting on the lectern is probably one of those rather pointlessly and religiously enforced school rules, the kind that seems to rival premeditated bloody murder as a Very Serious Offence. This does not escape the kids, but even so, as I meet their gazes, something inside me moves with emotion as I hear the bravado in their voices turn brittle. Only at this age is it apparently OK for a stranger to lecture you about sex, without you having first agreed to it. Some people rather like it, as a change from the norm, some are just pleased to get out of maths, but there are always quite a few who find the whole thing excruciating.

The lectern is proving surprisingly comfortable. I swing my legs and sit back to survey my subjects. Hairstyles, unpractised, yet containing within them hours of frustration, perhaps a few tears. The smell of deodorant, and over-used perfume, and the acid whiff of exhausted hairspray. The current trend is a mass of sticky, frizzy curls, (I make a mental note to go sleek for tomorrow). Mascara stabs angrily out from the ovals of rude, defiant, frightened eyes. There are the usual few, calm mouthed and placid, heavier perhaps than the others, and wearing no make-up. They are the ones who are popular with adults. They are the rejects, they are the sane.

They are often the saddest.

Small breasts heaving in rebellion, pushed up and together in deliberate black bras. They gleam from beneath the standard white shirt, they are a splash of colour, they are already a weapon. Red eyes, somebody has been crying. Someone else bears a graze, playground stunt or abuse? Those hands are nervous, they twitch at her skirt, she is covering a ladder in shiny black tights. These ears are still bleeding from some recent piercing, the metal bar pushed and pulled at and swivelled around. Beauty is pain, I think. Or punishment. Platinum blondes with black at the roots. Black hair with black make-up, (they will make her remove it). Mousy brown scraped back into ponytails, mousy brown unsuccessfully highlighted with gold. And – oh yes, the obligatory green - *that* one was definitely an accident. Ginger hair, pulled back roughly, apologetic, (don't worry too much, it gets better with age).

That girl looks like Tabby.

An invisible shard of something stabs through me. For a moment, I find I cannot breathe.

Tabby.

I see her for a minute, quick and bright, like strobe lighting. Long, pale delicate features. Bright hazel eyes flecked at random with orange. And those little dancing shadows of uncertainty. There always, at the back of her cautious little smile, in the shuffle of her feet, in the lights of her eyes. It is a dull ache but twisting, turning heavily in my stomach and then bolting upwards until I can taste it, like acid in my windpipe, bile in my mouth.

I swallow the bile. My mind, accustomed and trained for these moments, moves mechanically forward like some long conquered beast.

I do not think about Tabby.

"Right," I say "before we start let's get a few things sorted – first off - you are calling me Alice. Not Mrs Crayer, because I'm not married. And not Miss Crayer because, let's face it, you're ultimately going to end up calling me crapper because it's a lot more amusing." A few tentative giggles laced with possible scorn. They glance at each other. They are not sure yet. I know this. This is usual.

"Secondly, there are no right answers, you say what you like in here, assuming you're not deliberately trying to embarrass someone else." Appreciative murmurs. I hear a few expletives. Yes, they are experimenting. They are practising quietly.

"And finally," I pull out a banana from my bag and look at it dubiously, "I am not going to be teaching you to put condoms on this." A more general laughter. I feel them relaxing. "For one thing, it's embarrassing and for another, quite frankly," I hold up the banana, "if it looks like this, there's something wrong with it." They are laughing now, laughing with me and I ride with the moment, "Seriously girls, these things are not supposed to be bendy - if it's yellow and moon shaped get him down to the clinic..."

At lunchtime I burn my lips on school mugs full of scalding instant coffee. I discuss *Coronation Street* and *Eastenders*. I don't watch either of them. I know all the characters and the most recent plots purely from my time spent in staff-rooms across the country. In the corridor, I hear snatches of break time conversation, huddles of students cooped up indoors, away from the heavy rain which has been dowsing the playground so that it resembles a paddling pool more than a layer of tarmac. Cramped in classrooms, they are discussing Sadie's row with her boyfriend, Jason's crush on Maria, and the existence of ghosts. Inside we dissect *Emmerdale*.

"So, how's it going? Must be hard to know how to teach them really, I mean, if you're religious especially…"

Oh yes. And that. It always comes up, I can't escape it. This is because I have a brooch with a cross on it.

"I mean, obviously you've got to tell them the facts, but it must be difficult for you not to want to influence them morally, you know, with how you feel yourself…"

I struggle with an urge to make an immature joke about feeling myself and wonder whether perhaps I subconsciously enjoy these conversations. After all, I know what's coming, and I still wear the brooch.

Dear God,

Whoever these girls are, I pray that whatever they do with their bodies, they enjoy it the way you meant it for them, without getting it complicated.

I never know quite what I mean when I say that. I never know quite, in the light of the sterner, more rule driven sermons, which of course I don't pay attention to, whether I'm not actually uttering some kind of blasphemy. Praying they'll leave the place able to have fun and be sensible. When I ought to be fervently recommending that they go home clothed in righteousness, and reinforced chastity belts. What does it matter? I am talking to the God who designed it. He knows about sex, he'll sort out the details. I'm just here to explain the technicalities.

In the end I simply escape the staff-room altogether, with its heady aroma of coffee, and yogurt and anxious feet, and head for the computer suite, ignoring the fact I could perfectly easily check my emails on my phone. Amidst the bored computer whirr as the machine grinds wearily into action, as the deserted library creaks and grumbles, I find myself fighting an urge to escape. I can see myself doing it, rushing down the stairs and plunging, gasping into the dining hall. I have a fleeting, almost an aching impression of it. The giggling, the harsh, excited laughter, the bright, grating sound of young voices, the screech of chairs, the smell of tuna and vinegar and chocolate. My lungs, filled and swelling, with the glorious chaos, the utter hysterical frustrated cacophony. But instead I stay stolid in front of the screen, like a caught and cosseted goldfish, left out on the counter and heaving for breath.

It's strange though. Funny. The way no matter what institution I visit, *somebody* always looks like Tabby. Exhausted suddenly, I close my eyes.

I am standing on enormous gnarled tree roots, wobbling precariously. I clutch at the rough bark on the two tree trunks either side of me to steady myself. One of the trees is bleeding – its warm, sticky sap colours the tips of my fingers and I flinch and pull my hand away without thinking. Laughter pounds into my ears, above the audible thumping of the blood in my brain. They are standing at the front and back of me, trapping me between the two trees and I daren't look at them and I daren't turn my back on them.

And they say, "Go on…say something…just say something Twig Brain…look at her, she's so stupid…" and they lean in close to my face so that I can feel their breath on my hot cheeks and I wonder if its catching – their perfect skin and hair and the way they get away with bending the rules about uniform.

I am wondering if I could ever be like them and at the same time feeling the familiar tightening of my muscles, my bladder, in fear. And then I am saying, "No", I am saying "Go away," and my voice is thin and reedy and it shakes and of course I cannot manage the "No" and my throat closes and my eyes bulge and the tears I am trying so hard not to spill seem to boil behind them.

And they are laughing but there is also scorn, there is deep disdain and they say, "Twiglet? Tibby-Tabby-Twiglet, have you got ANY friends? Does anyone actually LIKE you?" and then my scalp seems to explode as they pull my hair back and I am looking up at the indifferent dry brown leaves of the tree. And my throat is closed and I cannot manage the "No"...

"If you wear tampons, does it mean you won't bleed?" I blink quickly and they swing fast into focus. Three of them, half giggling, in the harsh school standard issue strip lights next to my computer desk. "You know, like, on the first time?"

So they have sought me out at lunch time. I wonder what it is that worries them – the assumption of impurity on the part of the boyfriend? No, those ideas have moved on now. Perhaps the possible reprieve from embarrassment, from the necessary sheet washing and furtiveness. A sense of having made a mess. It's not too far from feeling dirty. Some ideas have not moved anywhere.

"Sarah says you don't if you've used tampons long enough."

"But I think she's wrong…"

"Yeah, as if *you'd* know."

"As if *you* would."

None of them do. I pretend to think about it to give them time to stop arguing and I push my chair back a bit and log off the computer.

"Well I think it depends," I say, "there are all kinds of factors, as well as just using tampons…"

And they listen so carefully I almost want them to take notes, just to reassure them. To carry about in their purses so they know it's all right.

"I'm not sure I'm free this evening," I say, "because I've just moved house." No one reacts. No one asks where or why or asks to see photos. "Those new builds," I tell them anyway, "the Brandon Homes development. Just up from the garage. On Gleedown Road. I thought today was just a preliminary session with the girls. Then half term and I'm back for the last four weeks."

It is their morals slot – I do a half term stint leading it. They call it PPS - Physical, Psychological and Social studies. They prefer 'Psychological' to 'Mental' because it makes for a less embarrassing acronym.

The headmaster does not frown – instead he looks at me with a slight smile which somehow manages to irritate me.

"Oh no, Miss Crayer," he says, "I am perfectly aware of that – we have half term next week – so this is a social outing. Just a few drinks tonight, after work."

Oh God I think – and mean it literally. I am asking him for some kind of an excuse.

"We always get together for mid-term drinks and we wondered if you would like to join us. You've run this course every year for a while now – you're one of the staff."

"Oh I only run the course for half a term..." My laugh is half hearted and some people frown. I realise I am about to offend everybody and my inner protests that its Valentine's day and town will be crowded, pink, plastic and overpriced are muffled somehow by my voice saying,

"Well that's lovely of you – that would be great. What time were you thinking, is it *straight* after school?"

Cath

14th February
The Day Of The Flood

When the water reaches the entrance of Patrick's shiny kitchen diner, high enough to spill over the raised wooden threshold and slide across the shiny laminate floor, I can no longer pretend it isn't here. Even so, I waste a great deal of time simply darting around uselessly before I finally regain enough control to seek help. Other people, I reason, must live in these flats, and we can work it out together. I am good with people. Or so I am told. I was. But when I knock on the door of the only other flat at ground level, diagonally opposite Patrick's, there is no response.

I am on my own in this.

Tentatively I open the external lobby door, so I can get a better idea of the scale of the flood. It takes some effort to heave it open and as soon as I do I realise my mistake. What little of the water was being held back by the door now surges inwards. I have little brown splashes on my legs. Hastily, I slam the door closed again, banging my elbow on the wall in the process. There is now nearly an inch of water in the lobby. I have made it much worse. Someone, I tell myself, would have done this anyway. Patrick might have done it when he came home. Another person, in another flat. Anyone might have done it. I catch sight of myself in the chrome finish of the mail lockers on the opposite wall. My reflection stares back at me. The chrome distorts it but even so. I see a blurred face, round and startled and gormless. The shoulders are bulky, hunched and gnome-like in a shapeless knitted cardigan that is comfortable to work in, and which saves Patrick's gas bill because we don't put the heating on unless we need to.

My elbow throbs and I pull back my sleeve to examine it. There is a neat little curl of skin, like a white chocolate shaving on a cake, and, in the place it has curled from, a slender, pink line. I look at the place where I knocked it. They have plastered the walls of the lobby, but either side of the door there is a sharp corner of brick and mortar before the perfect white line of the plastering begins. I stand there for a while, gazing at it. The edges of the brick are red and rough.

Slowly and deliberately I walk to the wall and place the slender pink line on my elbow back onto the brick. Then I lean into it, directing all of my weight into that beautiful sharp corner. It immediately stings. Very slowly, I drag my skin downwards across the jagged surface of the brick.

It feels good.

When I make my way back into the flat I feel miserable but somehow energised. I close the door and take off my bloodied cardigan, squeezing it down along the line of the door to soak up the water. I grab a tea towel from the rack and add it, for good measure. The progress of the water stops. Pleased, I go back to the sofa. If I sit here and watch it, I will see that it will go no further. The crisis will be averted.

When the inevitable happens and the encroaching liquid shows signs of reaching the legs of Patrick's shiny white sofa, I cross the room, pick up the phone, and call him.

"Cath, hi yes I know it's nearly nine, I went out with the guys after work. Can't you cope for an evening on your own?"

He sounds weary. I think he worked late before he joined the others. He worries about work. It leaves him sleepless. He thinks, though he has never once actually told me so, that he isn't as good as his promotion says he is. He is on a constant crusade to make sure it's not true.

"Patrick, hi. No it's not that. That's great. It's just..." My voice has become thin and I can't help but sound like a child caught breaking windows with a stolen football. "It's the flat, there's something wrong with it. Well not wrong, it's...I think it's flooding."

He is silent. I try again. I try hard not to make it sound as though it's because of something that I did. Somewhere inside me I have lost the conviction that it isn't.

"It's definitely coming from outside. I think it's the river. I looked at the washing machine and the sinks and the bath and things...all the obvious stuff. There isn't anything wrong inside -"

"- There isn't anything wrong. Except that there's water on the floor." He is curt and with it I feel the first swell of his alarm. Behind his voice I can hear the interior of the pub. Laughter and chatter and the clatter of tables.

There is a pause.

"I'm assuming? Cath? There is water on the floor. Is that right? In which rooms?"

"I -" I stop suddenly. The flat is very quiet. I can hear the ticking of the clock in the bedroom. My elbow pulses, as if filling in for the silence. It is raw and wet now. I turn it to look at it. There are little pieces of grit from the wall in the wound. I have deliberately not washed it. I press it on the table, for concentration, gritting my teeth as it stings. It galvanises me.

"I've tried to soak it up by the door but it's saturated the material," I say. "There's no-one else in the building at the moment. I'll move the furniture, get it out of the water. I might need a bit of help with the heavy bits..." I am gabbling now and I know it. Words tumbling over each other and falling through the radio waves onto the yeast stained varnish of the fashionably battered table tops in the Whistling Kitten.

"Oh God," he says wearily. I can almost see him putting his head in his hands and rubbing his forehead. I can hear a slight chuckle among his friends and I imagine the way it sounds to them and feel my cheeks burning. I have left a dark smear of blood on the table. I wipe it off with my shirt.

"I -"

"Forget it, Cath. I'm coming home."

"I didn't switch any lights on," I say in a rush. "I thought, with water around, it might be sensible..."

He had gone before I started the sentence. I sit at the table, listening to the dull tone of the phone and the rain on the window. Then I stand up, suddenly very decisive, and I begin, finally, to take action.

I go outside again. The door to the lobby swishes open when I push it, just a little too violently, and sends another wave of water surging in. I grit my teeth and splash my way through it. Rain pelts my face with fat, fast droplets and mingles with the blood on my elbow to make murky, reddish tracks down to drip off my wrist, and then back up again to pool in my armpit as I pick up bricks from the building site which will eventually be the second of these blocks of flats. It takes me several trips, and causes several more inches of water to slosh into the lobby each time I enter and exit, until I give up and shrug and simply wedge the lobby door open. Finally, soaked to the skin, I close it again and pick up one brick at a time from the pile I have amassed in the flat, and begin to heave and wedge them under the legs of the sofa, a corner at a time, until it perches there proudly, elevated grandly above the encroaching water. I heave the heavy table over to join it in the corner, against the inside wall, and I do the same with that. I begin to pile other things up on the table, books, CDs, all the contents of the bottom shelves of the cabinet. I put my laptop right at the top, very carefully. It's a precious item. Guiltily, I remember that I have not backed up my work. I can feel the adrenaline pumping inside me. It feels odd to be so active in this flat. It has always felt like a place of waiting. I clear shelves, remembering as I do it the process of filling them. Patrick consigning my sweet tin to the smaller bookshelves, tucked out of sight in the bedroom.

"A sweet tin? Cath? Seriously, how old are you? Do you really need a sweet tin?" His eyes on my stomach. My mouth stubborn and stupid. The tin, with its cavorting lambs and yellow daisies, an innocent in this situation. A memory of an easier life. Nowadays it contains loose change.

Patrick surveying the bookshelves, while I waited with armfuls of books, trying to decide which were the most impressive books to display. We put his *Descartes* and my *Collected Works of James Joyce* in prominent positions in the lounge. We consigned his crime novels, his old comics, my thesis and the Argos catalogue to the bedroom. I pick it all up and pile it together in the lounge. The first time we met was in a library. I was holding books then too. He bought me lunch.

The bright lights of a taxi, which must contain Patrick, swing like search beams into the carpark, briefly illuminating the mess. I panic suddenly. I should have acted much quicker. I've never been someone who could think of things fast. Patrick says I run like clockwork, just always a minute or two behind. And in that moment, maybe I lose some sort of focus, but my grip slightly slips on the chair I am holding and my feet follow suit, so that I wobble a little and stumble forward and, with a soft crunch I have put the chair leg through the plaster stud wall and into the study.

My breath temporarily stops. I can feel my heart pounding in my chest. When I finally pull myself together enough to extract the chair and put it back down in the water, my stomach drops sharply, as I survey the damage. A jagged hole about half way up in the plaster. It's not large but it's ugly. I feel slightly sick. There is a cold stone, radiating ice from my abdomen, and a coarse, dry feeling at the back of my throat.

I glance, instinctively, out of the window and I can see Patrick climbing out of the car, slamming the door and walking towards me. He is already soaked. There is a second in which I feel, oddly, as though I am falling and then without even thinking I have put the chair back on the top of the table, roughly in front of the hole in the plaster, and I have heaved the ratty throw I was using to soak up some of the water, up from the floor and over the chair and left it there, dripping. Soaking wet but at least now covering the section of wall in Patrick's beautiful new flat, which I have just mangled.

So that when he opens the door I am not a grown up, I am a guilty child and my mind goes blank and the first thing I do is say, "Hi Patrick!" in an overly cheerful voice as though nothing has happened and I fail to react to the fact that he is having trouble getting through the door because the door is wedged on a mass of saturated cardigan and towelling.

Alice

14th February
The Day Of The Flood

"It's a deep sort of green. That's the thing I really love about it. People never have their baths properly green – it's always white and chrome now. I wanted it different. But then that's the thing, because you actually *can*, I bought the whole place on plan and then they let you tell them – you choose it all, tiles and carpets and lighting and everything. You can buy these lights that angle out and just make a little pin prick – not wide light, the way you'd normally have it — and I got loads of them for the bedroom so on the wall it's like starlight..."

Of course I do not say all this. Actually I stop after I mention the carpet. It is about that time that I see that fleeting, tell-tale look – the ghost that passes across people's faces that whispers their boredom, or their bewilderment. In this case it is more a sense of detachment. As if the world in which we inhabit – the shared space of this bar, with its clinking and laughter, is an unwanted illusion. My voice and the ideas it expresses are a brief phenomenon of science, or a momentary spirit, passing coldly through. I plant a full stop firmly in the middle of my sentence. I engage with very convincing enthusiasm, in a discussion about nail care, and the scandal of oil prices. There is a pink plastic heart dangling above my head, close enough to clash with my hair. Glasses glint and clink and twinkle and a baseline reverberates like a machine in my chest. I say, "Yes" and "I know" and "You must be joking…no, really?" and I am shredding a beer mat and the room circles and swallows me.

Tabby had bright red hair like me on the day she was born. She was red faced and screaming the hour I first met her, and she was the length of my arm and she smelled of water and hospital. With greater experience of the world she seemed to grow calmer, and less fierce in her colours until eventually she was pale faced and slender, the fire in her hair and the blue in her eyes melted and agreed on a mutual hazel.

She was crawling by summer and took her first steps in the autumn. She liked cats and ice cream and the colour yellow. She never said much. And I was her favourite.

Tabby. I do not think about her.

Two teenagers get on the bus half way home. He is drunk, his eyes are rolling in alarm and his limbs, still somehow too long for his body, seem to run from him in panic in different directions. His girlfriend is worried, and half carrying him awkwardly. The bus driver is suspicious and she swears at him defensively, but they are both at his mercy and so it is under her breath. Less than a stop later her boyfriend has succumbed to a half comatose slumber and is lying heavily across her lap. I watch his head jerk with each lurch of the vehicle, whilst his girlfriend, chewing dangerously on her lower lip piercing tries, unskilfully, to support it with her hand. Eventually he gives in to the inevitable and throws up in the gangway.

"Right that's disgusting. Get off."

There are murmurs of assent from the handful of righteously indignant adults, who are swinging, hastily, to the other end of the bus.

"We'll clear it up." They have nothing to clear it with.

"Just get off. I've had enough of your lot."

"Come on, please, we've only got three stops left – it's too early."

A pause. Her panic turns to anger.

"How'm I s'posed to get him home?"

"Off!"

"What – you're gonna help me are you? You gonna help carry him or you gonna let us stay on?"

She scarcely pauses before she says it. She doesn't wait for his answer. She knows she's lost.

This time she doesn't say it under her breath. Then she says it a few more times, with a few variations.

"That is it. Off now or I call the police."

He has heard the word – but not the crack in it. When they get off I get off too.

Two hours later, when they are sleeping the evening into obscurity, I squelch round the corner to my development. I have blisters on my feet and his sick on my coat. And then I open the entrance door and realise the lobby is two inches deep in muddy water.

Cath

14ᵗʰ February
The Day Of The Flood

When Patrick eventually gets in the first thing he does is prowl the flat like a big, investigative cat, checking the carpets, the doors, the windows. I see his gaze rest for a minute on the wet throw, dripping water onto the furniture I have so carefully tried to keep dry, and there are waves of anxiety rising in me but also something else. I can see the panic in his eyes, the disappointment, always that perpetual disappointment, and I want to reach out to it and soothe it, and take him to a place more worthy of his fantastic expectations. A place with curved corners and definite outcomes. A place designed for him. A better world.

"Pat," I say softly, "are you OK? We can sit it out. There would always have been teething problems. You know how it is with new houses."

I reach out and put a tentative hand on his arm. He pauses briefly, his face crumpling, and then he shakes my hand off as though it burns him.

"You don't have any idea how it is with new houses."

He's right. I don't. He starts for the door, muttering something about checking the river, when he stops suddenly and picks up the tea towel I have put down.

"Cath! That's *my* towel. That was a present from my Nan. What is it doing on the floor in muddy water?"

I can't say anything.

He says, "Brilliant," picks it up, sighs heavily and lets it drop again. It makes a squelching sound. It makes me jump and, inexplicably, it makes me want to giggle. I cover my mouth. The irony, of course, which I could have predicted, is that it is precisely this exaggerated timidity, the unnecessary fear in me that makes him so impatient. I understand. It makes *me* impatient.

Twenty minutes later, when he squelches back in, soaked and angry, I try a new tack. I take hold of my shaking voice, bring it down a few octaves and try to be authoritative.

"Patrick, calm down. It's just a flat. We can deal with it."

From anyone else this would work, but I just can't carry it off. Patrick says it's because I lack edge. Definition. I automatically put a hand on my stomach, feel how it is soft and stodgy. A round face. Gormless. Blurring at the edges.

Right now, what Patrick says is, "Cath," in a voice of enormous patience, as though I am a child, unable to grasp a basic concept. "It's your flat too, Cath. That's your stuff that's going to get ruined. Your things as well. I mean, I assume you realise that?"

I realise, I just don't think it matters all that much, and for a moment I feel a sense of power. The manacles that tie him, I am free from, and I am seized by an ugly urge to flaunt that. To show him that I know some tricks he's not grasped yet, but before this resolves itself into some kind of action, or, more likely, dissipates into nothing, two things happen simultaneously.

Patrick says, "Cath, what on earth have you done to your elbow. You need to do something with that, it looks horrible," and there is a sound in the lobby. I grab my elbow with my other hand, sending fizzing bolts of pain through my arm as I touch it, and hurl myself past him and out into the lobby, another wave of water sloshing over the threshold. I leave him standing on the other side of the door in his flooded flat, next to the sodden mess that is his Grandmother's tea-towel.

She is standing in the lobby, keys in hand, surveying the water. She looks tired, but there is none of that panic in her eyes. When she meets mine as I half skid to a halt in front of her, she is looking at me mostly with a kind of calm curiosity.

"Hi," I say, breathlessly. "I'm really sorry."

There is a pause in which I realise this statement is difficult for her to follow, and so I add, "Not that it was me. But you know what I mean." I laugh, tensely and internally throttle myself. I used to be good with people.

To my surprise she laughs back, but properly. "Well, good!" she says, "Imagine if it *was* you!"

I must have looked baffled, because she says, as if by way of explanation, "That would have to be *the* most inconvenient superpower."

She laughs again. I wonder if she is a little drunk. It's late and I think I can smell something on her.

Then, "Sorry," she says, "I'm Alice." She gestures at the water. "This looks kind of...wet. It seems easier to laugh."

"I'm Cath," I say, relief flooding my veins and making my words tumble out over each other, "I live in that flat there – are you in the other one? The ground floor one I mean. Opposite? Not that I own it. The flat that is. It's Patrick's. He's my boyfriend. Partner. I don't know. Landlord." And I giggle.

Alice doesn't answer. She has red hair, though it's darker from the rain, small, elfin features and bright green eyes with pale eyelashes. And she is looking with concern at the mess on my elbow.

"Oh," I say nervously, "yes sorry about that. I banged it. It's a bit disgusting."

She looks at it for a long moment, and at me, and my brain goes numb with trying to work out a way to explain how I did it, but then she just shrugs and says simply,

"Not *that* disgusting. It just needs cleaning."

It takes a while, going into Alice's flat while she pulls out a roll of cotton wool and we wash the wound and then wipe it, excruciatingly, with alcohol. I wonder if Patrick has come out to find me, and feel an unexpected frisson, combining dizzyingly with the sting of my elbow, thinking of myself somehow hidden from him. Of him, left behind on the outside of a thing I am inside.

Alice doesn't have any plasters but we agree, together, that the fresh air will do it good, anyway, and it looks better already. She doesn't even look at the water on the floor of her flat. If she notices it, she doesn't show me. By the time we emerge and I bring her, gleefully, through the door into our flat to meet Patrick, I feel somehow as though I have made her. As though she is a marvellous thing I have created.

And Patrick has discovered the hole in the plaster.

Alice

14th and 15th February
The Night Of The Flood

I am staring at my shoes and noticing that some of the spit has landed inside the t bar onto my sock. As I look at it I can feel it suddenly, cold and gleeful against my skin. I consider bending down to wipe the shoe – to clean at least that gleaming patent, even if the socks were beyond redemption. But they are still behind me so I don't. I stay there, tense, and wonder how long it is until the bell, when they will surely have to leave. I wonder where the oboe teacher has vanished to. Does he realise? Does he know? For a fleeting moment I hope he goes home with his head in his hands, hope he is wracked with guilt and rendered sleepless. But I know that really he will drive himself home, and let himself in, kiss his wife and play jaunty, talented, lithe little pieces to entertain and show off to all his friends.

There is a sudden movement behind me and a music sheet is thrust in front of my face.

"Go on Twiglet, you'll only get good if you practise."

Jeering laughter.

"Go, on, off you go, like the teacher told us. Say the notes out. Nice and loudly."

I am silent. I wonder if it would be worse to cry now or to lift up my hands to wipe the spit off my face. Either way they will hoot with laughter. It will ring in my ears for the rest of the week.

"I can't hear you."

Collected sniggers. Have more people joined them? I dare not turn around. "Come on Twiglet. GBCD, GBCD, GBCDBGBA ...."

I am silent. Actually today I will even find it hard to do the "oh" sounds and the "ees". I will probably not say anything else now all day.

"Oh, I've found a bit more!"

And they shout again with laughter and advance with their instruments and I bend down very casually to close up my oboe case and try to pretend they are not shaking their collected spit out of their instruments onto my head.

When I pull myself back to reality I am standing, leaning against my closed door as if warding off danger. But, as I shake myself physically, and begin, sighing, to wade through the muddy brown water I know that the danger isn't out there, it's in here. Because this is what I do. This is the vice into which I pour myself. A series of moments, half memory, half nightmare, unnameable and unescapable. I've been doing it for years now. Every few months I tell myself firmly that it's over. That I will no longer indulge these ridiculous flights of nasty fancy. These borrowed memories which are not exactly thoughts of her, and so are somehow, reluctantly allowable. Except they're not all mine. My nightmare, perhaps. But not my memories. Half reconstructed, half imagined. I can't even be sure they were ever hers.

I jerk myself bodily away from the door and force myself into action. The water level is advancing, reaching up in the hope that it might lick, like freezing flames, at the very bottom rung of my book shelf, the lowest compartment of my TV cabinet, the bottom part of my beside table. My plug sockets are only slightly higher. I reach down behind the desk and contort myself grimly so that I can yank out the plug for my stereo system. I have assured Cath and Patrick that I am perfectly at ease with the flooding of my flat, these things happen, it's just a flat, it doesn't mean much to me. I will go and move the furniture, because that is just sensible but beyond that, well, it's life isn't it, really? I will probably clear up at bit, then get a bit of sleep. In the morning we can sort out the rest.

They sloped back into their flat, Cath with reluctance, and a quick flash of something in her eyes which was gone in a moment and which I shamefully ignored. I have seen that something somewhere before and it wasn't a place where I did anyone any good. Even so, that something swims, unbidden, in and out of my mind. It swims there a few times as the night progresses. But I am long accustomed to trespassing swimmers and have grown quite adept at seizing and drowning them. Patrick, on the other hand, appeared to be rather too obviously impressed. So he was able to get over the drowned rat look and the vomit on my coat then. I saw him note it before Cath had begun to introduce us. Sharp eyes, I think. And sharp tongue. Or perhaps not sharp. I recall the look on his face when we walked in, standing in front of some botch in the plaster. What was going on there I can't quite fathom but I suspect his tongue is not sharp at all. I think it is a blunt instrument and he lunges with it without thinking. Does it do any damage? To Cath, potentially. Not to me though. I yank another plug out. My tongue really *is* sharp. I move briskly, clipped steps sloshing ridiculously through the water, the fierce movement helping me to avoid proving my own deception. As long as I continue to shift furniture, I will not remember how shocked I am that my flat is flooded. I will not, if I am really lucky, even know that I am angry.

When Tabby was very young, we used to play together. She was oddly thin, small, even for her age and she nodded and smiled a lot.

I remember that at that time she used to smile a lot.

Furiously, I slam a chair down in the water. Breath explodes out of me like an angry bullet. I will not think about Tabby. But she keeps coming back. In every unguarded moment, an uneasy revelation, like the look on Cath's face as she followed Patrick back into their flat. Grimly, I become intense and organised about my work. I take a moment to stand back, and plan it, which parts will fit where and how I can assemble it so that it fits firmly and doesn't topple over. I pull on a pair of mould green Wellingtons and I roll up my sleeves and rummage around for a hair tie. I can't immediately find one. (I will discover them later, a whole box of them, floating about in the kitchen – I suppose I must have left it on the floor). Instead I grab a chopstick and clench it, pirate style, between my teeth while I pull together my mass of tangled redness and knot it up horribly at the nape of my neck, stabbing it mercilessly into place.

It's Cath of course. That little nod when we first met, a tick she doesn't know she possesses, that tiny sign of acquiescence, half eager, half broken, a rag doll programmed to agree. She did it three times just in our first conversation, too subtle to notice, if you were anyone else. But sending sharp stabs of something through my rib cage, rushing images, furiously stifled, but leaving me, each time, a little weaker. Admitting it enrages me.

I never did a lot of nodding. In fact I remember seeing my parents often through a grid of flashing red lines, as my hair swung emphatic in the force of my 'no'. I was always in trouble and always forbidden. When you say no a lot it starts to echo back at you. But Tabby was a gap toothed, smiling, 'yes'. And in the end it became the signal. I would describe the new game, each one wilder and more inventive, and she would listen, quite still, until I ran out of breath and then I would wait for that gesture, that decisive little jerk of her head and it was her nod, *only* her nod, that would launch it. One nod and together we would plunge, sprawling deliciously into whatever pool my imagination had led us, and there we would stay, immersed until teatime.

I am pulling things off shelves and out of cupboards. I have decided, after careful consideration, that my chairs and table should take the damage, they are the most fixable, and the least sentimental. Sacrificially they stand there, lined up neatly with their feet in the water. I have covered most of the wall with the tarpaulin I had left over from some youth camp, so that if mould should climb it, it will not touch my furniture. There are books, and ornaments, candles and CDs. There are also, at the back of the bedside cupboard, a couple of frames, face down against the wood. I take the frames out of the cupboard carefully and place them right at the top, on the underside of an upturned wicker chair. I make sure they remain very firmly face down. Even so, for the next couple of hours, as I haul cupboards, pile objects, heave boxes and rescue papers; as I wrap valuables in newspaper and chair legs in bin liners; and even as I catch myself, exhausted, in the mirror, face streaked blackly with newsprint and hair wildly escaping from its makeshift coiffure – all the time my mind keeps going back to them. The faces on the photo frames I so carefully ignored.

We had stuffed paper into our ballet shoes so our feet would look like we were on points. I don't think anyone was in the least taken in but adults are adept at deceiving children so they "oohed" and "ahhed" the way we had planned it. Of course children are adept at deceiving adults so we didn't let on that we knew that they knew.
A little hazel haired figure in lumpy ballet shoes, practising curtseys with that familiar nod.

I stop, very suddenly, with a rush of frustration, and then realise, in stopping, that I have done all I can. That every last thing is neatly stacked up and tidied and there is nothing else left now that I could conceivably do. Even the water seems, as I watch it, to be slowing. I am certain that I am not in any imminent danger. I am ever so slightly disappointed.

In the end I decide to have a bath. I stand in the water in the bathroom in my Wellingtons and watch the foaming, steaming water as it advances, stealthy up the inside of the tub. The irony neither entertains nor escapes me. I am a ridiculous, naked figure in green Wellingtons, stashing clothing on the top of piles of furniture and climbing, gingerly, into the lavender scented liquid that is so very far from its namesake, sloshing murkily around the skirting board.

I am bored of running and doubled over with stitch. I do not really care what they do with me, but on this occasion they too have lost interest. I peer through my legs as I catch my breath and they are strange and powerful, upside down figures laughing and strolling in the opposite direction. I turn back again so they don't catch me looking and I feel a sharp pain suddenly in the back of my ankle. A grey stone bounces off and rolls away to my left. I feel the same pain again a little higher on my calf. I fight a short battle with my pride and my fear and the fear wins.

As I run I hear one of them shout, "We'll be back".

It is supposed to sound menacing, but his voice is still breaking. Even I can hear the child in it. I can hear that we are all only kids in the park. In a moment some adult might stroll by indulgently, and calmly tell us to "break it up" or "play nicely".

My heart is still thumping wildly against my rib cage half an hour later as I return to the park to retrieve my bag from the tree. I find one of my shoes tied up over the railing. I am, at least, still wearing the other.

"We'll be back." It is childish but it is somehow still menacing.

I don't know if Tabby was always a fast runner. Perhaps she learned how to run at the same time she forgot how to smile. But whenever I think of it, even then, even before it, I always get a feeling that we were both always moving, always striving and straining to catch up with something. She was quiet and obliging, to make up for her silence, and the adults were sorry for her, and extra gentle to make up for the sympathy. And I was defiant against everybody, and loyal to her to make up for the defiance, and she depended on me, which made up for all the adults, who liked her so much more than me – and who didn't try to make up for it.

I have no idea of the actual time, but as I step out of the bath, now lukewarm and murky, it feels early now, rather than late. Sleep, predictably, has not so much escaped me, as never been caught in the first place. I switch on the old mechanics of my mind, and set to work on getting dressed. I re-discover lipstick and eye shadow, a hair brush and a belt from among my jigsaw puzzle piled belongings and I create a passable human being out of the wreckage. I have left Tabby, I think, left the images with the bathwater, but part of me, is shaking. Something's missing, somehow. A control I cannot quite put back.

I shiver and, on impulse, move fast, almost running, across the flat to grab the handle and haul open the front door. It's six o'clock and outside it's quiet. There's no one around but the water is gentle now, listening with me to my gradually slowing breath, lapping playfully against my open door.

Patrick and Cath have come round to visit me by seven. In fact I am amazed at how little time I need to leave my door just ever so little ajar before they are round, poking heads round the corner, furtive and conspiratorial, with a hint of apology. Patrick's eyes flicker perceptibly, up and down, taking in my newfound presentability, wondering perhaps, where I am hiding the vomit stains. His eyebrows raise in surprise, or appreciation, and I see Cath see him doing it, until she sees that I see her, and drops her eyes quickly, flushing pink in confusion, her head inclining in another, only just perceptible nod. I feel a surge of pain which somehow resolves itself into intense irritation.

For a moment we stand there, alternately spying on each other and then realising the spyee knows we are doing it and then Patrick says, "Scrubs up well for a girl in a flood, doesn't she?" and nudges Cath and somehow, even though it infuriates me, it breaks the ice and I see his cleverness, his drawing in of Cath so that she is part of his lechery, and disarming my likely indignation with deliberate unsubtlety, so that he becomes not rude, but amusing and boyish.

"Wow," says Cath, "you've sorted everything out so neatly. We just kind of...threw it all in a pile," and she blushes again but she is laughing and then suddenly all of us are consumed by hilarity. Unfortunately I kill the moment by looking daggers at Patrick who has had the nerve to cross the room and pick at my belongings.

"Chopsticks," he says, picking them up, and I am too late to stop him. They are inscribed with two figures with the proportions of sumo wrestlers, who are depicting position seventeen of the Karma Sutra. A present from a shrieking pair of emancipated teenagers.

"Ermm..." he says exaggeratedly, holding them up to the light at arm's length. Cath crosses the room to take a look. I laugh because it is the expected reaction and accidently meet his gaze over her head. There is a new look in his eyes now. Either he doesn't understand the picture – or he doesn't understand me. More likely the latter.

Cath looks at the chopsticks for just a little longer than is strictly appropriate.

I can't see her face.

Time passes. We stand around in my flat for a while, feeling pointless.

Cath says, "I love your hair," and, "So what brought you to East Grinstead?" and, "Shall we go out and get breakfast?"

Patrick says, "So, was this your first purchase?" and, "I got a great deal on the insurance," and, "Cath, it's too early, nowhere decent will be open."

And I say, "Thanks, I hate it," and, "Oh, the usual sort of reasons," and, "Why not, I'm just starving."

I say, "Yes, it was," and, "Oh, that's good," and, "I know a place," and I do not think about the fact that I did not get round to insurance.

M

Thursday 22nd May
2 hours and 51 minutes to go

Life is like reading through a foreign thesaurus.

It is the very idea of the existence of the thesaurus that is the greatest torture. The sheer, tantalising, irritating suggestion that everything you need to know just might be contained in one singular volume. That there really might be all that precious information, every nuance of every concept, every key to every metaphor, right in there between its dusty, plastic covers, in its tiny typeface and those little bold words and rounded pages. This could be it. The meaning of everything. The idea that you could possibly hold it in your insignificant, sweating fingers, the absolute and ultimate answer.

And the only limitation is your own ineptitude.

I have made some attempt at working. I know that I am expected now, to begin to shoulder some vestige of my part in the bargain. I am, technically, recovered or recovering – and apparently the subtleties within the tense of the word are not relevant here – other than that I am allowed a reduced workload. Neither I, nor they, can quantify this. Papers peep out from my lurking briefcase, smelling leathery and musty and suspiciously reassuring. In my email inbox, a letter of complaint, phrases jumping out at me, hanging in the air, swimming and circling and finally dissolving.

'Disgraceful', 'Appalling', 'Deplorable lack of customer service'.

They hover and die.

It started the day I found the 'wipe' button. There is a dark place in the organs of every computer which, if you type the right command, will gleefully exterminate everything on it. Every last particle of noxious information, or tedious data. Every record, every report, every potential promotion. A tired IT hack, responding as usual to an 'urgent' summons, to retrieve an 'essential' document which I had accidentally lost. He chatted, innocently, proud to know this command, enjoying my incredulity that something so simple could bring it all down.

The electronic workforce. The infrastructure. The mighty computer.

Little did he know that within six months, I would be spending hours each day just staring in fascination, fingers quivering over the enter key, the command tapped in, letter by letter.

Letter by electrifying letter.

Disgraceful: Contemptible
Contemptible: Mean
Mean: Miserly

Disgraceful: Shabby
Shabby: Bare
Bare: Naked

Papers piled around me. They spilled out of my desk, they made columns and pillars inside my office. The phone rang insistently and I sat there, unmoving, watching it warily, knowing I was its prey. Emails mounted until my beleaguered email client warned me hysterically that it had run out of space. But something in me wasn't moving. I had, suddenly and rather violently, collided with my inner wipe.

I had been, apparently, an unstoppable force. A god among giants. A giant among men. It took a very long time before someone, somewhere, crept into the space I had run out of, and gently led me away.

I retreated to recuperate and left behind me a faceless mass of brave diplomacy, while they began to unravel my tangled workload, make apologies and seek out angry creditors, exasperated colleagues, disgruntled or downright murderous customers. They worked, I imagine, inconceivable hours. They saved the company I created. *Unwell* was their battle cry.

But I never pressed enter. Because the fact is, even if I wiped the entire network, nothing would ultimately change. I would be out of course. *Out* in quite a significant proportion of the seventeen initial possible senses of the word. But the rest would carry on. And so would I.

That's the problem. There is no one who will carry you through this existence. This of all the infinite possible existences you could have chosen. That of course is the point.

You can't just read your way through the thesaurus.

Somehow, you are going to have to write it.

Cath

16th and 17th February
2 Days After The Flood

Patrick laughs at first. Which is unnerving. We walk Alice back across the corridor to her flat, largely I think to satisfy Patrick's urge to see that it is every bit as destroyed as ours, with the exception of course of a jagged hole in the internal wall from the lounge. We had asked if she wanted to stay. I imagined coffee and that kind of talking which, in the dark, becomes somehow immune to the usual politeness and is deliciously honest and open and bold. I imagined us firm friends within an evening. The flood becoming an indulged and comfortable memory, a catalyst for our closeness, a tale to recount. In my inner picture of that evening we sat around a crackling fire in a fireplace which neither of us actually have. I think Patrick had similar pictures though his may not have been quite so platonic. Mostly, I think we just wanted to avoid each other. But Alice would rather be alone.

Patrick and I slope reluctantly home. Wordless, we sit down on the brick elevated sofa, just because there is nothing else we can think of to do. For a while we stay there, silent, stiff and tense, the air crackling with the lack of conversation and the water sloshing about at our feet.

And then he laughs a sort of mirthless, exasperated laugh, "So, are we just going to sit here in silence?"

I say "No," and laugh in answer, but my laugh is scratchy and dry, like dead leaves.

He looks at me then and says, "Cath, just relax."

There is exasperation in his voice. He doesn't touch me. And then he stands up, looks meaningfully at the hole in the plaster and laughs again, a sort of explosive, breathy sound this time, and says, "Honestly, trust you, Cath."

His voice is indulgently frustrated, resigned to me. He turns away from the wall to face me and my eyes meeting his are nervous, trialling a dozen potential expressions, waiting, always waiting for his lead.

"I mean, there's a flood and a whole heap of really expensive damage, and you..."He pauses, laughs again, but it grows louder, and I sense, somewhere, some actual mirth in it and a taut string in me strains and twangs and snaps and I laugh with him, almost genuinely, but a little too high, and I can hear on the edge of it something hysterical.

"*You* decide to poke a hole in the wall! Typical!"

He stops laughing then, but gradually, as though running out of steam, and says again, on an exhalation,

"Trust you, Cath."

It sounds as though it is part of his breath pattern. In and out. In and out. As though it has been that way for centuries. *Trust you Cath. Trust you.*

I am struggling to pull all my reactions together, to make of them some sort of organised whole. He is really taking it very well. I am deeply relieved he can make a joke of it. But I still haven't relaxed and something inside me is hanging its head in shame, colouring my face, and my body is feeling heavier and even more bulky and lumpy and clumsy than usual.

"Patrick I am so sorry." There is a discernible and infuriating crack in my voice, "I really am sorry." And in that moment I remember his glee when he was first buying this place, poring over the plan. I remember his excitement and heart-breaking carefulness, choosing the tiles and the floor and the fittings. I remember that he hugged me, just a little too hard, in his exuberance on the day we first walked in and stood in the lounge, so that for a moment, what with the champagne bubbles still in my throat and his arms on me, I really couldn't actually breathe. I remember that everything hung on this place.

"*I feel like I'm home, Cath. I feel like I've finally grown up. I've made it. I've landed now, Cath. This is me.*"

This is me.

I look around at the water on the floor and the piled up furniture and the stupid, fraying hole in the plaster and it sweeps over me so fast I almost inhale it. A wave of misery. For him. For the flat. For me. I really am so sorry. I am so very, very sorry. And I say again, "I didn't mean to, Patrick. I really didn't. I was just packing the furniture up and I-"

"Cath it's *all right*." He looks at me strangely. "It's *fine*, Cath." It doesn't sound fine. But he is oddly gentle now, real concern in his eyes.

"Cath, what did you think I was going to do? Seriously? Who do you think I am?"

There is anger in that final question, and hurt. He had got up to walk over to the kitchen but now he returns to squat down in front of the sofa, on his hunches in front of me, his hands on my arms, "Cath, *listen* to me. I would never hurt you. OK?"

I nod, tears prickling and filling my eyes now and he stands up again quickly and walks back to the kitchen, saying over his shoulder, "Bloody hell Cath. I don't know what the hell ever happened to you, but you can't spend your life flinching away from everybody."

And he picks up the electric kettle and fills it. Puts it down again on the worktop and plugs it in. And I remember, suddenly, that I had moved it earlier, to clear room on the kitchen worktop to pile more things on it, and had accidentally dropped the kettle base, the part with the plug, into the water. I remember this too late and I almost call out in panic, but the kettle whirs away casually, as though nothing had happened, and I feel the words catch and die strangled in my throat.

I stare at his back and I think to myself that, in answer to his question, nothing like that had happened to me. Not ever. That of course I didn't really expect him to hit me.

But as I watch him I imagine his hand on the kettle. I can almost smell the sparks, see that small explosion and his hand, his body, thrown backwards and flailing, in jerky slow motion. Falling back, back, back, down into the water.

Trust you, Cath. Trust you. How typical.

I imagine him landing, bouncing slightly, his long body splayed out and fizzing in the water.

I wonder how I would feel if it actually happened.

Saturday is full of breakfast and small talk and then Patrick pacing around helplessly. I suggest we exchange email addresses with Alice, just in case, and Patrick laughs at me and tells me that nowadays people use Facebook.

"Oh I'm not on Facebook," Alice says, "too many kids in there asking me about sex." She insists on taking my email address first. The irony, if there was any, is lost on Patrick. I suspect he would rather like to ask Alice about sex.

We speak to the Flood Prevention Authority and we sweep and mop the water out of the flat in the hope that it isn't going to happen again. It is a soggily bright weekend, the sun glinting apologetically around the edges of the clouds and reflecting off the puddles of murky water and mud which are the evidence of the almost constant rainfall over the last five days. I know that statistic from Patrick, who follows these things and who has of course now researched every possible flood and weather related incident that could ever have been reported on Google. A lot of places have had much worse flooding, and much more consistently. East Grinstead has only a few patchy issues. We didn't even make the news. This is not a distinction that consoles Patrick. He spends the rest of the weekend perched with his laptop on the sofa until the early hours. I fall asleep next to him, something he takes, I know, as proof that I don't understand the significance of the great event and its impact on our lives. But we can do nothing about anything until Monday, when the insurers and the builders and whatever other services you call out when you're flooded, will yawn their way reluctantly into their offices or turn on their phones.

"I am very sorry Mr Leeson, but we have approached the developers and if they can prove they aren't liable, then we can't see how we can claim from them."

I am perched on the still elevated sofa, feet tucked up to let the floor dry, shrouded in a blanket against the cold air travelling past me through one open window and out of another. I have my laptop open but I'm not concentrating. What I have done so far is good, but I've had a sort of breakthrough, an idea which would make it even better, but would require me to completely rewrite what I have done so far. And there isn't a lot of time to do it in. Even so, it feels too important to be done less than perfectly. And the flat is not an easy place to study with Patrick, pacing in it.

"It's quite clear, Mr Leeson, it is there in their documentation. There's your signature on it. They really do have a very good case."

I can hear her voice as clearly as if it is me she is talking to, it is so piercing and nasal. I feel uncharitable and guilty, but, watching Patrick, I hate her. His responses are so full of bluster and fury they are barely comprehensive. It is painful to watch. She is probably rolling her eyes at her colleagues.

"I am sorry Mr Leeson, but as the flood possibility, though slight, (and of course, extremely unfortunate), was notified to you, and not communicated to us within our initial client inception form, we cannot cover you for this damage."

She says it quickly and firmly, and then she hangs up.

Patrick checks the contract. He spreads it on the underside of an upturned chair on top of the coffee table and scan reads it with such vehemence and such impatience that I doubt he understands a word of it. I make him a coffee. He complains it is too bitter. Then he reads the contract through again, slowly. He finishes the coffee.

He finds the small print.

"Cath, don't you have any kind of reaction to this apart from soppy platitudes? You act as though the whole thing has nothing to do with you and only bothers me. You know, don't you, that you're going to have to cough up half the costs of repairing this dump which we are now, thanks to the bloody lawyers and insurers, not to mention that slippery excuse for a house builder, going to have to meet ourselves? In full."

I have moved towards him, tried to put an arm around his shoulders, murmur something sympathetic. He shakes me off as though I have burned him.

My lack of reaction makes him cruel.

"You won't get to pay less this time, Cath, just because you don't earn much. It's not my fault you never got yourself a decent job."

Something in me pictures my finished article, in print, my precious argument and my promised dream.

Something else in me quashes it.

We go to tell Alice the news on Monday evening, me trailing uncomfortably behind Patrick, trying to send Alice some mollifying message, to soften his rather too obvious glee at the prospect of involving someone else in this drama.

I needn't have worried. In Alice's world, when faced with a problem, it seems you grin ironically and shrug at it.

"So, the insurers won't cover it because the house builders won't cover it – and the house builders won't cover us because they wrote it into our contracts..."

She must have signed without really reading it too. I can see Patrick's gaze on her, half pleased, half disappointed. Maybe he thought she would know some cunning way round it. A nimble, sardonic, clever way out of it.

"And the insurers blame you for not mentioning it in the first place..."

"Yes, yes!" Patrick is falling over himself in his eagerness to make sure that at least she, if not me, really understands the full impact of it, "And no law firm will cover us because the whole bloody thing was signed off by both of us, in blood, six months ago."

"Blood, eh?" That glint again – that giggle in her eye. "How posh. Mine was a biro I got free in the post."

I laugh in relief and in genuine amusement. Patrick steps back, physically in surprise. Alice just stands there, glinting incomprehensively at both of us and then, as if she has met Patrick, or somebody like him, on countless and wearying occasions before, "Oh don't worry too much, Patrick. They're thieving bastards. We're perfect. It's life."

As Patrick says later, it is almost as if she'd expected nothing more. Knew it all along and got one over on the lot of us.

I stand in that moment and I see us, both of us, the way that we look at her. Patrick with that hungry something I have seen on him many times before, even once or twice in relation to me, though certainly not in the last two years or so.

And me, with a horrible, raw kind of longing.

Patrick wants to take Alice, to have her, to touch her.

I want to *be* her.

It's the middle of Monday night. Or Tuesday morning. I'm not really sure. I'm lying in bed in the dark, tense and wakeful, while the room and the shape of Patrick in the bed next to me, settle mustily and morosely around me. It is as if the flat is groggy and hungover, intoxicated by its overindulgence in flood water. In the half darkness it is blurred and fuzzy, inhaling its own fruity aroma. Damp and brackish, like the after effects of an ill-advised kebab, breaking its journey, stumbling home. The carpets, rolled up and leaned against the wall in the corner, are like sentinels, ghostly and putrefying, the reanimated corpses of great, dark angels, guarding us against danger, or in case we escape. The walls, if I were to reach out and touch them, would be, very slightly, warm and wet, like fresh wounds.

I feel the bed bounce, suddenly, sharply. The restless heat of Patrick's body disappears, and a cold shock of air rushes in under the flap of the duvet and runs its fingers, comfortingly, down the length of my back. I stay very still. I close my eyes, but slowly, in case the hasty closure of my eyelids might somehow reveal my wakefulness. My body, curled up and round and away, is too stiff. I speak to all the folds of myself, force them to relax back into the soft, half melted form that looks the way I imagine I might look, asleep. I feel Patrick's eyes on me for a few minutes, then his angry steps to the window, and the wrench of it. I hear the sound of it protesting, violently slammed into the limits of itself, and a whoosh of cold air rushes into the room. Patrick takes a deep breath into it. I, though more quietly, do the same. I listen to him moving, for a while, swearing under his breath, then the bed heaves again, roughly, and I feel the haze and hair and scent of him, hurling himself viciously back onto the mattress, head thrust into the pillow, facing away from me.

And for a moment I want, I long, to turn and take him into my arms, to press the softness of my breasts against him, and murmur comfortingly, and stroke the damp curls of his hair. To have him turn to me, face in my shoulder, to feel him melting, sinking into me, consoled and restored.

But I know that this is impossible. And so I lie still, listening to the trees and the sound of his breath as it grows jagged and gasping, but doggedly muted. And I imagine the air as a white wisping being, swooping its elegant, snakelike body through the window and into the room, brightening the darkness of the patches of mould, soothing the bleeding walls, whispering hope into us.

Patrick's shape in the bed grows cooler, and his breathing more regular, but he isn't asleep. I stare at the patchy colouring across the wall just above the skirting board. It's closer to morning now, I can see more of the room. I lie and watch the shadows grow pale grey in the light.

How is it possible, I wonder, to be so close and so far from someone? To be so liable to do and say everything wrong. Does it happen slowly, a canker of time? Or is it a sudden realisation? Does one of you change?

My personal theory, is that one of you, me, is always faulty, like a toy purchased without the batteries. It is not until you have had time to go out and buy batteries, to put them in, to turn it on, that you realise it doesn't work the way that you wanted. Doesn't match what you hoped for. It never did.

I am a bright, broken thing that he lost the receipt for.

Patrick shifts slightly and I hold myself stiller. I would like to go into the kitchen, to open the fridge. I'd like to stand in the cold brilliance of it. I'd like to find something, anything, and cram it, with that mixed sense of deliciousness and discomfort, into my mouth. Cheese. Ham. Chocolate. I want to grab it and finish it all off without breathing. I don't want to stop until it isn't my stomach, but my throat that feels full. Until I am sore from swallowing.

I want to go and stand in front of that hole in the plaster. I want to regard it, solemnly, frayed and dark in the half light. I want to reach out, very slowly, and put my finger inside it. All the way through. To feel the air on the other side and the air in the lounge and the soft, fibrous hollow in-between. And then I want to tense that finger and rip it downwards, shredding great jagged lines in the wall, and sending big blocks of plasterboard clattering to the floor.

And tear the whole fucking building down around us.

I think it.

I really think that word, *fucking.*

And then I hear Patrick's breath growing quicker and faster, and the bed begins to quiver, with it. And I know that Patrick is employing his own cure for insomnia.

I curl up further, roll myself much, much tighter. Then I close my eyes and I concentrate very hard.

And I try to dream myself into the peace I am faking.

Brandon Homes

Extract from Contract of Sale of Flat 1, Ash Court, Gleesdown Road, "The Property"

Clause 20(iii) Brandon Homes regrets that it cannot take responsibility for any damage to the property, either directly or indirectly, arising out of natural events such as fire, flood, earthquake, severe weather or other such event as can be reasonably classified as 'natural disaster'. The buyer accepts that any such risk as he or she may encounter as a result, (either direct or indirect) of the situation, floor level or design of the property in the event of such 'natural disaster', except where it can be proved in good faith and beyond reasonable doubt that such risk was demonstrably worsened by some defect, as defined in the NHBC standard guidelines, in the construction or finishings of the property, with the exception of any such occurrence which can be shown to arise from the physical situation of the property, i.e. in its relation or proximity to a recognised site of natural risk

.

Alice

26th February
The Second Half Of The Spring Term

"OK. So we've talked about the whys and wherefores, we talked about how, we've talked about babies. What have we not yet talked about?"

A pause. They stare at me silently. Unsurprising. It's early in the session and they probably had geography before. Or home economics. I keep talking. It won't take too long to rehydrate their shrivelled brains. Teenagers get this abuse daily. They can bounce back.

"The thing we haven't discussed – the thing they never think of asking us to discuss, the thing that isn't even on the syllabus – is *when*. And I don't mean when to use contraception, ladies." I pause for effect. "I'm talking about when to use your vagina."

There is a collective but appreciative gasp. Sometimes I think I should write dirty monologues for murky backstreet theatre shows. Sometimes I think that is what I am doing.

"When," I smile wryly, "or maybe even *if* - you lose your virginity."

It's true. They really don't include it. You don't find it on any syllabus. That and how to make it fun. If I followed any of the recommended teaching structures I would cover foreplay as if it were some sort of rare and endangered animal species that you should probably give a bit of your pocket money towards saving, but which you're never actually going to come face to face with. All puns absolutely intended.

There are still a few of the more recognised parts of the syllabus in my teaching plan. We'll do the touch and feel session with the various contraceptive devices, and I'll talk about body image and the obligatory horror stories about STDs. I just like to mix things up with a few of my own ideas. The things I think the system forgot. These lesson plans are not usually available for head-teachers' approval. Today, according to the plans I submitted, I am facilitating an 'open and positive discussion on the benefits of safe sex and the effects of the body clock in reproduction and sexual liaison'. Nicely vague. And if you throw in the magic words 'safe sex', they rubber stamp it every time. All puns intended.

But actually we *are* talking about body clocks – not the menopause or the onset of a sudden wild and desperate broodiness when approaching thirty (a myth, by the way, it's a societal construct) - these things are miles away from the experience of these kids right now. They're not going to care about that stuff for decades. I'm talking about the other clock, the tyrant which begins in early teens. The incessant watch face, lurid and fluorescent, and with every metallic little tick, growing louder and more unbearable until, gradually and over a deceptively short time, its thundering clamour drives its owner to a state of nervous palpitation. So, then, a party, a public toilet, a sort of hurried thrust and shuffle which brings, with all its discomfort and embarrassment, a sense of crushing disappointment which pervades well into those aforementioned decades.

"You're going to get told a lot of things about timing. You probably already are. Parents who want you to wait for that doctor or banker or lawyer they've got planned out for you. Teachers who want you to wait till you're out of school. Priests – say no more. Boyfriends who want it right here right now and even if it is on your parents' sofa. Sound familiar?"

They are giggling a little and nodding. Actually it is a lot worse than that. There are the imaginary voices of future boyfriends, who expect some sort of experience or skill. There is the remembered disapproval of long dead grandparents who themselves probably harboured their own little secrets, their own dirty moments outside of wedlock, outside of the acceptable guidelines about race or colour or gender. There are always, *everywhere*, the inky tomes of the cackling witches who write for popular magazines about 'What to do if he is not satisfied', 'How to achieve orgasm' and 'What kind of lover are you?', seemingly with the sole intent of beating every last vestige of self-worth from every poor soul silly enough to buy them. I buy them every now and then. I don't know why. They have some sort of pull. You can loathe them and still really, really want to know how Jenny Pickering from Peckham lost sixty-four pounds of excess weight in two days, dumped her acne ridden dependable boyfriend for a younger, slimmer model, who promptly attacked her with a machete when she slept with his best friend – and guess what, reader? She lived to tell the tale. And presumably to become rich as well as sickeningly thin and beautiful – and, surely, deeply psychologically damaged.

Surely.

If there is any justice in the world.

"Right, well I don't know what your plan is and I'm not about to tell you when and where. The only thing I'm going to say girls, is that seriously – the loo at the back of the pub, up against a streetlight in the alleyway opposite his Mum's house, in the bus shelter or the underpass – is *not* romantic. If you think the smell of urine spices things up be my guest – but just don't do it for the first time. All right? Give yourself somewhere nice and make sure it's with someone you're not going to shriek and run from the second you come to your senses and realise he's actually Nigel from the Off Licence."

I pause for a moment and consider the practicalities. "Even if he is going to get you free booze."

They are laughing now. I sit back for a while and let the natural flow of conversation rise and fall. Young voices are so clear, so high and pure and dangerous. They can grate on you in their sheer exuberance, they can slice you in two even as you are seduced by their incisiveness.

Waves of laughter striking like boulders into the lumps of my retreating vertebrae. The hissing whisper of hatred, spiking like lightning. Hot enough to burn me, imperceptible to the teacher. Perhaps I can hear in another frequency. Perhaps when you're the target you gain extra strong senses. Powerful enough to hear every comment. Sharp enough to make certain you bleed.

I give myself a mental shake. I do not, I *will not*, think about Tabby. And yet, it seems increasingly recently, that I do. If I don't think *of* her, I find myself thinking *for* her. Ironic that a child who barely spoke can project herself so loudly across all the years I have tried to stretch between us.

The bell is going to ring at any moment. I make a slight movement and it's enough to take charge again.

"We'll discuss this more after break, I'll walk around and you can chat to me if you want to, or ignore me if you want, or play cards, I don't care – this is your time to use. You can use it as you want to. Just one word though - "I raise my voice above the newly swelling clamour. "Just one thing to remember. Sex is *great*. So don't waste your virginity. For God's sake don't do it just 'to get it over with'. That's the only reason I won't accept. It's the only choice in this whole series of sessions that I will categorically tell you not to make."

Once again, I reflect, as they squeeze themselves out of the door, I mean it literally. For the sake of the God who designed it.

He must be banging his head on the heavenly gates in frustration.

I'm not in the mood for adults today and I don't have the energy for another conversation about tampons, so I retreat to a quiet corner with my phone at lunchtime. I have one email from the company who have quoted for the work on my flat. The work which will bring it back to the state it was in when I bought it. Of course considering the fact that I bought it off plan this would require them to bulldoze it completely, which, given the size of the quote, is what they are considering doing. That and hiring a team of professional levitating fairies to hold the second floor up, for those people who were not so stupid as to buy on the ground.

I pause. I make myself sit back and close my eyes again. I manage to just about prevent myself from entering into a mad fantasy that by the time I re-open them, the email will have gone or it will be there but a few zeros will have been rubbed off the end of it, and I count calmly to twelve, by which time I have passed the moment in which I might have spent the entire lunch hour silently ranting. Still, I sit up a bit straighter just to reinforce the point, poise my fingers like the presidential secretary in some American war film, and clatter out with deadly precision a firm, clear email to the Brandon Homes enquiry box. I request an investigation into my difficulties. I accept that there is 'some contractual reference to inclement weather' but politely enquire as to whether this could reasonably be considered a warning specific to the site of this flat, reiterating calmly the distance of the river from the flat, and the assurances of clean surveys at the point of building. I point out how otherwise pleased I have been with the quality of the flat and wonder whether perhaps some compensation could be made in order to iron out this little difficulty. I inform them that I will, of course, now adapt my insurance to cover myself for my dwelling being in a 'high flood risk area', and would request that some consideration be given to the likely substantial raise in my premium as a result.

By the time I have finished I am very pleased with myself. I even copy Cath and Patrick in, as though to demonstrate to them that it is done now – I've solved it.

Back in class we are discussing first times. First times we heard that others had. First times we might have had. First times we refused. First times that apparently various celebrities, with varying degrees of celebrity credentials, had. First times we dream of.

"It's like in *Hollyoaks*. You know when Scott wants Lisa to sleep with him but she's like, not ready, yeah – and then–"

"-and then he makes her –"

"Yeah he makes her – but not like a rape – you know he says that, like, he's gonna leave her-"

"-and she does it but it's really horrible. And she feels like, all dirty?"

"Yeah but I would if I had to sleep with him – he's disgusting"

"He is though, isn't he? I don't know why she fancies him."

"No. She should be with Darren."

"And then he came back to kill her–"

"No he didn't! That's *East Enders*. How thick are you?"

They dissolve into laughter. I keep a wise silence. A dark haired girl looks at me worriedly,

"But what if everyone else has already done it and they're all talking about it and they ask you if you have?"

"Do what everyone else does. Lie," I say.

"If he really wants to – and you don't – you don't want to make him feel bad though, do you?" She's taller than the others, and stunning. It does not surprise me that she's in a relationship.

"Tell him you've got crabs," says her friend and giggles hysterically.

"Tell him he's the one," I say. "He'll wait."

Or he'll run. But I like to keep a little bit of optimism.

Somewhere amidst the general excitement someone stutters. I don't know how it is I can pick it out of the rest of the clamour. But I unfailingly do. In this case it goes unremarked upon. Either it isn't very common or they're getting to the stage now when that kind of thing just manages to pass. They might just be a group of particularly nice girls. Actually I genuinely think they are. Even so, it stays with me. The self-dismissal part of it. The 'never mind', the 'forget it', the 'it doesn't matter'.

That part always manages to come out so clearly.

Cath

Saturday 7th March
Three weeks Since The Flood
Just Over Three Weeks to Submission Deadline

We are at home. Wind dives and rushes through the rooms, darting and shooting into corners and up walls. Dust from the construction site of the second block of flats skitters in a fine haze across the surfaces of things. My laptop, his laptop. Our heads. It gives me the same feeling I get walking through ruined cathedrals or old roman remains. Beneath me, the swollen wood of the floor, above that, the green grey of the skirting boards, the piled up furniture while we wait for the builders. We still have all the windows open. Fine green lines define the gaps in the flooring. What it is feeding on after all this time, we don't know, but we are certain the green is alive and is growing. The rolled up carpets, unusable, remain standing in the corners. Patrick is still hoping we can get something from the insurance. He is keeping them, presumably, as some kind of evidence. They were removed hurriedly to assist in drying out the floor beneath them, and because they were unsalvageable. They were rolled up wet and now they ooze, horribly, with odours of hair and dirt and growing mould. We are huddled in blankets and hunched, separately, over separate machines.

Boredom and damp hangs heavily in the air.

From my vantage point on the sofa I can see Patrick, tense and hovering, like some kind of menacing bird of prey, over his computer. Everything about him is clenched. He barely touches the chair he is sitting on. As I watch him something mingles in me. Love and pity, and something else, something darker which I can't quite admit to. Something which is somehow bound up with my work, which is still only half complete, but which I am labouring over, lovingly, considering every word with a sort of intense joy I haven't felt about anything for a very long time. It's due at the end of March. I haven't mentioned the deadline to Patrick. I haven't even mentioned it to others at the university. Instead I've been working more and more from home, eschewing the commute to Brighton. Nobody really minds where you work, unless you've got teaching hours. And I want this piece of work to be mine. All mine. Even so, nothing about the atmosphere in the flat today is conducive to study. I feel like a cooped up, domestic animal, desperate to get out into the wild freedom of the wind.

Patrick stabs suddenly, angrily at his keyboard. He is hitting F5. *Refresh.* He woke in the night determined that he had made a mistake on some numbers he'd delivered to the managing director. He is concerned, perhaps correctly, that the decision by the MD, as to whether or not the business should take on a proposed project, will be based on these numbers. If the business takes on the project built on false numbers it might lose huge sums of money. Patrick woke seeing bankruptcy in his future, lawsuits in his inbox. He got up at five, and emailed his MD to ask him to hold his decision and to check his numbers.

Patrick has been pressing F5 every few minutes ever since for the reply.

It is Saturday. The decision is not actually likely to be made until next Tuesday. And Patrick has checked his numbers and can't find a mistake.

He remains convinced that a mistake has been made.

The day I first met him, a grey October four years ago when I was 25 years old and mid-way through my PhD, he was striding into the university library, looking harassed, and surrounded by a group of incongruous looking business suits. His colleagues from work. Come to support him, or, as he said later, more likely, to get out of the office for a bit and to please some sales team somewhere who wanted to grow the business' image as a community spirited venture. And to cream off the best students for future management. He said that without cynicism, almost with pride. And a hint of the pedagogue, giving me an insight into a world I neither knew, nor wished to live in.

At that moment, however, he was just a man in a library, carefully dressed in jeans and a shirt, so that he looked, if still a little out of place, not quite so much as his be-suited colleagues. Patrick always did his research, always carefully inhabited the necessary role. I didn't pay much attention then, just collected my books and piled them, just behind me, on the table next to my cardigan.

I was turning back to the shelves when I caught a brief movement in the corner of my eye. I was just finishing my thesis then, and had been lucky enough to secure a bit of teaching work for the next semester. I was doing some early prep, excited to have the opportunity, albeit only a handful of hours. Some of the books in the library seemed to crop up on every English Literature module. On the top of my pile was one of these. Key reading material. The library never stocked enough copies. It had been the last one on the shelves.

The movement turned out to be a small, dark haired girl, who had been hanging furtively around near the table, and who had darted over and grabbed it from my pile of books. I noticed, but decided, in the circumstances, to ignore it. I would buy the book if I really needed it, and I knew the text well anyway.

"Hey!"

There was an outraged male voice, which I swung round to discover emanating from the harassed looking man who had flustered his way into the library earlier. There was absolute indignation in his face.

"She just deliberately stole one of your books as soon as you turned away!"

He was looking at me, slightly open mouthed, in the way people do when they expect a certain reaction. In those moments I am never sure what reaction they want. It's not always clear to me if I should be impressed or disgusted, cynical or surprised. I try to guess, to do whatever it is they hope for, but I don't always get it right. The dark haired student had frozen, like a child half way into the biscuit tin, holding the book and looking fearfully at both of us. She looked a lot younger than eighteen.

I made a decision instinctively.

"Don't worry," I said to her, "which course are you doing?"

She mumbled something incoherent. I don't know if she had identified me as a tutor, I'd hardly done any teaching until now, but either way she was bright red from neck to forehead.

"Wartime literature? First or second? Although really that book is quite interesting for either." I paused, "Actually I would recommend Thatcherson's *Smoke and Mirrors: Literature as Propaganda*. No one really thinks of that angle, but it'll give you a good edge."

The student managed to say thank you. Then repeated it a few times. Both she and the man were gazing at me as though I was Mother Theresa.

"That was amazing!" said the man, approaching me in the wake of the student's embarrassed retreat. "That was so nice of you. You didn't have to do that."

I shrugged. It wasn't a particularly big gesture. I didn't need the book especially desperately and I had felt horribly sorry for her. She looked like the kind of student who suffered from headaches and nervous tension. In fact, looking at him, so did the man who was now standing looking at me with something akin to accusation.

"So what brings you here?" I asked, because I was bright and cheery, I was good with people.

Back then.

He, on the other hand, was hopelessly and obviously out of his territory. He didn't even live in Brighton, he had commuted from East Grinstead. He looked at me sheepishly. It sat strangely on his face, because generally he exuded confidence. He had a charisma which drew you to him, even now, in a library he clearly couldn't navigate. "I'm meant to be delivering a...speech."

"A lecture?"

"Yes. A lecture. I work at Transhaw Limited. Business Analysis. We're doing a talk, a... lecture, on business metrics to the further maths students. Part of a series on applying it to the real world, you know, from theory to actually producing something."

He spoke with the slight disdain for academia that is common among people who don't enjoy it. Or who are unable to do it. I stifled a smile. This man was wearing so many disguises. The only thing that was clearly him was the natural charisma, the power of him. And the palpable tension. I had, for a sudden and unexpected second, a rare urge to touch him, but whether to soothe or arouse him I was not quite certain. The rarity, and ludicrousness of this feeling made me smile further. The smile did not please him.

"What?" he said, half laughing but only to partially cover the genuine concern that he was somehow ridiculous. I knew him. I felt I knew him so very well then.

So very well, so very early.

So very young, so very reckless.

"Nothing," I said, "so when's the lecture?"

"In about twenty minutes?" he said it with an upward inflection, and a wry smile of his own, the twitching muscle in his jaw relaxing marginally.

I smiled back, "You're nervous?"

He shrugged, "Well I don't really do this public speaking malarkey. Not to students anyway." He looked around the library vaguely. "Popped in for a bit of peace and quiet. Psych myself up. I guess it doesn't matter. They'll probably talk or sleep through most of it anyway."

"They won't talk or sleep." It is an old, old formula, which I have found, and still find, works every time. "You have a natural command and you're charismatic. They'll listen instinctively."

You reach in, you take whatever it is, the thing that they have, even if only a germ of a thing, even if its half buried in bluster and misery, and you open your hands to show it to them.

"Really? Well, thanks...yes. And I'm well prepared for it." He corrected his slight slouch, rebalanced himself, planted his feet a little more firmly apart.

You show it to them, and then you hand it back.

"Anyway, thanks. I guess I'd better go and do it then!" I agreed, wholeheartedly, "You better had. Oh, and students don't always talk through their lectures," I smiled to soften it for him, "some of them really do actually work." A shadow of that sheepishness passed across him, but he smiled back and turned round to leave.

"Oh – and one other thing," suddenly I was anxious to delay him. To hold him with me. To keep feeing that delicious sense of discomfort, the dizzy impulse to do things not befitting my library. My sacred place of calm and study. To put my hand beneath his shirt and feel the warmth of his chest.

"Yes?"

"The key is to know your opening. Open confident and with something that grabs their interest." It was obvious advice, and I'd only done one sessional lecture a couple of terms before, but it gone very well and I'd enjoyed it immensely, "After that you barely know you're talking. The enthusiasm just takes you."

"OK. Will do. Thanks."

And he did. I couldn't curb my interest, and I waited ten minutes and then checked out my books and carried them with me to the mathematics block and into the lecture theatre. I slipped in at the back and I knew that he saw me. Felt suddenly in his gaze an echo of myself. A faint reciprocal something, covered quickly over by another of his adept and multiple disguises.

He introduced himself as Patrick Leeson and, as it turned out, Patrick Leeson was amusing, wry, inspiring and confident. He began his lecture with a work place anecdote, told so perfectly it felt like a drama performance. Which I suppose it all was. The students, his colleagues and I, listened silently and attentively the whole way through. He had a charisma but also, perhaps grown out of that palpable tension beneath the surface, a danger in him. A formidability.

When he had finished I waited for the students to leave. He strolled up, flushed and pleased with his success, and I saw as he neared me that his collar was wet with sweat, and his hands were shaking.

"Thanks for coming," he said, to me, formally, as though I had been an invited dignitary. I could see the hairs on his neck, alert and listening, hyper aware of his colleagues, milling around like pin striped hyenas, a little way behind him. I understood, for a moment, why he might need to do it, to layer himself with so much social weaponry. He didn't acknowledge my advice. He just looked at me a little bit longer than necessary, then, sensing a shift in the tribe behind him, he turned to join them.

"Wait." It was rare for me to want this. To want somebody. I had a career that I loved. I had plenty of friends. I was good, as I have said, with people. I just didn't need it. "The fact is, I quite like you..." I was courageous then. I never believed in the usual game. Largely because I'd never quite understood the rules and it seemed people always played it differently and in the end both somehow ended up losing. "So I was wondering if you want to go for coffee?"

Somewhere, blurrily behind him, I saw a ripple of interest and something akin to a school boy "oooh!" among his be-suited colleagues. There was a hint of macho laughter, but mostly they were impressed. I could still see that in those days. I could still merit it then. Patrick, shifty, pleased but bewildered, heard it too.

"Wow! Um...yes, the er...the Bell Inn is nice for lunch."

Because it needed to have been largely his idea. Which never bothered me. It didn't matter to me how we arranged it. I said, "Sounds good!"

He said, "Thanks. I'll look forward to it."

Perhaps that was Patrick's mistake. Not the numbers he sent to the dreaded MD. The numbers were perfect.

I too, would like to press *refresh*.

Brandon Homes

"Thank you for calling Brandon Homes. In order that we may transfer your call to the correct department, so that your query may be dealt with quickly, please choose from the following options:

If you are calling to enquire as to the nearest Brandon Homes development, please press 1.

If you would like a quote on the cost of having Brandon Homes take the hassle out of your house purchase by handling the conveyancing on your behalf, please press 2.

If you are calling to query the progress of your purchase, please press 3.

If you would like to speak to our media and marketing department, or you are a member of the press, please press 4.

If you would like to join our dedicated team of professionals, please press 5 for the Human Resources department.

If you are one of our valued Brandon Homes investors, please press 6.

At Brandon Homes, we understand how important a home can be, and for this reason we put all our effort into ensuring that the process of purchasing a Brandon property runs smoothly and that your Brandon Home is every bit as wonderful and unique as you are. Therefore, you should not need to raise a complaint, but if you do have any concerns at all, please press 7 and we will do our very best to resolve the problem.

Customers should note that Brandon Homes do not provide financial advice, though we can refer you to one of our carefully selected service providers in this area.

To hear these choices again, please press 0 or alternatively, you can find all this information and more by consulting our website at www.BrandonHomes.com.

Thank you for calling Brandon Homes."

M.

Thursday 22nd May
2 hours and 46 minutes to go

Nothing is simply one thing only. The word *care*, if you look it up in the English thesaurus, has any one of six possible meanings. It can be *mind* or *be bothered, worry*; *attention, custody, caution,* or *treatment.*

Before I was *unwell*, every quarter I would sit there, in a brown boardroom full of officious brown furniture, breathing air which was filled with passionate brown words. And at the same point in the meeting every quarter, the Chairman of the Reputational Risk Forum would arrive and tell us, with ghoulish enthusiasm, all the potential reputational damage, all the slander he had found that quarter on the Internet.

Eventually, when the Risk Chairman had breathlessly concluded, it would be necessary for the Board to give him permission to take the necessary legal action, where such action was possible, and to consider whether the complaining customer was enough of a threat to make it worth the expense. Legal action was most often recommended in cases in which, though this was never openly admitted, it might possibly turn out that the company was in fact quite deserving of the slander in question.

Out of all those six meanings of the word *care* only a few could potentially apply to the way I felt about the Reputational Damage report from the Chairman of the Internal Risk Committee. And one of them wasn't *be bothered.*

In a rational world, one which made sense, in which one could simply pursue one path to one end, it would not be possible to *worry* but not necessarily *mind.* It would not be possible to care nothing about the reputation of the company, but still feel those fingers, those cold squeezing fingers of tension, probing at your temples, running freezing through your veins.

Sometimes you can't even choose the way you read the thesaurus – you can't even select the most reasonable meaning.

Worry: concern, trouble, problem, anxiety, fear, tension, mind.
Mind: be bothered, be concerned, think about, heed – worry.

Nothing is simply one thing only. And everything always takes you back to the start.

Cath

Later, Saturday 7th March
Three weeks Since The Flood
Just Over Three Weeks to Submission Deadline

I have turned off my computer, and am hopelessly fiddling about with the sound system. All I am trying to do is turn the radio on. When we first moved in, Patrick connected it to the smart TV screen, and then to his new speakers and now I can feel him bristling quietly, watching me. He is not going to tell me how to do it. Not again. He thinks I should know. Should know *by now*. The last time I asked him to remind me he wondered aloud how I could possibly get on in life without him. Whether he ought to be following me around, checking I was breathing and cleaning my teeth. I laughed, tensely. He didn't.

In a grim, trapped sort of resignation I begin pressing some of the myriad of buttons experimentally. There is a deafening blast of white noise from the speakers. I jump and squeak a little, accidentally. I have found the radio but have managed, in the process, to reset the tuning. I tense against the onslaught and begin, hastily, to manually readjust it, twiddling the button so that the flat is treated to a series of fuzzy half sentences and blurry melodies.

It mingles sourly with the sound of the wind.

"For goodness sake," Patrick's voice is so clipped and his teeth so gritted the words are barely making their way through the gaps in them, "leave the tuning button alone. What's the point in doing it manually?"

I feel a slow pink colour begin to climb up my face from my breastbone.

"But...how do I do it the other way?"

Wordlessly he crosses the room and picks up the remote. I hold my hand out for it, taking care not to flinch. He stabs his finger at the 'automatic tuning' button.

"Automatic tuning," he says.

He watches while I press the button and the digital display finds Radio 1, Sports24, Classic FM, Radio 4.

"Cath you need to get to know the place, OK? You should learn how to use stuff. You can't just *live* here without noticing anything."

There is a pause.

Patrick presses F5.

I say, "Shall we go out?"

Alice

Saturday, 7th March
Three Weeks Since the Flood

For some reason, when I put all the rest of my furniture back, I left the picture out. The one with the ballet shoes. I didn't put it back in the cupboard where it used to be. There were other pictures, and I put them away fine, picked them up, put them in, didn't turn them over, no problem. But this one somehow made its way to the shelf.

I got it when I was thirteen. And Tabby was eleven. She bought it. Went out proudly and chose the frame. It was a special present because it was the first birthday I was 'teen'. She is ten in the picture. The frame is quite scratched now. It's been face down for so long on so many surfaces. I don't know why I kept it really. I don't know why I still keep it. I don't know why it isn't back in the cupboard.

I walk to the shelf, look at it for a moment, and then turn it face down. Then stand it up again. I've done this several times already today. Irritated, I slap my hands hard against my thighs in frustration. I need to settle to something. I don't know what. A distraction.

I make myself walk away into the kitchen. I flick the kettle on and listen to it rumble, batting a teaspoon against the palm of my hand, pointlessly.

The picture and the frame. They were a special present.

Cath

Later Still, Saturday 7th March
Getting Out

"We should invite someone else," I say to Patrick, watching him press F5 again. "How about Alice?"

"Why not?" He visibly straightens. I see a light in his eyes. Like a hunter. I see all that charisma and charm and power being collected up inside him ready to be shot like bullets out of his body. It still has all the strength it used to. He saves it, now, for people like Alice. For other people. Who are not me. It makes me want him still, just the way it did that first day in the university library. It makes me want to touch him. And it makes me want to run from him.

But this time, there is something else in me. I want to go out. I want to go out with Alice. Patrick can come too. If he likes.

"I'll go and knock on her door," says Patrick and instantly, smoothly, it has always been his suggestion. "That'll give you time to get ready."

I hadn't been thinking about changing. I shrug, "Oh, I'll probably go as I am."

"Are you sure?" he says and I feel his eyes flicker over me, burning me from the inside outwards. Past him, in the mirror, in the hallway, I can see myself and I am blurred and pale. I have light brown hair and a light grey top and light blue trousers on. I look as though somebody forgot to

87

colour me in. My face is pink, pastel and insipid and round. It looks awkward and hesitant. And a little bit stupid.

I don't want to go out. I want to stay here, blending slowly into the green-grey mould and the dust and the carpets. I haven't written that last section of my argument, I remind myself savagely. I haven't finished anything yet. The deadline is in just over three weeks' time. It seems to me suddenly that I have too much to do. That the whole argument probably needs rewriting. It seems to me suddenly that I should just delete it. I should accept my limitations. I should cancel the contract.

Patrick is looking at me strangely. Half amused. Half exasperated.

"Earth to Cath," he says, shaking his head and half smiling, "you seriously do just lose it sometimes."

I laugh slightly, but I am distracted. I think he has finished, that he is turning to go, but he stops and turns back again,

"Really," he says, "do you *know* that you do that?" I say nothing in the heat of his gaze. I'm not sure if he requires an answer, or what it would be if I gave one. Increasingly, recently, there has been a new something deep inside me which is struggling to get past the rest of me, to get out there and to tell him to just fuck off.

It really thinks that. It thinks that word *fuck*.

I slip my hand inside the opposite sleeve of my top and scrape my fingers slowly across the wound on my elbow. That something has nothing to do with the rest of me. The pain doesn't help. There isn't any. I have let it heal over.

"Well you do," says Patrick.

He sounds a little defeated.

I *am* going out.

I am going out. With Alice.

"I guess you don't *have* to change," says Patrick. "Suit yourself."

He walks out of the door and I stare, for a moment, at the ghost of myself looking back at me in the mirror.

I flick the shower on.

"She's up for it. She says she'll be ready in ten minutes," Patrick announces as he strides back through the door, finding me wrapped in a towel and searching frantically through piles of clothing excavated from the back of the wardrobe. Things I forgot about. Things that I just haven't worn for a while.

"Ten minutes!" says Patrick, kissing my forehead as I straighten up, outfit hanging in crumples over my forearm, "So quick! How long does it take you? Ten hours?"

The blur of activity which is my transformation from ghost to substance, actually takes less than ten minutes. My heart is beating wildly in my urge to go and collect Alice before Patrick thinks to do it. I slip out while he is standing in the lounge with his back to me. Frowning at his computer and pressing F5.

Her door is open and I have walked halfway into the room before I realise she doesn't seem to have noticed me. She is standing in the middle of the room with her back to me and a photograph of a young girl in her hands.

For a long and awkward moment I am looking at it with her, and then she starts and pulls the photo away and I am saying, "Sorry. Sorry. I didn't mean to...I was just coming to get...ahh. Is that your niece? Looks like a smaller you."

I have said 'ahh' only because usually a photograph of a child is supposed to elicit this response. Even as I say it I know, somehow, that this is different. Know by the way she is looking at it. By the odd, dramatic air in her stance. By the stiffness in her shoulders.

And then she says, "No-one. No-one anymore." And there is such bitterness in her voice that I step back, physically, and at the same time fight an impulse to step forward again and touch her. To put my warm hand through the ice that so suddenly encases her.

"Oh," I say.

There is a pause.

Something I don't understand hangs in the air until I think it is going to take shape any moment and slap me, hard across the face. Then she moves, quickly, in one swift action, grabbing the frame and throwing it into a cupboard, and then whirling round to face me. "So, come on then. Are we painting the town red?"

And she bites her lip and rearranges her face until she is meeting my gaze.

Patrick appears in the doorway.

"Hello, oh, hi Cath. Wow. Aren't you a little overdressed?"

I am wearing a deep red dress, high heels and lipstick. I glance down at myself, at the plunging neckline and find my hands clasped together over my cleavage. Alice is wearing tight jeans and boots and an olive green T-shirt. Patrick wears jeans and a shirt and aftershave.

I haven't worn this dress for a while. It clings.

I pull my stomach in, remove one clenched fist from my cleavage and press it uncertainly, into my midriff.

"Overdressed? I don't think so." Alice moves her gaze from mine, meets Patricks and destroys it. "But we might need a stick."

I am briefly confused. For a moment I think she means to attack him. I look up from my cleavage, blush abating, and see that her face is full of life and sparkle. And underneath it, her eyes still on Patrick, I can see a hint of something cruel.

"You know," she says, "to beat off all the men."

I shout with a laughter which is loud and unexpected and sudden. With it comes a great rush of air, as though, for some time, I haven't been breathing. I look up, habitually, for Patrick's reaction, and I see, for a moment, a deep discomfort, a fearfulness on his face. My laughter still rushing at him, like smoke in his eyes.

I feel a rush of adrenaline and then we are leaving and I realise that somehow, Alice and I are in front. And Patrick is bringing up the rear.

Alice

Later Still, Saturday 7th March

We are huddled around a sticky table in a bar. Cath's eyes are bright, she is laughing and leaning forward in her enthusiasm to catch something I am saying and if I look down all I can see is ample, soft cleavage and, somewhere deep within, a glint of black satin. I note with some amusement that I, predictably, am not the only one to have noticed this, and if I turn round at any point in the conversation I could meet any number of masculine eyes, straying in this direction and ranging from furtive to blindingly, pelvis thrustingly obvious. Cath, of course, is blissfully unaware. Either she is used to it or she just doesn't speak that language. Patrick, interestingly, is studiously ignoring it. And he, I am certain, is fluent.

He sits diagonally across from me, legs far apart, face flushed, talking quickly, and just a little too loudly. I decide my hair has escaped far enough, and I move my hands up to fix it. One of the grips pings across the table, and lands in Cath's lap. There is uncontrollable hilarity. Everything everyone says is so witty. We have freed our inner children. We are incisive and clever.

We have all had at least five different cocktails.

For the last hour and a half we have been happily swapping side-splitting stories about the flood – none of which were even slightly amusing at the time.

"I bet Brandon Homes would have a laugh."

"Of course. If we could ever get through to them."

"We should leave it as a message on their answer-phone."

I have a warm, fuzzy feeling, though thanks to the last cocktail (which I think contained absinthe), it is a little queasy at the edges.

We are all friends.

Cath tips her drink a little too excitedly and douses her chest and the table, causing a palpable stir from her numerous watchers. She giggles delightedly and I join her. Patrick doesn't laugh until I do.

Well. We are all *something*.

"Right." He puts his elbow on the table, questioning. Little flurries of *Mohito Magic* scuttle around it. "Answer me this one though, because I'll never get it. Why do Brandon Homes put locks on every door? They've got them on the cupboards and the internal doors, for crying out loud."

It's true. You can actually lock the bathroom door from the outside. I suggest it's because they are so frighteningly expensive they assume you can only afford one if you share – and if you share you might want to lock your stuff away from your housemates. Of course you'd never want to live with someone you actually *trust*. Patrick thinks maybe they got a deal with the lock supplier and they had to use up a certain quota of locks. I suggest the houses were built by a fetishist.

Cath has not noticed there are locks on the doors. Patrick is exasperated.

"You pay no attention to anything! Didn't you ever wonder? Didn't you even see them? I mean – have you actually ever locked the *front* door?"

"It locks itself. Or you're with me and I let you do the double locking thing. I don't think anyone is really going to break in anyway right now, I mean, who would want it?"

A good point.

"Actually, Cath," he is suddenly serious, "you probably *should* lock them."

"What, even the inside ones?"

I sit quietly and wait for his answer. I am as incredulous as she is.

"Yes. You should. For the insurance."

"The insurance!" She is laughing. "What against? You think someone's going to break in from *inside* the house and steal what? The loo roll?" She growls menacingly and makes a stabbing motion with her fist in the air in front of her. "The carving knife?" She makes a conciliatory attempt to kiss him affectionately, which he doesn't co-operate with.

I giggle.

"No, seriously." For some reason he is addressing me, eyes a little too bright, a tiny bit feverish, religiously keen to outline his next point. I rearrange my face so it regards him with solemn interest. It is all part of the social contract. He pretends I agree with him, and I help him pretend. "Seriously, because Cath doesn't own the house."

I am genuinely surprised. "She doesn't co-own?"

"No. She's my lodger."

I start to laugh and then realise, hazily, that he's serious.

"We're not officially 'co-habiting'. I own the house and Cath – Cath just lives there..." He pauses and then winks.

"And grants sexual favours."

I am a little too stunned to react but Cath is still laughing. She kisses him full on the lips. He recoils slightly, and looks around him, as though her action is at the very least embarrassing, at the worst, somehow scandalous. Cath is either used to it or oblivious.

"I'm just the cleaner!"

Patrick doesn't laugh.

There is an enthusiastic rendition of 'Happy Birthday' from a nearby table, followed by a heady chorus of whooping and table slapping.

A barman writes his number on somebody's hand.

A girl says, "So I told him-" and someone asks where the loos are. My arm sticks to the table where another party, weeks ago, must have spilled something sugary.

Cath starts telling a story about a mad academic and Patrick is laughing. He says, "I can't believe the people you work with. I can't believe the people she works with."

There is an old man bent over his pint in the corner. His fingers are yellowed and curled around the glass. A thin sliver of dribble extends from his open mouth onto the table, little diamonds of saliva strung along it like beads. With every breath his head drops lower. I look at him and I know that any minute now that man is going to pitch forward into his pint glass. And no-one is going to do anything about it.

M

Thursday 22nd May
Exactly 2 Hours To Go

Love is surprisingly simple. We hunt it like prey, to consume it, to discredit it or simply to open our arms to it and allow it to consume us. Western society is fixated by it, music inspired by it, film and literature revolves around it. It is the thread through every narrative, be it fact or fiction, public or personal.

And yet, though there are hundreds of words for it, all of them go in one direction. *Passion, zeal, ardour, devotion.* They don't circle back to something entirely different, it takes a search through many meanings before you reach that stage, and even then the furthest you can get is *vehemence,* which is not absolutely unconnected.

Maybe that is why we seek it so fervently, we who through the ages have been so seduced by the idea of an oracle. A single, guaranteed, straightforward truth. One word, the solution to every riddle. A path through the relentless muddle. A bookmark in the thesaurus. A start or an end to it.

I returned, or, more accurately, was delivered home to my wife after my brief incarceration, a gradually eroded parcel of parts. She must have been tracking it, the progress of this erosion, watching fearfully as it approached us, but she said nothing. She knew, perhaps, her own inability to stand in its way, understood its inevitability, its status as the only way out. When it came she simply opened her arms and accepted me into them, all the broken parts of me. When I refused, entirely, to leave the house, when I sat for hours, red eyed and staring, she simply carried me like a burden or a child on her hip, and continued with life on behalf of us both.

"I'm sorry," I said to her, and she said,

"I love you."

She must also have hated me. But love is simple. It is an instinct. It goes in only one direction.

Sex, of course, is another matter.

Cath

14th March
One Month Since The Flood
Just Over Two Weeks To Submission

I remember.

I remember the way he touched me then, his long fingers, smooth and gentle with pale neat fingernails, short but somehow oddly feminine on the ends of his tall and self-consciously masculine body. I loved those hands. They were my access point, his vulnerability in the midst of so much striding confidence, so many layers of obvious defence. He was a walking kaleidoscope of carefully constructed personas. I could see through them, I felt, so lightly, so easily. I was sure that, given time, I could somehow peel back the blustering, swaggering skin of him and find underneath something sweet tasting and beautiful. I thought, I suppose, that I could cure him.

And that something at the heart of him *was* there. *Is* there. I was only wrong about my own ability to discover it. It required someone incisive and sharp and quick. Someone charismatic and clever and strong. And I am a jaded, blurring figure, blending into the background like a faded stain. So that gradually, like some sort of horrible fairy tale, more and more layers grew around him. Perhaps I even helped construct them. Until he became a blunt stone object, impenetrable and weighty and that edge of excitement, that hint of danger, became something darker and dirtier and angrier and cruel.

But still, I remember. I like to remember.

His body, hot and tense over mine, his breath in my ear and the weight of him after, when he collapsed onto me, gasping out his love. We would lie for a while, then, silent and sated, his hair soft and tickling against my skin.

I remember how often we were late for appointments, turned up tousled with thrown together clothing and hair awry. That flush through my body, talking, laughing as usual but with a delicious sense of naughtiness. A secret smile. His eyes on mine across the table. A special connection. Patrick and me.

I remember. And it is the remembering which holds me. Captive and hoping. Always. Hoping.

Alice

14th March
Second Half Of The Spring Term

Junior School. Always an odd one.

A small child approaches me at the end of question time.

"I understand how the seed gets in." he says, "but when Mummies and Daddies aren't having babies, why do they do it then?"

"Because they love each other," I say.

There is a pause.

"Usually. Usually it's because they love each other."

Brandon Homes

"Thank you for calling Brandon Homes. You are through to the Complaints Department. We are sorry but our offices are closed at the moment. Opening hours are from 10.30 a.m. to 12.30 p.m. and from 2.30 p.m. to 4.30 p.m. Please call back later."

Cath

Thursday 20th March
Ten Days To Submission

He must have come in very quietly. Stood at the door for some time. Closed it slowly, so that it made only the tiniest little 'phut' as it shut. He must have been listening to us for a while.

I have been talking to Mike, one of the workers who are sorting out the mess that is Patrick's flat. He's taking a break and the others have gone out to their van for something. Mike is only young, he's just a little younger than I am and he wants to be a photographer. He has a dark room and a small business selling prints from his home, but it doesn't make ends meet, so he works as a builder in the day time, just to pay the bills.

"I know the feeling," I say, "I have friends who are actors..." I trail off suddenly, because I don't actually. I don't anymore.

Mike hasn't noticed.

"I guess," he says sadly. "But it would be nice to move out, you know, from my parents."

His shoulders hang. Mike is always slightly apologetic. He didn't mean to get into this really. We just got talking. Or I asked him. I don't remember.

"Just seems a bit pathetic," says Mike.

"No," I say firmly, "I think it's brave. You're a strong person. You don't give up. Pathetic would be if you just caved in and got a desk job. You're the opposite of pathetic. You have proper integrity."

You reach in, you take whatever it is, the thing that they have, and you open your hands to show it to them.

Mike's shoulders lift a little, in a shrug which somehow becomes an invitation. "Thanks!" he says. "But I'm not that great." Even so, he laughs a little and his eyes, usually so skittish, briefly meet mine.

I smile encouragingly.

"Perhaps I could bring a few pictures round, you know. To show you." He drops his gaze quickly. "If you wouldn't mind."

I am touched that he would consider doing this. Mike seems a very private person and I'm not sure how I've managed to get into this deep a conversation with him. I would love to see his photographs. I am convinced that they are probably amazing. Mike is red in the face and shuffling uneasily. There is a blotchy rash on his neck.

I put my hand lightly on his arm. "I would love that!" I say.

He laughs nervously. "Cool," he says.

"Cool," I agree. And then I am laughing too, and as our laughter grows I tip my head back, and several things happen at once. I catch my reflection in the mirror and, for once, I really don't want to smash it. I look pink and lively. My hair is shining and my eyes are bright. And as I blink, surprised, I see him standing there.

Patrick. In the doorway. Silent and intense.

I jump, violently. He laughs. Mike starts to laugh back, but it's strangled into a cough.

"Sorry!" I say. "I didn't see you...Um...Patrick, this is Mike."

Mike nods and, nervously, begins to stretch out his hand.

"Cath, I know that," says Patrick, "I hired him, remember?" His voice is light, confident, and easy.

Mike snaps his hand back.

I make a staccato sound which should be laughter. I realise too late that I should have just said, "Oh yeah." Should have led the moment. Should have somehow joined in.

"Oh yeah," I say, "Ha! Trust me."

My voice sounds deep and forced and dull. It doesn't leap lightly over phrases like Patrick's. It's as lumpy and as slow as I am.

"How's it going?" says Patrick, to Mike.

"Good thanks," says Mike. There is a pause. I seem to have frozen but I can't remember why.

"You on a break?" says Patrick. "Did she offer you a coffee? Cath, haven't you even offered Mike a coffee?" He turns to Mike, ruefully, over my instant, stumbling apologies, "How long have you been here? All day? Cath! Honestly!" and he laughs indulgently and somehow Mike joins him and they are comrades in arms, and I am laughing too, but shamefacedly, and there in the mirror I see that my face is pasty and my shoulders are fat, and everything else just a trick of the light.

I retreat to the kitchen area, aware of their eyes on me, and with exaggerated busyness I open cupboards. I can't remember immediately, what I'm supposed to be doing. Behind me, Mike and Patrick shuffle their feet and cough a little.

"So. Photography." Patrick says eventually.

"Yes." Mike jumps on the new found social cue but I hear the reluctance in his voice. "Yes, I'm trying to actually make a living out of it. But hey, who knows if it'll work."

"Who knows," Patrick agrees.

There is a pause.

Then there is a crash, and somehow, my fat fingers have dropped something, or knocked something and there is coffee everywhere. All over the top and all over the floor. And I don't do anything about it initially. I whirl round, eyes wide and mouth hanging gormless and open. I stare at Patrick.

"Cath! CATH! Behind you! Pick it up at least...oh for God's sake, I'll do it."

The cafetiere is rolling gently, slowly but surely towards the edge of the worktop.

Things happen. In no particular order.

Mike looks horribly embarrassed. Patrick strides towards me, then stops suddenly, and smacks his head into his hands in a gesture that manages to be both despairing and violent. The cafetiere rolls off the worktop and smashes, still pouring coffee onto the mouldering flagstones.

"Sorry," I say. "I just...it got knocked..." I sound small and nervous. There is a rapidly growing lump in my throat that is threatening to stop my breathing.

"No problem," says Patrick in a voice which tells us all it is. The cafetiere was expensive. Patrick was proud of it.

"I was trying to do it carefully," I don't know why I am still talking or what it is I am saying. My eyes are blurring and there is coffee dripping down my leg. Somehow, only my mouth is moving. "I just...I think I kind of just knocked it..."

"It's fine, just – Cath – can you please get out of the way so I can get the cloth."

I scuttle back like a rat or a cockroach. I make my excuses. I mutter something nonsensical about it having been nice to meet Mike. And I reach the bathroom just in time. I keep it, from practice, very quiet. I don't exit until I have lost the flush from my cheeks, the tears from my eyes, and the contents of my stomach.

Alice

Thursday 27th March

I am sitting on the train on my way to a conference. *'The Annual Congress of Youth Workers and Teachers; Celebrating Childhood'* to be exact. The pamphlet for it reads like an advert for adulthood. Somewhat half-heartedly, I am staring at my laptop, reading through all the marketing claptrap and the timetable and noting those speakers I might actually want to listen to. Typically these are all crammed into the same slot after lunchtime, and in venues as far apart as physically possible.

To be honest I am simply pleased to be out of the flat. The Annual Congress of Smug Middle Agedness represents a night in a hotel, all white tiling and room service. I cannot wait to flop down on my crisp white, puffed up pillows, and breathe deeply.

I minimise the conference site and open my email. Nothing. Even having paid through the nose for a train Wi-Fi connection, I still cannot muster up a response from Brandon Homes. Fuelled by a sort of weary irritation, I begin a new message.

Dear Sirs,

Next to me, a man with a large paunch and a missing shirt button is clearly reading my email as I type. Unless he is from Brandon Homes and can give me an immediate answer, this is not something which, in today's mood, I really appreciate. I angle myself away from him. The tiny flap on the seat in front of me, which apparently constitutes a table, does not really allow me to re-angle the computer.

Despite several attempts to contact your offices, including numerous phone calls and three emails (attached), I still have not received a response from you.

The man next to me actually changes position to better see my screen. He was a lot less excited when I was reading about the Moral Advancement of the Youth of the Nation. I look at him pointedly and clear my throat.

I am writing again in the hope that you have now had time to consider my position.

He is still reading. I can see his pupils moving with the letters as I type. I delete the last sentence. I watch his gaze move with it. Slowly, I retype it. Against the black of the tunnel we have just been plunged into, I can see the reflection of his face in the screen.

Some rebellious instinct takes over and I arrange my face impassively and type him a message. I ask him how he is enjoying reading my emails. There is no gasp, no sudden, embarrassed rustle as he shifts his posture. We emerge into daylight and I can't tell any more whether he is still following. Disappointed at this lack of reaction, I turn to him impatiently. He is gazing out of the window. Sheep amble about on a green hill in the distance. A miniscule man is walking his dog.

When I turn back I realise I have accidentally hit the 'send' button.

Cath

Thursday 27 March
Nearly 6 Weeks Since The Flood
Only 4 Days To Submission

Patrick is darting in and out of rooms like a big stray cat. He is flying out to Switzerland tonight on some conference with work, and he won't be back until Monday. Secretly, tantalisingly, I am waiting for him to leave. Tonight I will write the last sentence of my manuscript, save it and send it to my publishers. I am a whole four days ahead of the deadline.

The manuscript, saved onto my laptop, is like a warming pulse inside me. I have checked and double checked it, proof read it four times, and then again, more slowly. Despite all this, I am still deliberately holding that last sentence back. I want to savour the act of typing those last few words in. I know exactly what they are. But I want to write them with a flourish. I want a fanfare. Even if it's only me. I have told Patrick nothing at all about it.

Patrick has been on edge for the last week or so, even more than usual. There are builders in the house each day, rectifying, repairing. I look at them with relief. They are lively and jovial and nice to have around. And they are making things better. They are physically, discernibly, improving Patrick's coveted house. His long awaited Brandon Home.

"Be careful," Patrick keeps telling me, "don't leave your stuff around."

The presence of the builders makes him tense and unhappy. His shoulders stoop and stiffen and his voice is taut, as though it is being played on a string which might snap. I want to reassure him, but he thinks I am naïve. Patrick stops darting and comes over to give me a perfunctory goodbye kiss. Then he reminds me, for the third time today, how to use the DVD player.

"This," he tells me, "is a television recording device, colloquially known as a DVD player. You have to press record at the time the programme starts. The programme I want you to record begins at 8.30 tonight, so you should press record at 8.20, just to be sure. Yes? Cath? Put your finger on the button and push. At 8.20. Are you going to remember? Do you understand? Cath?"

I nod. The DVD player is mine. I brought it from my house when we moved in. Patrick snorted and put it up high in the cupboard and we used the massive TV screen with internet enabled. And then it flooded and the cable had to be fixed. And so we go back, as Patrick puts it, to the Stone Age. We go back to the way I lived, not so long ago, when I was a real person.

"Cath? CATH? Earth to Cath. Seriously, where do you GO when you do that?" Patrick is standing, one hand on the front door, bag in the other, rolling his eyes at me. "I'm going now. Lock me out. Don't forget to record that programme."

M

Thursday 22nd May
1 hour 52 minutes to go

Life demands attention everywhere.

From the moment of birth, pink and screaming, eyes accosted by bright white hospital lighting, the shock of the cold air on your skin. Your skin itself, so new, so tender, reflecting the light back at you, responding to your kick, the very movement of your foot so strange out here. So sudden and violent after the warm resistance in your fluid filled growth chamber. Even then, you are so occupied with that first crucial gasp, the air inflating your lungs, blood busily carrying it to your brand new organs, drinking it in. Even then there are faces, voices, nurses, hands measuring, weighing, soothing, caressing. And for the first, bewildering months of life there are targets to meet, skills to master. First smiles, first words, first solids, first steps. You have to hold a knife and fork and wield them correctly, have to breathe and eat simultaneously, but without opening your mouth. You have to learn to time the needs of your body so that they match with social niceties and available facilities. Everything at the same time as everything else.

When I first came home, to recover from my *illness*, I was a lump of something which plodded, aimlessly around the house. I sat still for hours, staring at nothing, losing time. But you can't afford to do that. It's what I did in my office for six, featureless months. It's what nearly bankrupted my company, it was punishable by exile.

Exile can mean *Outcast, Banishment* or *Expel*. It can also mean *Separate*. I liked exile. The first few weeks contained nothing. Time slowed a little, but it didn't stop. And the more it slowed inside, the faster it went outside, until the movement through the lines was indistinguishable, a blur moving too fast for my eyes to focus on it. But I couldn't ignore it forever. There is no suspension, no pause button, no mute. My wife went out to work. She came back. Gradually, her patience grew thinner, her vocal chords tighter. She was alone in this furious accelerating existence. I loved my wife. I love her still.

"I'll help," I said. "I'll do the fridge."

She looked at me oddly.

For a few days, I had been watching the fridge. It's a solid, reassuring block on the outside. But inside, it is changing constantly. The trick, I realised, was to grasp at existence, to order it so that it can be held in one hand.

I began with the fridge. I made a list of everything in it. I noted how much there was of each item, and in which position it sat on which shelf. I re-read my inventory. I allowed myself to relax. I would conquer this madness one item at a time. But the contents of the fridge kept changing. Things moved, things grew smaller, things ran out. I was angry. I asked my wife to stop changing things. She pointed out, with cold patience, that if she did that, we wouldn't eat. You have to eat to exist. You have to keep on eating.

"Perhaps," said my wife, "you need a different system."

I updated my list. I kept track of the contents. I rated items according to importance. I devised a complex spreadsheet system which warned me when we needed supplies. I don't know how long I needed to do that, before one day I realised the system had grown out of date. And then realised I didn't mind any longer.

You can control other things with a bit of effort. But you, yourself, are not a constant. Everything changes. Nothing stays the same. That's what you don't realise when you first come, screaming, into existence.

That the world is only going to get faster.

Cath

Later the same evening
27th March
Four Days to submission

I set the table up exactly. I can't immediately find my laptop so I work on perfecting the other details. I put some music on, light some candles and some incense. I will have to open the windows later. Patrick hates the smell of burning incense. But for now I want it - and I am allowing myself to have it. I am giddy with the pleasure of delayed euphoria. I make a pot of coffee, place it carefully beside my notes. I still can't find the laptop but I pull the half bottle of champagne from my bag. Bought for this purpose, I have kept it hidden. Patrick knows nothing of it. I don't even intend to drop in on Alice. This moment must be, needs to be, all mine. I slip the bottle into the freezer to make it cold quickly. It's a half bottle because it isn't meant to be shared. I take a step back and look at everything. I have even prepared a makeshift ice bucket for the wine, when it's time. I have planned this carefully. It has to be perfect.

All I need is the laptop. Everything is saved on there. It's all ready. Even the email to the publisher is prepared and waiting in my drafts folder. Just that final, ceremonial sentence and it's done. It's finished. Attach and send.

I must have put the computer in the bedroom, which confuses me because I'm sure I used it last in the lounge. I look in my bedside table, in the wardrobe, on the desk. Then I try the floor by my bedside, my other handbag, Patrick's bedside. Panicking a little, I check the duvet, the laundry basket, under the mattress.

I walk back into the lounge. I go through it carefully, lifting things, moving things, checking underneath furniture. The lounge is cluttered with dust blankets and piled up furniture and paint. The rolled up carpets remain in the corners, damp and sour, Patrick still saving them in the hope he might get some kind of compensation. Alice's flat is almost back to normal already, though I think she took out a big loan on top of her mortgage to pay for it. For a sudden, wild moment it occurs to me that she needs a lodger and I entertain a brief fantasy of moving in. I chase it away guiltily.

The laptop is not in the lounge.

I abandon logic. I check the kitchen and the bathroom. I try the door to the utility cupboard but it seems to be jammed. I have been biting my lips so they feel sore and swollen and I am dusty from scrabbling about on the recently flooded floors. My heart is thumping in my rib cage and there is a cold hard lump in my throat. I force myself to think calmly. I don't like to think that Patrick is right about the builders. But the thought makes me wonder, suddenly, about that jammed utility cupboard.

I try the door again. It doesn't move.

"You need to be a bit more careful, Cath. There are builders in the house. Just be a bit sensible, OK? Try not to leave your stuff around."

I grab the phone and dial Patrick's number. His recorded voice invites me to leave a message. It's studied in its professional joviality. I was there when he got the new phone and recorded it. I think it was the seventh version. "Patrick, it's Cath. I can't find my laptop. Did you lock it away by any chance? Maybe in the utility cupboard? Do you know where the key is? Um....OK, well if you could ring me back soon... to let me I know it's safe. That would be great. Hope you're... hope you're having fun...um. OK. Bye."

He is probably still travelling. I am a jabbering idiot, fat and swollen, flapping about in the house like a lost fish. I wait fifteen agonising minutes. Then I call him again. I get the answer phone again. I don't leave a message.

After an hour, in which I have gradually abandoned all dignity, and called Patrick no less than eight separate times, sometimes leaving other messages, I finally admit defeat. I pour the cold coffee down the sink. I turn off the CD. I blow out the candles. The flat resounds with silence. I have a momentary sanity, in which I cross the corridor on impulse and knock on Alice's door. There is equal silence. She must be out, or away. I go back to the flat. I pour the melted ice from the ice bucket into the sink.

I stand. I am filled with crushing disappointment. I am a useless creature without my laptop. I don't have everything saved anywhere else and there is a horrible cold dread in the pit of my stomach that Patrick has not moved it and that really, it is gone forever.

I stand there and I make myself listen to Patrick's voice in my head. I should have backed my work up somewhere.

I should have taken more care of my laptop. I should have written that last sentence when I finished the rest of it and sent it to the publishers as soon as it was finished, not waited for some pathetic, finalisation ceremony all on my own.

A familiar frustration courses through me. I want to take my blurred body, my blotchy skin and above all, the stupid, blundering contents of my head and I want to run the whole package at top speed into the wall. I press my fingernails into my palms. I concentrate hard on pressing, I aim to draw blood. But I can't even manage to successfully do that. I look around the kitchen for something, anything. I pull open the freezer. I push the palms of my hands directly onto the sharp, shocking cold of the ice at the back. I hold them there.

It burns.

"Cath," Patrick is fond of telling strangers, *"is seriously prone to accidents."*

I look at my palms. They are bright red. I hesitate and then I put them back.

"Aren't you, Cath? You always seem to be doing something. Tripping up, banging your head, you're a walking disaster zone!"

I press my palms into the back of the freezer until the ice begins to pool at my feet.

Later, I drain the contents of the champagne straight out of the bottle. It was a stupid idea anyway. The bubbles, drunk with punishing speed, prick painfully at the back of my throat and fizz through my nose. I gasp. I make myself keep gulping until the bottle is empty and my throat is sore, my head spinning. Then I pick up the phone and order a takeaway. I put the TV on quite loudly to cover the absence of other voices and when the doorbell rings I shout to my imagined accomplices, "Don't worry guys, I'll get it. We can sort the money out later."

I am adept at pretending.

I take the food and dump it all into the largest bowl I can find and I pick up a spoon. I put it down on the table where my evening began and I silence the still gabbling TV.

The room is damp. And very empty.

Brandon Homes

To: info@brandonhomes.com
From: Alice.Crayer@yahoo.co.uk
Subject: **URGENT**

Dear Sirs,
Despite several attempts to contact your offices, including numerous phone calls and three emails (attached), I have still not received a response from you. I am writing again in the hope that you have now had time to consider my position.

Is this interesting? Are you enjoying reading my emails?

It must be fascinating for you.

Hello.

Hello?

Alice

A Long Time Ago

"Who's that? Looks like a smaller you."

Tabby, inevitably, reached ten and three quarters and the state demanded that she continue her schooling at secondary school. She, and the other thirty ten and three quarter year olds in her class at Belmore Juniors were scooped up by their respective families and descended on the town centre. They swarmed on the one sanctioned school uniform shop, and the countless Marks & Spencers and BHS Stores and other such helpful purveyors of regulation non-descript navy blue clothing. They were herded around like bewildered sheep by countless hassled parents, talking constantly to the shop keepers, to the children, to each other.

"Come on now, we haven't got much time."

"That'll do – he'll grow into it."

"Oh no – shoes are a nightmare, we never can get anything to fit."

Tabby was obedient to the point of catatonia. She followed or was pushed, she was dragged through crowds of thrusting elbows, she squeezed into lifts, she climbed up stationary escalators. She looked out at the world with huge eyes as usual, and maybe it is only now that I notice it, but was that growing apprehension in them? Maybe I did notice at the time. Maybe we all should have known even then.

We helped her into numerous navy blue jumpers. We laughed with callous familial jocularity as each one seemed huger than the other, each *XX Small* dwarfing her tiny frame, each set of sleeves a little bit closer to dragging on the floor. She laughed with us, nervously. She peeped out sideways to see if anyone was watching. There were a lot of other children in the changing rooms. There were Mothers, everywhere, briskly, casually, yanking down trousers and forcing fumbling feet into yet another pair. There were children everywhere, arms up, jumpers over their heads, a moment of blessed anonymity, face covered, chest or knickers bared. Our Mother was no exception, and I had been through the same experience myself two years earlier. I stood in front of Tabby and spread my arms and legs as far apart as I could to cover her up. When another child, momentarily relieved from her own routine exposure, looked over and laughed at Tabby's latest skirt, falling down as soon as it was zipped up and buttoned, I turned round to face her and gave her the fiercest, the most threatening stare I could possibly manage. She turned away and sniffled. Tabby looked at the floor. Did she expect it? Did Tabby know, if not the rest of us?

She was tiny for her age. Tiny and bony. Now she was older it had become more obvious, and in the last year or so people had started to stare. She had a way of holding her head on one side, like a bird. The nodding habit had become a compulsion. She blushed bright red when people looked at her. She stuttered when she spoke.

"It's going to be fun now, in big school," we said. "Just think of all the new friends you can make!"

We tried on the jogging bottoms and T-shirts in the fashion shops. They wouldn't fit. In the end we purchased the regulation gym kit, the one no one else would be wearing, the one that could be more easily adjusted to fit her.

"It's great in the gym hall," I said. "They've got a proper climbing wall and everything – and basketball hoops." She was terrible at sports.

"These will be nice and hard wearing," said our Mother.

We didn't have a lot of money left by the time we'd bought everything. Tabby's school bag from the junior school was still in one piece, so it was decided that she would simply keep using that till we could replace it. It was bright pink and had My Little Ponies on it.

"You could put stickers over it," I said. "I've got some cool ones."

"That will ruin it," said our Mother, "I'm sure lots of people will have these."

She nodded silently, unconvinced and compliant. I don't think junior school had been especially comfortable. Certainly her stutter had got worse after Infants.

I thought of our school, of the chewing gum and non-regulation sports jackets, the graffiti and the shouting. I thought of the fun I had racing after footballs, or throwing offensive notes in paper airplanes to my classmates. I thought of the smokers in the toilets, and the things which went on in the gap behind the shed. I thought of the shrieking, giddy pleasure in the yelling of swear words, in the leaping in puddles. I thought of the crowds of chanting children, 'Fight, fight, fight,' gathered, excited around a pair of flailing fourth years, until the teachers broke it up. Of the rumours afterwards. The tales of Jonny Keating being caught with cocaine or of Jennifer Lawson having gone all the way with Mike Benson in the toilets. I thought of the mixed rugby sessions, the exhilarated passion for the winning, the fevered, if short-lived hatred for the team member who missed a try.

We were sending her out there like a lamb to the slaughter.

M

Thursday 22nd May
1 hour and 48 minutes to go

I will have to go out. There is no milk in the fridge.

I look outside. Still whirling past in the thin sliver of blind at my window. Advertising, newsflashes, corporate jargon, pinstripes. Screams of fun, screams of pain. Shrieks of fear, shrieks of laughter. Two girls in short skirts and tight T-shirts. One makes you a lucky man, the other a paedophile. It is increasingly difficult to tell one from the other. We are heroes in wartime and mass murderers outside of it. The coin donated to the homeless on a freezing winter's day can be spent acceptably on junk food but not on alcohol. The lines of life are not simply a little ambiguous. They have been drawn by us in the first place. They might not even exist.

The word *outside* can mean *exterior*, *slight*, *faint* and *remote*. None of those possible interpretations sound good. I don't think I want to go there.

Life is like a thesaurus. My concern is we might not have all of the pages.

Alice

A Long Time Ago

It took about three weeks for her to become more or less wordless. In those three weeks, every day I watched her. I craned my neck in assembly, I looked for her out of the window when we were in English and she was in rounders, I spent break times scouring the playgrounds, searching for her. I spent every single day pointlessly watching. Watching her. Watching out for her. It didn't make any difference. Schools are full of little hiding holes, physical or otherwise, little knots in the structure where things can be done, things can be said, strikes can be made.

Every evening I walked her home. Slightly strained, but still nodding, still forcing a smile out. Missing her lunchbox, or her bag, something taped to her cardigan. I chatted brightly, then asked questions, then tried to bully it out of her. She never told me anything. She never complained. She made excuses, or she simply didn't answer.

After a while I was wordless too.

Cath

Friday 28th March
Three days to Submission

The flat is full of empty spaces. Cupboards hanging open, contents across the floor. I have looked in our bed, felt across the top of high kitchen cupboards, even, in a moment of half hysterical mirthlessness, checked inside the kettle. I have to tiptoe like a tight rope artist in the tiny spaces on the floor between the spilled and excavated contents of boxes, shelves, cupboards, bags. The only things I haven't moved are the speakers, the TV and the DVD player. They are Patrick's devices. They feel forbidden and unfriendly. And, despite my hopeless search in the kettle, I know there is no way my laptop can be inside them.

I have been searching since five o' clock this morning. I am wired so tightly I feel as though I might snap into pieces at any moment, broken bits of bone flying out across the rooms, smashing the crockery laid out on the floorboards. The flat is so full of stuff I can barely move in it. And yet the air seems full of nothing but emptiness. All I can see are the insides of emptied storage, the aching absence of my laptop. It is a loss that catches in my throat continually, choking my airways in alternating panic and bitter disappointment. I have not lost my laptop. I have lost my chance.

By the time the day has passed and the night grown dark and, finally, I fall into bed, the flat is spotless. I have emptied and restacked every cupboard. I am exhausted and defeated, and my shoulders and wrists ache from trying, continually, to force the utility cupboard door. The builders are not here today and the flat is only made emptier by the presence of me in it.

I lie, spent, eyes dry, staring up at the ceiling, experimenting with possible scenarios which might mean I still have a chance of sending my manuscript in time to meet the publisher's deadline. I remember, in agonising detail, every second of that original conversation. It used to be my triumph, I have recalled and rehearsed each moment of that contract for months, it has warmed me in every icy moment, it has been my hope. The way I was Patrick's. The way Patrick, still, so cruelly, is mine.

Now each repetition, each stress on the importance of submission by that crucial date, of that crucial first draft, floats through the musty air to confront me with the horrible realisation that it is quite possible that all is lost. I cringe, seeing my own flushed face in the darkness, my eager assurances that I would, that I could easily, meet that deadline. That one requirement.

I don't sleep.

Katie Hall-May

Alice

Friday 28th March
Second half of the spring Term

School, today, is not going well. They are a bunch of sixty fourteen year olds. Sixty is too many. I said this to the head-teacher at the outset, but this is a school I haven't been to before and I wasn't prepared for what I might have to do battle on. She is a brisk, tight-lipped fifty year old with a starchy blonde bob. She speaks as though she's expecting a challenge, so she clatters out her sentences in rapid fire like some ancient, merciless typewriter in the assumption that no challenger can find a gap to stick the wedge into.

"We like to do the whole year group in one go, so you'll have sixty of them. It should be fine. I'm going to take the LSAs out to do some maths work with the bottom class. I don't think that class are ready for sex education yet. We'll cover it with them briefly later in the year."

I wonder when the bottom class is going to be considered "ready" for sex education. When they are pregnant perhaps? Or worse? She clip clopped off in her high heels before I could answer. It wouldn't have done any good. You have to go in prepared, and I wasn't.

I survey my crowd of defensive faces. A good proportion of them look back at me with little insolent smiles. They mask the fear, not of this session but other things. Usually I see that. Today, when I open the session I accidentally drop something out of my bag, to barely stifled scorn which ripples and grows as it catches on through the crowd. Sixty is far too many. Somehow my humour, reserved for such occasions, and guaranteed to break down defences, deserts me and, thrown off balance, I screw up the first part of my speech.

"Hi," I say, "my name is Miss Crayer."

They instantly christen me "Crapper".

Twenty minutes later I am no closer to reaching a rapport. In fact I am dangerously close to enmity. I am pitting myself against them, getting one up on them. I am alarmingly unbothered about what kind of a mess these little clusters of hairspray and puberty might make of their sex lives.

"Miss?"

A tall girl, a half smile, dyed black hair and a nose ring. She is a ring leader of sorts. I can tell it in her posture. Something in me bypasses my sympathy. The impulse to empathise simply isn't there. I can't help it. Instinctively, I dislike her.

"Yes?"

"When is lunch?"

A chorus of giggles. They escalate rapidly into full scale laughter, then a buzz of chatter. Instinct, the other one, the professionally learned one, kicks in and I make myself laugh with them.

"Sweetheart, I don't go to this school – you do. I don't know when lunch is. Actually though – if you could tell me I would be grateful, I'm starving. Is the canteen any good?"

It's still not quite right – I can't remove the final traces of gritted teeth from my tone, but it has softened it slightly. There is a renewed wave of giggling but a few of them are answering, grinning, genuine.

"It's crap, Miss."

"Yeah, if you like burned baked beans then it's great."

"Why, you gonna come and sit with us Miss? Miss? Are you, like, trying to be one of us?"

She is too clever. For her own good. She is going to be so clever she will cut herself on the edge of her own knife and no one who matters, no one who will employ her or potentially cut her a break, is going to trust her. Right now she is too clever for *my* good.

"It's crap, Miss Crapper."

I have lost them.

All around the room I can see it. Girls sniggering, girls laughing, girls whispering, a wall of sound too loud for me to penetrate. My professional senses know it is lost. I can pull them back to order but I will not make them care.

Sex, in my voice, in my lesson today, will be a dull, uninviting boring thing, and I won't be able to help it, and they won't believe it. Nothing I say will matter now. I can feel it in my bones. I can almost smell it. That acid whiff.

It has been a long time since I last caught it. The scent of hollow victory. The stench of school.

Pencil sharpenings.

Hair.

Vomit.

Dust.

Blood.

Cath

Saturday 29th March
Two days to Submission

After a night in which I seem simply to have waited, stiffly, for the first sign of daylight, I get up with the dawn chorus. Birds sing heedlessly into the bleak replication of the previous day which I immediately throw myself back into. I go through every inch of the house again. I pick up every cushion, I open every drawer, every cupboard, and every box. The laptop is no more there than it was when I looked 12 hours ago.

I punctuate this with calls to Patrick's mobile. It's off. Of course it is. This is an offsite meeting held annually by his work and he gets incredibly stressed about it every time. He does not turn his personal mobile on when he is at work, it's a rule he has. And rules, for Patrick, are non-negotiable, neither by him nor anyone else. Even so, I suspect the offsite contains plenty of drinking and dining, when he could, potentially, turn his phone on. But he won't. I still call him four times in three hours. Every time, I leave a message.

Several times I hold my phone in my hands, debating whether to report the lost laptop to the police. A few times I go as far as to look up the local number and even to dial it. But I never press 'call'. I don't know how to explain that the laptop is lost, that there are no signs of a break in, that there is one cupboard I haven't looked in because that cupboard is locked and I have not been provided with a key by my partner. And I know, deep down, that this is Patrick's New Flat. I cannot bring myself to call the police to it.

When, at lunchtime, I get in the car and drive the hour's journey to work, I know in my heart that I have finally given up. I haven't been to the university for months. When I moved to East Grinstead with Patrick I put distance of several different kinds between myself and the youthful, buzzing, shared office with which I used to feel such an affinity, so long ago. When I no longer had teaching hours I devoted myself to research. And somehow, it seemed more and more difficult to go in. That place, full of clatter and clutter and bright young minds seemed, somehow, to get further and further away until I realised I no longer believed I belonged. I worked at home on my research, I threw myself into my article, I pinned everything on one tiny hope and one publisher. Eventually it wasn't just difficult to go to work. It was difficult to leave the flat at all.

The office is empty, and uncharacteristically still. I walk to my desk with the lights flickering on with my movement. I blaze a forlorn trail to my desk and my lockers, and finally to the cupboard where I know there is a spare laptop for staff use. No one uses it, I don't believe many people even know it is there and it is a heavy, slow machine, out of date and out of use. I stand there for a moment, holding it in my arms and it feels, overwhelmingly, like a metaphor for me.

My own laptop, containing the only recent copy of my article, and the culmination of countless hours of work and countless moments of misplaced hope - is not here. But of course I knew that. I tried anyway, but I knew. It doesn't belong here and neither do I. I am not a bright young thing. I am here out of turn and out of place.

When I walk back out with the spare laptop it feels like stealing. I spend a panicky few minutes explaining to the porter, who is uninterested and impatient for me to leave again. He didn't recognise me when I arrived, and my staff pass, corrupted or just out of practice, didn't work on the turnstiles so he had to get up to admit me.

And when I get back in the car and pull away I feel as though the building physically sighs with relief.

Alice

Friday 28th March
Six Weeks Since the Flood

"Hi, my name is Alice Crayer. Yes ... No, I'm calling about a flood in my flat ... No, not now ... well the thing is ... oh. Well, will he be in later? ... OK ... It's just that ... No ...I have left others ... Emails. And phone messages ... Yes ... Recently ... Oh, several ... You haven't? I did send - ... no, of course ... well yes, but ... Ok well- ... I - ... thank you for your time."

I put the phone down. I swear viciously. Then I apologise for God. Assuming He, at least, is listening.

M

Thursday 22nd May
1 hour and 43 minutes to go

Outside is a place I have to go. I know this. And I have been there before. Even since this strange limbo, this *unwell*. I have to get milk because I love my wife and because I have put her through hell. I have put her through a cold and lonely hell and I know that now she is hopeful. She, the doctor, even those heroic worker ants left behind in my offices. They have begun to send me some 'light work' home. But I don't know which definition they are using.

Light can mean *Bright, Nimble, Easy, Buoyant, Fluffy, Frothy, Flimsy, Gentle, Pale, Blithe, Frivolous* or *Muted*.

I think my favourite would be *nimble*. The last thing I want is *muted*. *Muted* is the sound that the world makes through my carefully closed windows, my heavy curtains, which I shut every day as soon as my wife leaves the house. And open again, blinking, before she returns. *Muted* is an ominous sound, of chaos held only just at bay. Outside is scratching at my windows, clamouring to seep in through the cracks. It moves too fast to focus on it. I know. I've been out there. And it's a different place now to the one I went out in before I was *unwell*.

The first time I went Out, I was so tense I could barely move or speak. I was trying to pull everything somehow into order, to mentally prioritise the birds, the billboards, the shop windows, the cars, the occupants of the cars, the car interior, the movement of each wheel, the smell of rubber, the wet brown of the puddle, the grainy dirt within it, the individual garments worn by individual people, all passing each other at speed, yet somehow, so rarely colliding.

It was better the second time. And the third. I tried, as I had been told by my doctor, who seems to be an expert at handling this chaos, to focus just on one thing. On the thing I am doing. Noticing a leaf. Waking down steps. Crossing the road. Buying milk. I could do it then. I could handle Outside. But it worries me. All that information, all that matter left unordered, unprocessed. What happens to all that when nobody looks at it? Does it simply pass by? Does it cease to exist? I think what I am afraid of is that it might gather together, like dust, and form some kind of a monster, rising up to roar and consume us all.

What we need is to get ourselves properly organised. Just think what the human race could do if it just worked together. If it just followed a carefully logical order. We could assign everybody one thing to be doing. One thing to notice, to record and write down. One page, per person, of the mass thesaurus. And then maybe we could find one final route through it.

I have to go out. And buy some milk. To make coffee for my wife because I love her. It is simple. And I have done it before.

But it would be so much nicer to keep it muted.

Cath

Sunday 30ᵗʰ March
One Day To Submission

I sit and stare at the screen. It flickers every now and then, noticeably, and it makes my eyes hurt.

I have been trying since yesterday. I hauled it home, threw it onto the table and opened it and began, almost before I had sat down, to type. There is, on my university account, a very old draft. At some point, perhaps before it became so important, perhaps before I began to feel quite as fearful of leaving the house for the foreign climes of the university office, I had saved a version of the original article, the one I had written for the journal, and been asked to extend and rewrite for a layperson.

I tried adding words here and there, editing hurriedly, trying to transform this raw material into the piece I had become so proud of, by a sort of combination of speed and desperation. But in the end I had to admit the truth - the path by which I had originally written the new article, by abandoning the original and starting from scratch, was the only way back.

So I tried. I know the argument, I know some of the text off by heart. I have read it, loved it, reviewed it and nurtured it daily for months. I have rewritten it twice from scratch. It germinated in me like a secret, illegitimate child. An offspring only of mine.

I remembered the title. And some whole sentences of the opening paragraph, read over and over, so many times. But it wouldn't flow. I had less than two days, from the point I arrived home with the spare work laptop, to recreate a work of art. And something in my brain was hard and lumpy, like a held in sob. Something in my heart wouldn't give me over to it. I scraped and laboured over one paragraph all day. And each time I re-read it, it became more and more clear that it wasn't right. I went to bed well after midnight, dejected and exhausted. Today, I woke up again well before dawn. I have spent most of the day in a flurry, writing feverishly, painfully against the clock. It's now after four in the afternoon. My back aches, my eyes sting, my fat white legs bear the imprint of the chair I have sat on for over twelve hours. There is text on the page. Not enough text. And not good enough. I read it back with a sort of numb depression. There is no hope that this can be sent to the publishers tomorrow. It is smeared with my haste, and it smells of frustration and a solid, stabbing sort of pointlessness. It doesn't read well. I cannot bring myself to submit this. It is not a first draft I would consider worthy potential for publication. It is not a first draft that I would even consider a worthy first draft.

And now I am sitting. Solidly, doggedly, on the chair, still staring at the flickering screen, and knowing, deep down, that I gave it up hours ago. I am sitting, clock ticking, the flat growing colder and darker around me, and I am silently watching something die.

For the millionth time, I summon the last shreds of hope inside me and I walk to the utility cupboard door and I try it.

It's locked. And I realise for the millionth time how stupid, how utterly pointless each action I have taken has been. It can't be in the cupboard, because Patrick would have mentioned it. I know I didn't put it there. And I've looked, ten times over, everywhere else. The laptop is gone. The manuscript is finished. It's over. And it's my fault. All mine. Everything that ever went sour was mine.

I realise I am still tugging, viciously, at the door and then hopelessness swells and rushes over me and I lean my head against the door of the cupboard, sadly, gently, and simultaneously bring my fist down hard on the hardwood of the door. The effort makes me bump my head. I bring my forehead up and turn, numbly to view my hand. It throbs. There is blood on my wrist bone. I rest my head back on the door. I rest my injured hand there too. I leave a small smear of blood on the door. It feels right. It feels fitting that I have bled into this flat. Into this stinking, dusty, dingy flat with its hopeless occupants and its locks to imprison them. With its lies and its gloss and its shallow, false hope. I close my eyes. Memories dance on the inside of my eyelids.

I feel Patrick's hand in mine, back in June last year, the first day we viewed it. He was shaking with excitement.

"This is it Cath! This is it! We're going to own it."

We. Us.

Later, I remember Patrick signing the deeds, that characteristic flourish at the end of his signature. Patrick opening champagne to celebrate. Later still, both of us, standing, in the empty lounge on the concrete, before it even had carpet. Popping champagne and laughing.

Bubbles in my nose. His hands on my hips. His lips on my neck.

"It'll be different here, Cath. It'll be so much better. I can feel it, Cath. We've finally made it."

Bubbles in the bath. My skin. His hands.

I remember early on after we moved in, when we took what he called the 'snagging' tour. His physical slumping with each new defect he forced himself to notice. His corresponding elation when the builders came and fixed it.

I remember the first month. Bubbles in the sink. My hands washing dishes, cooking still fragrant in the kitchen. His hands unexpected, on my waist.

"This is it, Cath. We've made it."

I open my eyes and the memories flicker and die. They smell of blood and they taste of salt.

I am filled, suddenly, with a violent rage. I want to smash this flat. I want to take every last little scrap of it and break it, thoroughly and viciously, into tinier and tinier pieces. I want to scream with all my lungs, to gather all the tear stained, battered pieces of this flat, every sliver of wood, every twisted bit of steel, every fibre of plaster, every last bit of brick dust, and stamp on them with all my solid, lumpen might. I want to take it and grind it into the ground so hard you'd never know it was ever there.

I reach into this rage and I hold it against me. I feel better, somehow, taller. I grasp it, fuel it, and it makes my skin tingle and my sense buzz, like a shot of caffeine or a needle full of drugs. I haven't felt this good in ages. My anger is hot and sharp and heavy, like a weapon. It feels strong. It feels potent.

It feels like power.

I walk back to the laptop. I close the page I am uselessly working on. I open the browser and type 'CEO Brandon Homes'. A list of search results appears. I click on one. It's a link to Companies House. There is a button entitled, 'click here to download documents'. I do. There's a fee but I'm not really caring. I type in my credit card number and I pay them £1. The document is entitled *Annual Return*. It contains share details, registered office and the names and addresses of all the directors. Funny, I thought they could be anonymous nowadays. I read an article recently. They changed the law. Brandon Homes must be a little slow on the uptake.

Name: David Brandon Marsden

Address: 42 Canterbury Drive, Manchester, MA12 3PW

Occupation: Chief Executive Director

I have never heard his name before. But I think he was the founder. He built it. He built this company that built this flat that collapsed and smothered the life we had left in us. David Marsden. David *Brandon* Marsden. So he named it after himself. How arrogant.

I stare at the form for a very long time. The anger is warm and round and comforting. I encircle it, cradle it, hug it in close.

David Brandon Marsden.

It seems like a name I could hate.

M.

Thursday 22nd May
1 hour and 39 minutes to go

Search: Hunt, Explore, Investigate, Rifle, Comb
Hunt: Pursue, Chase, Rummage, Track, Hound
Hound: Wolfhound, Harass, Pester, Persecute, Bully

We don't spend very long in this world. Not enough to know it. To understand. We are not masters of our lives, but tourists. Navigating the world with an incomplete map. Maybe we could know more, could even make sense of our torn thesaurus, if we shared our respective germs of understanding. But we don't speak the same language. We don't know what it is we are supposed to be looking for.

And if we go the wrong way we only lose ourselves deeper.

Cath

Monday 31st March
Six hours to Submission

Patrick gets back at 6 am, grey faced and blood eyed from his course, and, I suspect, from the drinking which occupied much of the weekend. I hear him come in, and despite the fact that I have given up, I can't quite stop myself from leaping, restless, out of bed to ask him. At the door to the bedroom I pause for a moment and collect myself. It doesn't do to corner Patrick. I attempt a casual, loving stroll towards him and open my arms.

"Hello stranger," I say, brightly, "How were the bright lights of Switzerland?"

"Cath," he steps around my open arms, "I've only just got in. I need a shower and some coffee. Then I've got to somehow turn myself back around and get out to work again. Could you please just give me a bit of space?"

Wordless, I let him pass, and stand around in the hallway, uselessly, listening to the reproachful sound of the shower. Eventually I try to be useful and make some coffee. I know he'll eat breakfast at work so I don't bother with food. But I smashed the cafetiere and he doesn't like instant, so I end up hovering about in agonies of indecision, before making him a cup of tea and leaving it like a peace offering on the table, myself forming a nervous backdrop to it twisting my hands in my stomach, then realising and sitting on them.

He comes out of the shower still pulling his shirt on, walks in, takes a swig of tea, grimaces, picks up his bag and heads for the door, checking his watch on the way. I leap up off the chair as though there are ants on it.

"Patrick," I say desperately, "Do you know where my laptop is? Did you move it?"

He pauses, door open, half out in the lobby, and something moves in his face. It is so inexplicable and so conflicting that I cannot begin to interpret it. Even so, encouraged, a tiny shiver of relief begins within me and I continue, quickly, before he can move,

"Only... I couldn't find it last night and I also couldn't open the utility cupboard. So I thought maybe..."

I trail off. The thing on Patrick's face has changed suddenly. It is harder and there is something in it which I still can't place but which reaches for that germ of relief inside me, grasps it and quickly breaks its neck.

"Patrick? Do you...um. Do you know? Or maybe...do you know where the key to the utility cupboard is?"

"Cath." His voice drips, thickly, with exasperation. He doesn't so much speak the words as incorporate them into a heavy sigh, performed in perfect harmony with the movement of him stepping out of the door and letting it swing shut behind him.

"Cath. You didn't remember, did you? You didn't record that programme."

Alice

Monday 31st March
The Last Week of the Spring Term

It is the usual touch and feel session. I am trying to inaugurate year 9 into the ways, wiles and wherefores of various forms of contraceptive. A girl in a short black skirt fumbles with a condom packet. She finally opens it and look questioningly at me.

"Urgh," says her friend, "It's slimy."

Later this particular condom will find itself face down in some puddle on the outskirts of the school grounds, having been blown up, catapulted, filled with water, thrown at passers-by and generally destroyed. Another girl is stretching hers between her fingers. It pings off suddenly and hits her neighbour in the face.

"Eeeergh! That's disgusting" There is a chorus of squealing and giggling and a rash of similar "accidental" condom flights aimed at various class members around the room. Behind me, a pale blonde has stretched hers right over her bunched fist and half way down her arm. It splits.

"Shit," she says.

Katie Hall-May

Brandon Homes

Letter to A. Crayer dated Thursday 3rd April

Dear Miss Crayer,

Thank you for your emails. I note with concern that you have had some trouble with your new Brandon home and am very sorry to hear about the unfortunate flooding incident you have suffered during the recent period of unseasonably inclement weather.

Regrettably, however, I am unable to help you in this regard. You will note in Clause 15 of the contract, that Brandon Homes cannot accept liability for unforeseeable natural events of this type. As the development is situated in an area, which may, in some exceptional circumstances, be liable to flooding, you should find you are covered under your insurance policy, which will normally allow for this, assuming you have informed them of the risk at the outset. I am not, I am afraid, in a position to advise you as to the provisions of your personal insurance policy, but would suggest that you take the matter up with them.

I wish you a long and happy residency in your new home and would be grateful if you would please ensure that any future contact with Brandon Homes is made through your insurers.

Yours sincerely,

(Electronically reproduced, unreadable signature)

D. B. Marsden, CEO"

Cath

Friday 4th April
Four Days After Submission Deadline

I don't call the publishers. I don't call them on Monday. I don't call them on Tuesday. I have spent all week not calling the publishers.

I don't know what I am going to say.

Instead I say nothing. I remain silent. I turn off my phone and I ignore my emails. I stay, as much as possible, away from Patrick, but I don't leave the house. I catch him looking at me strangely once or twice, but he says nothing. Most of the time he goes out himself. I suppose he would prefer to have stayed away on his conference.

I wander around the house. I am aimless and lethargic but I can bring myself to do nothing. I hesitate sometimes near hard surfaces and sharp edges, but I can't find the energy to do anything with them. Instead I simply press, every now and again, against old bruises. Literal and metaphorical. And google *David Brandon Marsden*.

Alice

Saturday 5th April
Start Of The Easter Holidays

I stand, leaning against the wall listening to the tirade from Patrick. The letter he has received from Brandon Homes lies on my table, and he picks it up every now and then, waving it about to illustrate his point.

"'*Regrettably*'. As if they regret it. They don't give a damn. They just sit up there in their bloody paper castles shuffling files about, typing out one sodding letter and then reproducing it for every stupid idiot who buys one of their useless houses and then finds it falls down around their ears. I mean he couldn't even be bothered to sign it himself for fuck's sake. That's just some electronic signature he prepared earlier. He probably hasn't even read it. Probably written by some underpaid minion who gives even less of a toss than he does."

Needless to say, Patrick's letter is identical to mine, the only difference being the address on the envelope. I am not especially surprised by this. Patrick is livid. Also, they have spelled his name wrong.

"I mean, what, do they produce so many of the damn things every day the poor bloody director would get cramp in his poor bloody, little hand if he had to actually lift a finger to put his mark on the bottom?"

"Perhaps his fountain pen ran out," I say, mildly. My mind, as is the case so often these days, is not really in it. I missed the opportunity to mention 'indelible ink'. I couldn't be bothered to suggest anything amusing. I feel weary and worn down. Perhaps it's just the end of term.

There is a short pause in which Patrick looks at me, oddly, opening his mouth to consider a retort, half not hearing me, half not understanding. Into the pause I mutter, "Sorry," and then, somewhat nonsensically, "Yes."

It's the Easter holidays now, I tell myself. I can rest. I will be fine.

"And what really annoys me, what really, really gets my goat is that they can't even shell out fifty bloody quid in a goodwill gesture, and these guys, in fact this guy right here with the illegible electronic scrawl – this guy probably earns double both our combined salaries – and that's just in benefits. I mean, you'd think they could at least, at the *very* least..."

I am not sure whether Patrick actually stops speaking, or if I simply stop listening. Either way, what happens is that we both end up silent, staring at the door.

Cath has entered abruptly, swinging the door on its hinges so hard it bangs on the wall. She neither apologises, nor seems to notice.

"He earns four hundred thousand pounds," she says, "that's his base salary."

She throws a Brandon Homes Annual Report and Accounts onto the table. It lands on the letter, crumpling it at the corner, and with such force it nearly knocks the book I was reading right off the table and onto the floor. The room reverberates with the bang of the door, the sudden crash of the report on the table, and the look on Cath's face. There is an unhealthy sheen to her pale skin, her eyes are red and she is wearing no makeup. She looks, for the first time since I have known her, genuinely unattractive. But it isn't her skin or her hair that is doing it. It's the expression on her face.

"It's probably rounded down, of course. It'll be that plus a few hundred. They don't count the hundreds. If you earn hundreds of thousands, you don't notice a hundred."

She laughs, hollowly. Her lips make the briefest of shapes, vaguely approximating a smile. She snaps the shape away as soon as she draws it.

"I guess you don't notice much of anything. On four hundred thousand."

Cath's hair is scraped back into a vicious looking ponytail at the base of her neck. The combination of the severity of the style, and the fact that it seems, if not quite greasy, at least not newly shampooed, means that her usually rather jubilant, disobedient mane looks somehow defeated. Like an animal tamed by cruelty. Like Cath herself. Except this, I realise, is what we are surprised by. Cath looks odd, unlike herself. And she doesn't look tame. I try to remember, with a flash of guilt, how long it has been since the last time I saw her.

If she can feel the atmosphere she has so shockingly created, she doesn't respond to it. We stand, frozen, mouths open, watching. Into the silence, tight voiced and grim faced, Cath continues speaking.

"In bonuses and benefits there's a further five hundred and seventeen thousand, seven hundred and eighty two. That's on top of his base salary."

There is a shiver of recognition inside me. Something in Cath's eyes stares out into mine. Something I've never stood and looked into before. Not in Cath. Not in anyone. A deep, surging anger, frustrated and sore. The kind that burns and stings inside you, like a spark you intend to fire out like a rocket but which, inexplicably, you keep holding, keep stoking. The kind that only grows redder and rawer and sorer. The kind that you scratch at and pick at and pull at. Until finally, you become it. It is all there is left. I have never looked out at it before. But I've felt it.

"So it's not quite a million pounds a year. But nearly."

She looks at us expectantly. I realise, suddenly, that it is imperative that we respond. That it is crucial that somebody *must* say something. Right now. I look into Cath's pale, set face, arrange mine into as casual a mixture of outrage and wry amusement that I can muster, and stride across the room to join her.

"They're just such *bastards*, aren't they?"

I say it lightly, conversationally, the same way I might comment on the state of the weather. Or the bedroom antics of a minor politician. I say it as I take her arm and guide her, gently, strollingly, over to a chair, and then perch on the arm of it.

"Impressive that you got their Annual Report. Don't know if I could even be bothered. I can barely be arsed to buy a newspaper."

Whether it is the praise, the support, or the profanity, I don't know. I may have felt Cath's anger. But I've never known how to solve it. But I watch her face relax, even smile a little, the hard line of her jaw soften.

"Oh I don't read newspapers either," she says, and if her tone hasn't quite matched my careful levity, it is certainly getting there.

"Oh I know," I say, "I mean they're just... *so. Boring.* Who *cares* if Bryony Whats-her-face has had a boob job?"

"*Has* she?" says Patrick.

"Or the cabinet's had another completely random reshuffle and some more really dull people are in charge of some more really pointless things."

Cath is giggling. Her body melts a little into the back of the seat cushion.

"Or if the minister of agriculture got caught doing it on video with some girl he got to dress up as a milkmaid," she says.

There is a pause.

"Actually," I say, "that IS quite interesting."

And suddenly we are all laughing. Patrick, standing by the table, hands itching to pick up the Brandon Homes report again, me hyper aware and watchful, feeling the creping warnings in my brain and somehow, valiantly trying to ignore them. And she, flushed and slightly feverish, giggling a little too violently so that the chair shakes and nearly knocks me, clown-like, off my perch.

Thank God, I think, and then – *Really, God, thank you.*

Patrick asks whether the video is set in a cow shed.

Cath says, if it is, she feels sorry for the cows.

I wonder whether the apparently random assignment of politicians to causes is actually based on their sexual proclivities.

"But," says Cath, splutteringly, "how would they *know?*"

"Oh please, Cath," says Patrick, "you are *soooo* innocent."

"Yeah, Cath," I say, in mock amazement, "how could you not know? It's all part of the selection process."

"God," says Patrick comically, sending Cath into fits of hysterical giggles again. "Just imagine that."

And more to the point, God, I think, watching the high spots of colour on Cath's cheeks, *whatever's going on, just sort it out.*

What I don't say is that I don't really want to have to deal with it. That I don't want to be responsible for someone else's mental wellbeing. Not again. That I've seen it and done it and I don't want to go back there. And I wasn't exactly successful the first time. And I feel a sharp pang which cuts me so deep and so fast I gasp with the impact of it. Now, giggling with nervous hysteria, once again so eager to please, Cath reminds me of Tabby more than ever. My gasp is lost in the general noise.

I don't want to think about it, I tell myself fiercely. I don't want to get involved with it. I don't want anything to do with it.

"I'd rather not imagine that," says Cath, "but thanks for the image."

I try hard not to notice that I have a sudden and desperate urge to get rid of them. Both of them. Out of my flat.

"Cup of tea?" I say into the now subsiding laughter.

I flick the kettle on without listening to whatever the response is. When I have finished clinking about, unnecessarily, with cups and cupboards and teaspoons and bags, the atmosphere in the lounge is subdued again.

Patrick is back in his stride. He thumbs through the Report and Accounts on the table, runs his finger down the names on the page headed Board of Directors' Remuneration.

"Well he's definitely going to retire on millions. Sitting in his mansion sipping champagne. *He's* not going hungry. *He'll* be fine"

"Fat cat," I say, distractedly.

"Exactly!" says Patrick, and takes a breath.

"People are feral," says Cath. And then, "People are animals."

Cath

Wednesday 16th April
Over Two Weeks After Submission Deadline

I call the publishers.

I tell them the article is lost.

I tell them I can't meet their deadline.

They express sympathy. They tell me that they are very sorry, but they cannot wait indefinitely for a new article. They explain that the publication timetable was very tight, and that my article was not essential, and so they have already begun the process of taking the rest of the compilation to print.

I thank them for their time,

I tell them I understand their position.

I do not tell them that the article, to me, was essential.

I do not tell them that I have not, for days now, even tried to look for my laptop.

I do not tell them that I have not, for days now, really bothered to eat. Or to have a shower.

I do not tell them, because I do not quite know, exactly what I have spent my time doing.

Instead, I only apologise, numbly.

I wish them a happy Easter.

And hang up.

Katie Hall-May

Alice

The Early Hours of Easter Sunday, 20th April
And Somewhere Before

I lie in bed, caught in that shadow world between sleep and waking. I haven't seen Cath for a few days but I am sure now that it is she who has triggered it. Something in her mannerisms, something in her face, brings my careful blockades crashing down and Tabby stumbling into the forefront of my brain. And I can't seem to stop it. For someone so silent, Tabby's voice is alarmingly insistent in my mind. It summons me, demands my attention. It tells me her story in aching detail, it fills in spaces in the narrative, adds colour in those places where her pain was only ever a blurry shape to me. I never knew how it was for her, exactly. She never told me. I knew better than to ask. And now, years later, I presume to imagine it.

There are three of them and I should have turned back and I didn't. And they are sitting, drinking on the swings that I wanted to swing on and they are in my year but they are bigger than me and they are tougher. My mind is howling at me, screaming to turn round, to go back, to do something, but I stand like an imbecile and even now as I am standing, I see them seeing me and they nudge each other and grin. I have to move. I have to move now and turn tail and run and instead I am standing here, too stupid to go anywhere. *It's probably pointless. It will happen anyway. It will happen tomorrow. Or it will happen the next day.*

"Oh well, look who it is! It's little twiglet."

"Awww, did the little baby want to play on the swings?"

I did actually. I actually did. Somehow, ridiculously, it is only now that I find the will from somewhere to move my limbs but I only manage a pathetic stumble backwards and it is the cue they were waiting for.

"What's wrong, twiglet? Running away?"

In the chorus of their voices I feel my feet sinking backwards into something soft and sludgy. The large patch of mud at the corner of the playground. The one that always seems to be there.

"Whoops a daisy!"

"That's a lovely outfit, twiggy – wouldn't want it to get dirty."

They have surrounded me. Their laughter is high and harsh and it stings my ears and I want to join it. I want to be one of them.

"So what's your real name, twiglet?"

"Yeah, come on, don't be shy, tell us your name."

I keep my lips firmly closed. The waiting tears make them quiver.

"Oh, that's not very friendly – only asked you your name, didn't we?"

"Yeah. Come on, twiglet. It's not a hard question. Tell us your name"

I look into their grinning faces and my mouth, my useless, treacherous mouth ignores the shouting inside my head and I say,

"T...Tab...mb..."

"Mb?" They are almost hysterical with scorn. "What's an 'mb'?"

I do not try again. It doesn't matter. It doesn't take long before I am sinking, still fighting to keep from sobbing, one knee, then the other, into the mud patch until I am kneeling there, sniffling, obeying blindly their laughing instructions – one hand, then the other until I am down on all fours, panting and hiccupping in the mud. They toss their heads and laugh and casually leave. They have not, at any point, even touched me. They didn't have to move a finger. They don't really have to try any more.

I stay there for a while. I hear them go and I just can't be bothered to make the effort to get up.

And I think, when they made me, they didn't do it properly. They made my voice all screwed up and my body all scrawny, and then, just to make it especially impossible, they gave me the most difficult name in all the world to pronounce. 'Tabitha Crayer.' All plosives and fricatives.

And one day somebody is going to injure me properly and if anyone bothers to come afterwards to rescue me, I won't even be able to tell them my name.

I shake my head. I shake away the fantasy and the accompanying, creeping feeling which pervades in the wake of it. I stand up, feel the chill air on my clammy bare skin and cover it, instantly with a pulled on dressing gown.

It's late, but I don't want to go to sleep now. I pad into the kitchen and flick on the kettle.

Memories pour into my mind, uninvited, chasing each other in their eagerness to invade. I sigh even as I try to push them away but, now, at least, the memories are mine. The view of the house from upside down on the climbing frame. The passwords to skip levels of ancient computer games written carefully in our best handwriting in a battered old exercise book. Pirate ship sails made out of old living room curtains. Plasticine creatures, hers always so much more lifelike. The delicious, shocking cold of the leafy water in the old blow up paddling pool, riddled with punctures, patched and re-patched. Wet footprints all over the garden path.

I shake my head again and the images flash and flee but now new ones chase them and these ones have sound.

Adult voices, calling us in from the garden. Her clean face and my dirty one. My Mother, exasperated.

My own voice now, high and breathless and excited, telling stories across the dinner table. My Father saying, "Alice, settle down."

"Yes sweetheart. Just eat your dinner. Let your sister talk."

Her silence.

"There you go, darling, now you can get a word in edgeways." Their encouraging smiles. Her look of panic. The reluctant, fleeing, unformed words catching and blocking in her windpipe. The almost physical ache in my own head, all those words so ready to escape, so eager to be said, so many stories, so desperate to be told. Battling silently to keep them in against the sound of awkward, scraping cutlery. An age passing and then my mouth losing the battle.

"So anyway – what happened was–"

"-Alice – you talk too much." My Mother.

With a gargantuan effort I awake to the present, move myself physically. The kettle boils. I pour it over a several heaped spoons of hot chocolate powder. And some sugar for good measure. It bubbles. Lumps of powder, miraculously dry, bob to the surface. I crush them viciously against the side of the mug.

In my cupboard, there is a picture of a little girl with hazel eyes.

She is gone. I will not think about her.

Perhaps now it's me who cannot say her name.

Cath

Wednesday 23rd April
Nearly One Month After the Submission Deadline

I try the utility cupboard door, in passing.

It opens.

There is a hoover and a mop.

There are some spare towels and a sleeping bag.

There is also my laptop.

M.

Thursday 22nd May
1 Hour And 34 minutes to go

I stand in the middle of the lounge. I rock on my heels but it seems I cannot easily move my feet. There are papers spilling out of my briefcase on the table. There is milk in the corner shop. Just across the road. I need to do something. I am rendered incapable by the need to do something.

Action can mean:
Deed
Exploit
Combat
Lawsuit

Or *War*.

Patrick

Wednesday 23rd April
Home

It comes out of nowhere. One minute I'm sitting on the sofa, surveying our newly put back together lounge and trying to work out where the furniture used to go - what's left of it, and the next she's in there, banging the door on its hinges against the paintwork. She's red in the face and screaming at me, and nothing she says is making sense.

"You...you...just...how *could* you?? I can't believe you would...you *had* it. You fucking...you *had* it."

I have never heard Cath swear. Even she's taken aback. She trails off in shock. But in seconds she's back at it – and I don't know what the hell is going on.

"You took it...and you hid it....and you...I mean....you just...*why?*"

She is asking the last in genuine bewilderment, but right now she knows more than I do. I can't think what would get her this worked up. She's never like this. She's standing over me, and she's bright red from neck to face and shivering with hysteria, or rage – I don't know what. She's actually scaring me. I stand up abruptly. I'm taller than her but it doesn't make me feel any better. It's like she hasn't even noticed. It's like she's possessed.

"Cath," I say, trying to calm her. "Cath, darling, what's up?"

It's a mistake because I never call her darling. I never have. It sets us both back a few seconds and I think maybe it's enough to soften her so I can work out what's happened. But she's staring at me open mouthed.

"Seriously? Patrick...you actually don't know."

She says it flatly. It's not a question and I get a sinking feeling that this is going to be one of those women things where you are supposed to know what you've done and if you don't they won't tell you and then you just can't win and you never could, which I suppose is the point. It ends in the man grovelling for months and then never actually knowing what happened in the first place. But Cath doesn't usually play those games. Cath is sensible. All right, so she's been a bit weird in the last few weeks, but generally she's pretty patient. I mean she's so bloody saintly you can't get a grip. You feel like a lowlife the whole time in comparison and you know every single person you meet shakes your hand thinking, "she could do better".

I pause for a moment. I realise, apart from Alice, that I can't remember the last time we met someone. Not together. In fact I'm not sure I can remember the last time Cath has spoken to anyone else at all. Shit. She must have done. Surely.

"No," I say firmly, trying to get some sort of control into the situation. "Cath, I don't know what's wrong so I suggest that you take a breath, and sit down and then you can tell me what the matter is, calmly."

"*You took my laptop! You hid it and even when I asked where it was ...you didn't tell me...*"

Oh hell, the laptop. I forgot about the laptop.

She shouted with such force her voice broke and now she is trailing off, miserably. She's not shouting anymore and she's about to start crying, which is worse. I feel awful. But I still don't get it.

"Cath, I'm sorry, I moved it a while back and I meant to tell you but I-"

"-and now I lost my publishing contract because I missed the deadline..."

She is fully crying now. Numbly, I put out a hand to her shoulder but she flinches away violently and just stands there, sobbing. Big gasping sobs like she's not getting enough air, and her whole body is shaking and trembling and juddering. She looks crazy. I haven't got a clue what to do. I think about going to get Alice, but I don't know how I'm going to explain to her that I'm not a complete bastard.

I didn't know she had a deadline. I think a while back she might have said something about having a contract for something to do with her research or something, but she never once mentioned a timescale. In fact I don't even know if that was the same thing. I don't think she mentioned it again. I didn't even know she'd finished it. Didn't she have it backed up somewhere?

"Didn't you have it backed up?" I say. "On cloud strorage or your email or..." I trail off. I guess not. She is Cath. Cath is saintly and lovely but she's not exactly practical. You only have to look at the sodding programme she was meant to record which is what started all this.

She just looks at me. I want to recoil physically from the look on her face. It's like she's slapped me. It's like she wants to slap me. I've never seen this. I don't know what I'm supposed to do with it.

"Sit down," I say. Something in the command or in my voice gets through to her and she finally does, perching on the edge of the sofa as far from me as possible and wiping tears and snot and hair off her face with her forearm. She's still crying. It's horrendous. She's not even bothering to sob now, it's like her eyes are just pouring water automatically. She's not even trying to stop it. But at least now she's quieter.

"OK, Cath," I say, trying to keep my voice as level as possible. It wants to shake and I'm not having that. I'll apologise if she wants but I'm not going to join in with this ridiculous hysteria. It's not going to help and I'll lose whatever last shreds of self-respect I still have on me. Living with Cath doesn't leave you with much. She's always the victim, you're always the bastard. She's the victim even when nothing has actually happened. You don't have to touch her, it's there in the maddening defeated look she always gets in her eyes and I want to be sympathetic, I want to be sorry, but at the same time I can't help thinking, 'get a grip'. I mean she's an adult now. She should be able to stand on her own two feet and get on with things by now. Surely. Or grow up and face up to me if I'm really that much of a monster.

Thinking this is riling me up. I take a breath carefully, before I speak again. Because this is the thing. She can scream all she likes but if I lose my temper now, I'm the big baddie. I'm the violent boyfriend, even if I don't lay a finger on her. All her friends, back when she still seemed to have them, hated me on first sight. I see the disbelief in the eyes of strangers, shop assistants, bar staff, anyone who sees me with her. It's not easy, being the one everyone thinks isn't good enough.

"Cath – I didn't know about the publishing thing, OK? Or I knew but I didn't know you were supposed to be submitting it. I really didn't know – you never mentioned...I mean...when was it anyway?"

"End of March?" Now she does have that tone – that rising tone, like the kids and the American sitcoms. It's not unsure though - it's accusatory. End of March. Shit.

"OK. Cath? I'm sorry. OK? I'm sorry. I picked up your laptop because you had left it on the sofa, and the builders were in and I didn't want you to lose it. OK? So I locked it in the cupboard."

She is silent. It's unnerving. There's nothing worse than talking to someone who's silent. She's not saying anything. She's not even looking at me. I'm sorry that she lost her thing - really sorry. But how was I supposed to know, if she didn't tell me? And why didn't she tell me, for heaven's sake? What was I going to do, steal it? Publish it in my own name? My voice is growing crisper to match the sharp edges inside me and to try to convince myself I don't feel like an arsewipe.

"You were in the shower or something. Somewhere. And I had to leave the key somewhere you would find it because I didn't want to shout out where I'd put it or the builders would hear. I didn't want - what's his name? Mike? Or someone to decide they could earn a bit of extra cash on the side. You know, help buy film or something - support their photography business…"

I am trying to make her laugh, raise a smile even but she just gets angry.

"Mike would never take my laptop."

OK. No humour then. Fine. Why did that get a rise out of her? At least she's speaking.

Is she having a thing with Mike?

"All right, well, whatever. Anyway. So I put the key where I knew you'd find it."

She looks at me now. There is curiosity, finally, mixed with the loathing. I pause a little for dramatic effect because I still think this was pretty clever. I was disappointed when she didn't find it. Not just for the missed programme. I thought we could have a laugh about it. You know, a mini treasure hunt for Cath. It's the sort of thing she'd go for. Or it was once.

"I left the key on top of the DVD player. Because I knew then you'd see it, because you were supposed to be recording that thing for me. So you'd see the player and see the key and then you'd work it out from there. You know, like a mini…"

"It was there all the time?"

"Yes…um. Yes. Cath, it was there all the time."

There is a pause. She looks at the floor. I don't know what to say but I'm not sure whether she gets it, so I carry on explaining.

"Because you would have found it, wouldn't you? But then you didn't record it…"

"I didn't record your programme, so I didn't see the key."

Her voice is flat. I can't tell if it's admitting defeat in this argument, or if she's just defeated generally. She does that. I don't remember if she always did. It feels like Cath was probably born defeated. I feel annoyance swell in me. For goodness sake. She needs to toughen up.

"Yes. You didn't record it. So you didn't see the key."

Maybe she wasn't like it always. Not when we first met, anyway. Was she putting on some kind of act to get me? Or did she just start to crumble as soon as we were together? You can't keep doing that though. It's no way to live. She'll realise that if she gets together with Arty Mikey. Even he'll get fed up if she's always a martyr.

She never actually apologised for missing that recording.

"But I asked you," she says, "and you ignored my messages."

"I was away. You know what these things are like, I was working twenty four seven. I wouldn't have time to call you, even if I could get decent reception, which most of the time I couldn't"

And I turned my phone off. I always do when I'm away. She knows that. And God knows I needed a break. I needed a break from *her*. I feel a stab of guilt which I push away angrily. I didn't regret turning my phone off. I didn't miss her. I was relieved to have an excuse to be out of contact.

"Yes but after. You never called back or…"

"For fuck's sake, Cath." I am losing it. I lower my voice again, hastily. Last thing I want is the neighbours any more interested than they probably already are. I bet Alice is having a field day. Thinking up smart comments. "Cath.

I was tired, OK? It was early in the morning and I live with you. I had to get out to go to work. When you asked me I remembered but then I was annoyed because you didn't record the programme for me. If you'd done that, you'd have found the key and then you'd have found your laptop. I meant to send you a text or something from work a bit later, but it slipped my mind. OK? I didn't know it was that important, because you never bloody said. And by the way, it's not normal to leave twenty two messages on someone's phone."

"I…"

"Some of them weren't even five minutes apart. I mean, bloody hell, Cath, that's a bit psychopathic."

"But after that though…"

She trails off. She knows it and I know it. She didn't actually ask me. After that one conversation she didn't ask me again. It was crucial, apparently, and she didn't even ask me. Apart from the twenty two phone messages. And I guess I forgot.

I forgot. I wasn't being cruel. I wasn't trying to punish her. I am sure that I forgot.

"Well, that morning, I asked you straight up and you could have just told me and instead you only went on again about the recording…"

She knows but she's not letting go yet. I'm going to have to spell it out.

"Yes. Get it? That was my clue. I thought at least then you might look at the recorder."

There is a pause.

"It was also your cue to apologise for missing the recording." I say, unable to keep the bitterness out of my tone.

There is another pause.

"Look," I say, realising I am floundering like an idiot, and fighting another impulse to shout in frustration, because I haven't actually done anything wrong. "I didn't know – I had no way of knowing that you had something on that laptop that for some unknown reason you didn't back up. I thought you'd found it. I saw you, afterwards, tapping away on one."

"It was a spare," she says, flatly, "I borrowed it from work."

And then one day, when I needed something out of the cupboard, I unlocked it. I didn't really think much about it.

"I lost my article," she says.

I am losing patience. "Cath, you didn't. OK. You have it now."

"I lost my chance."

I just stand there. I don't know what to say.

"I lost my chance   and it was the only thing I....it was my one....."

She can't vocalise it, whatever it is. I feel utterly spent. I feel useless and crappy and I am angry with her for making me feel this. Damn it, I am angry with her for always making me feel this. Cath is great for listening to people. Or she used to be. When I first met her I could see it, she was everyone's agony aunt. Cath loves to solve someone's problem. She loves to play counsellor. But she can't do anything practical. She can't save a document. She can't remember a recording. And you can't live like that and expect people to run after you, sorting your life out.

"Cath," I say, "I'm sorry about the laptop, OK? But you've got to get with the picture. Get on the same planet as everyone else. Look around a bit. Live a little."

She looks directly at me.

"I think maybe I hate you."

And she's gone. She's up and out of the door and for a moment I think she's gone forever but then I realise she hasn't even put her shoes on. So she'll be back. She'll return later and presumably there'll be some sort of stand-off, or more likely, knowing Cath, she'll pretend it's all fine. She'll apologise in that way she has, looking doe-eyed up at me, like she's being big for saying sorry but she knows it's my fault.

And she leaves me standing in this room where we once drank champagne. Where I thought things were going to be so much better. Before the flood. Before the builders. Before this. There is liquid in my eyes and I gulp it back, somehow, into my throat. I was just beginning to believe things were about to get better. Before the damp and the piles of furniture and the stinking rolls of carpet.

Oh yes. Because everything's always about to get better.

Alice

Wednesday 23rd April
First Half Of The Summer Term

"Suzie Grant's a lezza," says a plump girl with ruined dyed blonde hair and black roots. She has a nose stud which they've let her keep. Good. It's nice when the school system deigns to allow them to express themselves. They spend enough time trying to express each other – we should be encouraging every last vestige of potential individuality. The nose stud is shaped like a tiny skull. Even better. I like this girl. A self-styled hard case. But still. Self-styled. I presume the piercing is one of those which is perpetually 'only just done' and must be kept in to stop the hole re-closing. For a brief moment I remember school when it was something heady and exhilarating. When I ran in the centre of it, shouting.

"Would you get away with behaving like that at home, Alice Crayer?"
　　"No, Miss. That's why I have to do it here."
　　Followed, of course, by the usual detention.

Ah, school. I grin to myself for a moment.
　　"Yeah. And you're a dyke!"
　　"Fuck you."

Homosexuality. It's actually one of my favourite ones. I am supposed to teach tolerance.

"OK," I say to the skull girl. "So how do you know that? Did she tell you?"

"No," she says defensively, "but you can just tell."

"Oh OK," I say mildly, then turn to the second accuser, "so how did you know that *she* was a dyke?"

There is a roar of hilarity at this. I press on. No-one has the wit to make the obvious wisecrack so I make it for them, "Could you just tell?"

"Yeah!" says the second girl, ginning widely. "Yeah I could just tell!"

"Mmm hmmm." I turn to skull girl who is glaring at me. "So, are you a dyke?"

"No!"

"Ahhh." I am thoughtful. "So maybe you *can't* tell?"

There is a flurry of discussion.

"You can't tell," says someone firmly, "no one knows except the person."

"You could ask them."

"Yeah, right. Like they're gonna tell you."

"Good point," I say quickly, "why should they tell you? Do you go round telling people you're straight?" I don't really like the word 'straight' with its implications that anything else is 'bent', but I use it here because it's easier. 'Heterosexual' sounds like some sort of homeopathic remedy.

"No," says a skinny girl with a hole in her tights and bitten black nail varnish, amid giggles.

"Yeah, but you *do* need to know," says skull girl defiantly. She is a little sullen now. I hesitate slightly, listening to her tone. Perhaps that illustration was ill chosen. I thought she could take it. She had the look of a fighter. *Self-styled* though, remember. I curse myself inwardly. She continues. "You need to know because what if they're like, in your changing rooms, and you're getting changed in front of them."

"Euurgh."

"That's disgusting."

"I think I'm gonna puke."

The last voice has a particular ring of sheep-like nastiness that makes *me* nauseous. I pounce on that comment.

"What makes you want to puke? The idea of someone being a lesbian or the idea of you lot getting changed?"

There is laughter. I ride it.

"Because if you think about it – how many of the boys in your class would you actually *like* to see naked?"

More laughter. More euurghs.

"But they *fancy* girls." The skull girl is persistent. She's intelligent. She understands what I'm getting at. But there are some battles she desperately wants to win. And I am sorry, I tell her silently. But I can't let it be this one.

"Are you that irresistible?" I say. "Do you fancy every single man that you come across? Do you hang around in their changing rooms gawping at them?"

It's the killer comment. But I've misjudged this girl. She blushes bright red and looks at the floor and all around her the class erupts.

"Yeah. Pervy Ali!"

"Ali fancies all the boys she can get!"

"Go Ali! Get your leg over!"

She even has the same name as me. Shit.

"Hey!" I shout over the din, my voice made harsher by the sense that I've started something I don't want to be responsible for. "Get a grip."

I am so intense that they do. The noise settles to the odd giggle. Skull girl still stares at the floor.

"Nobody really looks in changing rooms," I say, trying desperately, to soften the blow, "because everybody's too busy trying to cover themselves up."

I have never understood why they insist on forcing open plan changing rooms. Adults get the dignity of a curtain or a cubicle to choose from if they're not happy to get naked with strangers. Why not teenagers? *Especially* teenagers.

They take my point. The class proceeds. I may or may not have taught them tolerance.

I try not to notice the harshness in the laughter that still follows skull girl as they squeeze out of the door when it's over.

I get home earlier than normal. It's the only class I have today, and I normally hang around to talk to the Deputy Head about tomorrow's session. She thinks I am running things past her. I think I am getting information on the kids. But today I don't have the heart any more. I want out.

As I open the door that is home and walk through the still damp scented lobby I can hear raised voices, and it takes me a while to register that it's Cath. Cath. I feel a guilty trip in my stomach. I haven't seen her since her outburst over that letter. Her voice sounds all wrong, raised up into a shout. I unlock my door hastily, get in and close it. I can still hear muted shouting, Patrick's low rumble, by turns conciliatory and angry, Cath furious. Something about a laptop.

I don't want to listen. I don't want to know. I don't want to hear the break in Cath's voice, or the confusion in Patrick's.

I move into the kitchen and make myself the longest, most involved cup of tea I can possibly manage. I clatter every cup, jangle every spoon, and boil my noisy kettle twice.

When I've finished I listen. Things seem a little quieter. I move, relieved, to stand with my tea by the patio doors, facing out into the entrance to the development.

Suddenly Cath comes hurtling out of the door to the lobby. She is sobbing and running, barefoot, across the tarmac. I seem to be frozen, looking at her. As she nears the front gates she slows, uncertain. I try to move, to look away, but I am somehow stuck. Cath stops, hesitant, just by the entrance. To the right of the gates there is a patch of stinging nettles, waiting to be cleared when they finish the landscaping. It's going, apparently, to be a "pentagonal planting area". Whatever that involves.

Cath stares at the nettles.

No.

I watch her, like a child captivated by bloody roadkill, morbidly fascinated. I need to move now. I need to go out there and get her. Bring her in. Give her tea. Cry it out.

Calm her down. But I don't. I just can't. I can't push myself into it. Everything in me feels unfeasibly exhausted.

Cath takes a step towards the nettles. I see resolve in the set of her shoulders. Back in her flat I think I can hear gasping, grunting sobs. I try not to notice. I ache with trying not to notice.

Cath speeds up. I turn away.

From her picture frame, which I haven't put away but am trying not to notice, Tabby gazes out at me, eternally disapproving.

Cath

Wednesday 23rd April
And The Following Week

Because nothing ever really finishes. There is no bang, no sharp relief, like watching fireworks or being shot. I don't march out, he doesn't evict me. Instead I limp home, sore and chastened. And I have never been further than the gate.

He greets me nervously, scanning me for signs of further hysteria. But I am too tired. I am so intensely tired of all of it. So I simply go to bed. Hours later he joins me, careful, tentative, picking up the bedclothes by the corner, and climbing in, as though I am a bomb which might, on contact, explode. But I do not explode. I do nothing.

In the morning I get up and I simply carry on.

Days pass. Small things change. Only small things. Patrick is quiet but I can feel he is angry. Something simmers in him, as though if I could slice him open he would bleed indignation. I am quiet too. We are polite and careful. We have an uneasy truce. Quietly, I abandon my research. Since I never go to the campus, nobody notices. I have no further contact with the publishing company and little by little the raw red loss becomes a sort of muted ache. Brandon Homes continue to refuse to answer phone calls. I write letters. I write emails. Brandon Homes do not reply. The swelling in my feet subsides gradually, along with the violent and interminable itching. Patrick thinks I have some form of eczema. Alice goes out in gloves and wellingtons and chops down the nettle patch. I watch her, furtively, under the pretence of checking my mail box in the lobby. There is an angry set to her shoulders. I don't mention it afterwards and neither does she. I wonder, numbly, how she knows.

On Saturday night. Patrick has a friend round. They are meeting here for a drink before they go out. I take a shower beforehand and put on makeup. When I appear in the kitchen I am artfully arranged in a small towel.

"Oh, hi Darren," I say casually, as though I hadn't been aware that Darren would be here.

"Hi Cath, alright?" says Darren.

He blushes uncomfortably, feeling Patrick's eyes on him, but it's too late to stop his gaze from travelling over me. I imagine Darren's eyes are his hands on me, trembling, stroking marshmallows. My hair is a wet rope, draped over one shoulder, dripping small rivulets of water down into my cleavage. I meet Darren's roaming eyes deliberately and smile. This too, is a small thing that has changed.

When I can no longer find reason to be in the kitchen, I return to the bedroom and take care getting dressed. Clad in tight jeans and a low cut fitted blouse I stroll back in, brushing my hair casually, mermaid style. They are eating Chinese takeaway.

"Sorry, we didn't order any for you," says Patrick, eyes on my blouse, "because you said you were on a diet."

My hand rushes immediately back to my stomach, feels it like a hot, gelatinous mass. I ball my fist up and squeeze in.

"No problem," I say, my voice squeaked and high, as though it is being squeezed out of a hole much too small for it.

"Cath is trying to lose weight," says Patrick, confidingly, to Darren. He turns to me, "Two stone, was it?"

"One stone," I say haltingly, but already I can see Darren's embarrassed gaze resting, by reflex, on my stomach.

"Oh," says Patrick, "I was sure it was two. Oh well."

I make my excuses and flee.

Later, when they have left, I creep back out again. The door to the kitchen is locked. I look for the key in the bathroom, the bedroom, on the windowsills, in the waste bins, and then finally I find it. In the utility cupboard. I unlock the door and let myself in. There is a large bar of chocolate waiting for me on the table. Next to it there is a note.

Well done for finding the key! Enjoy!
Patrick

M.

Thursday 22nd May
1 hour and 25 minutes to go

Indecision leads to panic. Always. I have yet to meet a person who can face indecision without a rush of panic. There is a deadline, always, whether set out for you or not. An internal deadline. One moment of awkward silence feels like half an hour. Half an hour of wavering, caught between two alternatives, feels like a life sentence. Some people make quick, snap decisions with confidence and incisive certainty. The wrong decision, they say, is better than no decision at all. They never fail to act. They never fail to move quickly. They also never get it wrong. How do they do that? How do they navigate that minefield of potential calamity, of opportunities lost, of slopes slid down and too steep to clamber back up again? They just don't seem to think about it. Those people.

I used to be one of them.

I have told myself that whatever I do, it has to be better than this standing. It has to be productive. To be something I can later be proud of. It's what the doctor told me. It's what normal people do. Unthinking. Every day. That crowd of normality, of people who can cope. I don't know when I left it. Or how to get back. They talk about baby steps, but they don't spell out a clear path. There is no one path. There is no one meaning. Life is like reading through a foreign thesaurus. You look up one word and you find another twenty.

Inside, but working. Tackling that email. I printed it off this morning. That was the first step. It was the first thing in my inbox. Dated Wednesday 20 May. Yesterday. They sent it quite late at night. An email of complaint. But still, when I scanned it, there was something about it I liked.

Inside, but working. Or outside, buying milk. I have not allowed myself a third option. I have kept things neat. Kept things simple. But still, there is no obvious pathway. No right or wrong. Outside, the world is bathed in dappled sunshine. The work on my desk is only a scattering of pieces of paper, so light that when I brush them with my elbow off the edge of the table, they don't actually fall in a straight line. They only drift, unhurried, to the ground.

But the sunshine makes me blink and the non-uniform fall of the paper worries me.

Alice

Thursday 1st May
First Half Of The Summer Term

"AIDS is not restricted to monkeys and gay men," I say.

"And sluts," says someone to a chorus of cackles.

"And sluts." I agree.

I am tired today. My eyes feel dry and sore, as though I have been crying. I haven't been crying. It's because I didn't sleep well. I dreamed I was naked in class. Text book anxiety. Only I wasn't the teacher. I was the child.

"Anyone can get it," says a tall blonde, knowledgably. She looks at me for confirmation, and I feel, fleetingly, as though she is coaxing me, helping me along. She is supplying a line which I forgot.

"Exactly. Anyone. It could be your first partner or your millionth one. You could be promiscuous, or gay, or straight, or just unlucky."

I never cry. Even so, it feels a little as though it might be quite nice now, just to put my arms on the lectern and sob a little. To let my mouth grow lumpy and my eyes grow wet. Tiredness. That's what I tell myself.

I realise they are all looking at me, a mixture of impatience and unease.

"Assuming," I say quickly, "that you didn't use a condom."

It occurs to me suddenly that sex is simple. If you don't want complications then you just use a condom. A reassuring barrier of rubber between yourself and all the mess and veins and hair of that ridiculous thing that is a penis. In real life everything is blurred. You can't protect any part of your life from anything else that might stroll in. My life, right now, feels blurred and shapeless. I can't distinguish Cath from Tabby. I can't distinguish now from then. There is a hazel haired child in a photo in my living room and I can't distinguish my history from hers.

"OOOOH! Look at Twiglet! No socks today, Twiggy? Trying to be sexy?"

I am on my way out of the changing rooms. I am on my way home. We had gym last session. I didn't put my socks on without really thinking. It didn't seem important because it's hot. I feel my face burn. I am so stupid.

"Phwoooargh, Twiglet! Look at those legs."

There is a chorus of wolf whistles. They are a crowd of boys, waiting outside for their friends or their girlfriends. They move towards me like a pack and I feel that familiar fear, but I also think, forget it. There's no point in running. I only have to walk back into it tomorrow.

I look down at my skinny ankles. I walked into it tonight.

"Let's have a feel then...oooh lovely!"

One of them has his hand on my leg. He rubs it up and down. I flinch but I am too slow to move. I am frozen inside and I am too used to it. Too weary. I'd like to move but my legs won't do it. I'm scared he'll grip my leg and I'll fall

down the concrete steps and finally, actually, hurt myself.
And I don't want to do that. In front of them.
   "Ha! Look at that! She's not even moving! Hey Twiggy,
feeling frisky? Fancy a shag? You getting desperate
because no one will have you?"
Some of the girls coming out of the changing room have
stopped to watch. They are carrying gym bags. Some of
them still have their shorts on. Some aren't wearing their
socks. For them, the rules are different. And I am stupid
and should have known it.
   I make a sudden move, a jerky, half thought out, clumsy
break for it, and in the same movement he reaches up and
grasps the waistband of my skirt. And I don't know if he
means to or if it happens accidentally, but my skirt is too
loose and when he pulls it comes down. My knickers, pink
with a Barbie motif because I have to wear children's size,
come down with it.
   And now. Now when my skirt is round my knees, when I
am pulling my underwear up and stumbling down the
steps, without caring any more if I fall or I hurt myself, with
surprised and delighted laughter blaring, deafening in my
ears - now, finally - I run.

"Miss?"
   I blink. I meet the gaze of thirty two curious faces.
   "Miss, are you all right?"

Cath

Wednesday 7th May
Home

We are late to bed. Very late. Because it is past two in the morning when I find the key.

Patrick is giggly and excited, like a child. He has been watching me sideways all evening, as though there were some secret he wanted to share with me. I spend the evening studiously trying to ignore it, but my heart is pumping hard in my rib cage, my mouth dry. I never know what it is I am afraid of. But I am always so afraid. I sat at my laptop, opening that document again and again.

Name: David Brandon Marsden, Occupation: CEO.

Patrick watches me. He thinks I am writing notes. In reality I haven't written a sentence of my research for weeks now. I haven't even reviewed what I've already done. I get up each day and I stare at the screen. I eat, I sleep, I stare. I lose time. I'm not sure at any moment what I did for the last hour. It's been a long time since I got a thrill from my work, it is the first time I have regarded it so entirely without passion.

Address: 42 Canterbury Drive, Manchester, MA12 3PW

I could leave the university. I could start again somewhere else. Try to recover that other Cath that I half remember. But I can't afford a financial risk at the moment. The flood was expensive.

187

*David Brandon **Bloody** Marsden.*

And what if I never *was* that Cath? What if she never existed?

Eventually I give up, snap the laptop closed and head for bed. Patrick is behind me, crackling like static, fired with some sort of secret glee. It is a game of course. He was skipping with delight when I couldn't open the bedroom door, eyes sparkling with the delicious, shared fun we were having, and an edge of hysteria that I recognise because I know that my eyes, when I meet his, which is increasingly seldom, contain the same edge. Sharp and prickling.

I want it to be a game. I want that shared fun. I want everything to transform itself into an extended, breezy joke. The way others would see it. The way Alice would. But I feel as though everything has been carved out of me, my sense of humour a lost thing, dead on a slab. Morticians searching through it, trying to find something, anything, they could work with. I tramp dutifully through the house, looking for the key under rugs and behind cupboards, a thick, stupid smile pasted painfully onto my pale round face.

For a while we both keep up the pretence. I even try to laugh, though it comes out thin and reedy, like something strangled at birth.

I pause every now and then, put my hands on my hips and say, "Patrick, come on. How old are you?"

My voice is teasing, playful. Strangled.

It's excruciating for us both. I keep waiting for him to finally drop it. I think he is waiting for it too, but he can't find the moment. And eventually, as the clock creeps past one, neither of us pretends to laugh any more.

"Patrick, please." I am close to tears.

He is dogged.

"Come on Cath, this is our way of getting you to know the place." He tries for a smile. It doesn't come. He tries again. "Don't give up now, I'll give you a clue, you're getting warmer."

I find the key in the teapot. He probably put it there intending to make us laugh. I simply pull it out, wipe old tea leaves from it with his Grandmothers' tea towel, and we both form a miserable crocodile of two, and trudge down what seems like an endless hallway, to bed.

Alice

Thursday 15th May

Cath comes round in the evening. I've been home about an hour, wandering uselessly around in the flat.

"Hi," says Cath.

"Hi," I say. There is a pause. "Sorry," I add, with a shallow little laugh, "I was doing something but then I forgot!"

She laughs too, dutifully. Then waits, expectantly. I am not sure why she is here.

I hold up the CD in my hand, "Ah! A clue! I was putting some music on. Ha! Going senile…"

We both smile though we know it is slim pickings and I, for want of anything else to say, cross the room and slot the CD into position. Something indie, angry and doleful fills the room. I move again to switch it off.

"Don't," says Cath, "I like it."

I look at her. Paler even than yesterday.

"You OK?" I ask.

"Yep," she says.

There is another pause.

"You?"

"Yep."

Whatever we are, we are not conversationalists. And whatever we are, we are neither of us OK. There is a longer pause.

"Um," says Cath, "could I...is it really rude to ask for a drink?"

"Course," I say automatically, "I was about to offer – tea, coffee, juice?"

"Coffee," she says flatly, and then, "need the caffeine!" and she laughs. It's not so much a laugh as a sudden exhalation of air. I wonder why she doesn't make a coffee at home. I busy myself making it and then curiosity gets the better of me.

"Ran out of instant?" I guess, jovially, handing her the cup.

"Oh! No. Um. But Patrick's gone out and I can't get into the kitchen..." She trails off. The explanation doesn't really follow.

"Cath," I say, "are you and Patrick – "

"-She's so sweet."

She says it so suddenly and with such quick intensity that at first I don't know what she's talking about.

"The little girl in the picture," says Cath. "She's beautiful."

A rush of emotion hits me so hard that for a moment I can't catch my breath. I stare at the floor, half turned away from her, battling to get myself under control. *Get a grip Alice Crayer*, I tell myself furiously. *Get a handle on yourself. Pull it together. Now.*

And as Patrick suddenly blunders in at the doorway, all false heartiness and 'yellos!', so that I glance up, startled, blood pumping and pooling in my face and my mouth still working to regain control, I see her, watching me closely. And I see that she knows.

191

I want to open my mouth and pour it all out at her feet like vomit.

"All right?" says Patrick, without waiting for an answer, "is our Cath bothering you again?" He extends one arm jovially and catches Cath in it like a rugby tackle. She stumbles a little, but her eyes are on me.

He's been doing that a lot lately. Not the rugby tackle. Turning up. It's as though he doesn't want to leave us alone. But beneath his arm I meet Cath's gaze and I know, for sure, that in the end she'll be too clever for him. She may not be anything as aggressive as 'sharp'. But she's bright. And she's worn out.

Cath

Monday 19 May
Home

I don't sleep much. Nowadays I never seem to. The bed, even the weight of the duvet feels the way this flat, this stinking, grubby hell hole of a flat, feels.

Like a trap.

Next to me is a shape that is Patrick, huddled right over to the edge of the mattress. It seems to quiver and shake every night, until the early hours. The sound of stifled machine gun sobs, like spasms through his body, fill the still air. Neither of us mentions this. Sometimes I get up and open the window, as if to release it somehow, to let the sound out so it is no longer in here. But nothing escapes from this flat.

I am tired. When I turn my head my vision blurs. My eyes feel dry and red and my face is even more podgy and pasty than usual. I wander around the house like a restless spirit, catching sight of myself suddenly in mirrors, making myself jump.

After Patrick gets up, wordless, and goes off to work, I spend all morning searching for the key to the lounge. Only I don't really search any more. I wander aimless. Often, nowadays, I don't care if I find it or not. We have dropped the pretence that it is some kind of game. Neither of us gets any pleasure out of it. And yet. And yet.

After a while I pause, expressionless, emotionless, in front of the lounge door. Then I move back a few steps and run and slam my whole body weight into it. Amazingly it holds.

I knew it would. I've tried it before.

Brandon Homes would of course make the doors to their prison as solid as possible. Even if they made the walls out of paper and plaster.

David Brandon Bloody Marsden. David Bloody Brandon Marsden. Bloody David Bloody Brandon Bloody Marsden. It is my mantra. It's what I use now, to get to sleep.

Perhaps I should simply knock down the walls.

I consider going out but I don't have the energy. And Patrick has done something with the double lock on the front door on his way out. I'm probably supposed to know how to work it.

Funny. He hasn't gone that far before.

I pause at the bathroom door. I haven't eaten so I would bring up only bile. But it might be something. I consider. I think about running into the door again, just for the impact, but the bruises, blossoming purple on my sides from repeated attempts that stopped, a while ago, being actual attempts any more, aren't really doing much for me. There are razors and a place where the head board has splintered and any number of possibilities in the kitchen. But the kitchen, unfortunately, is also the lounge. And anyway. That doesn't really work anymore.

In the end I go back and pick up the phone in the bedroom.

"Good afternoon, Brandon Homes. May I help you?...Hello?...Hello?"

She sounds harried now. And tired. I wonder who she is. A secretary perhaps? A switchboard operator? I google the name every day, to look for updates. There have been no changes since the first time. Something about him taking a break for ill health. And about a hundred articles about his fervour, his flair. Him being a 'self-made man'.

Quietly, I hang up.

I have done this before too.

Alice

Wednesday 21st May
The Last Week Before The Summer Half Term
And A Long Time Ago

The cardigan was our secret. Because she was afraid of what our Mother would say. Of what she might do. Our Mother. A middle aged vigilante warrior. But it never works. Adults messing with the world of children. I knew it. Tabby knew it.

The cardigan was a mess. Chewing gum glued it, viciously and fibrously, to itself, 'Twiglet' scribbled on the inside label. An attempt to tear it hadn't really worked so there were holes punched in it with a compass. Even a couple of neat squares cut out of it with scissors.

I would have cut some neat squares out of them. If she would only tell me who. But I knew as well as she did, there was no 'who'. No one person. It never worked that way. Things were never so clear cut. There is no 'someone'. There is only 'everyone'. School kids are highly unique individuals. But they move like a pack when they have their sights on a target.

I am standing in the school hall, watching the class filing in. They are sniggering, laughing, and shouting things from one end of the line to the other. Fanning out around the chairs, tipping them back, turning them round to perch defiantly astride them. Eyes beneath heavy kohl and mascara, willing me, daring me to do something about it. It doesn't work. I don't care how they sit.

"Laura!" says the teacher. "Put that chair back and sit properly."

Ah. So it's not me they are defying. She is tall and prim, twin set clad, even though that went out of fashion years ago. Worse, she is a 'sitter in'. I hate that. Usually I can get the teachers to leave for a while, get a much needed coffee. Either they understand or they want the break.

"Oh," I say, with carefully faked surprise as she fusses around them, "I don't seem to have a projector. Is there any chance I could get one?"

I don't need a projector. Nobody uses projectors anymore. But you can be guaranteed to find one in a school. Even so, locating it, booking it out, and wheeling it in...with a bit of luck it'll take her all session.

"Oh dear," she says, her eyes disapproving, "well if you'd told me before..."

I wait, willing her to go and fetch it, knowing, because I had seen the one and only battered old specimen being carted off into some science classroom, that it wouldn't be available.

"Jennie," she says, eventually, addressing her bark at one of the students, "go and ask reception if they can send in a projector."

Damn.

"Alice Crayer, you were doing *what*?" said our Mother.
"You were trying on your sister's cardigan? Why on earth were you doing that?"

"To see if it fit?"

Her eyes burned, "That's enough of your lip."

"It didn't though." I said, belligerently. "Fit, that is."

"Well no, you ridiculous child, it wouldn't." A pause. Her eyes closed for a moment in exasperation. "So where is it?"

"I tore it," I said, "so I threw it away."

Recalling myself to the dubious present, I realise that the class is finally assembled, but is still being coerced, herded and screamed at by the teacher, who seems not to have noticed that she has already wasted about fifteen minutes of my time, on whether or not the class is 'sitting properly'.

"We are talking," I want to tell her, "about sex. It's not finishing school. I'm not teaching deportment."

I don't tell her that. In the end I just barge in and begin, raising my voice a little to talk over her.

"How can you tell," I ask, "if someone's lost their virginity?"

There are a few muttered comments about bleeding and hymens but I've dispelled that particular myth earlier in the term so they mostly run down into silence.

"They tell you?" suggests someone.

"Maybe," I say, "but what if they're lying?"

Later, when I had been duly shouted at, lectured, grounded and exiled, I asked Tabby if she tried to fight them.

"N...no," she said, eyes filling with tears, "just...w...just...w..."

A pause.

"Just watched them."

The class are talking more openly now, forgetting the teacher.

"Josie Smith reckons she's had sex," says someone, "but she hasn't."

"Yeah there's no way. She's well ugly!"

There is a chorus of laugher and a swell of voices.

"Yeah Janey took her picture with her phone and put, like, a voice bubble? Saying, 'I'm a munter.' And put it up all over school!"

Everyone laughs loudly.

"Laura!" begins the sitter in.

"Janey," I say over her, "sounds like a little shit."

Later, Cath finds me in the carpark of our flats, head in hands at the steering wheel, the evening setting in around me.

"You OK?" she says, and then, "Would you like to come over for dinner?"

I have been hauled, of course, in front of the head-teacher, rather like a naughty child. That is, apparently, unacceptable language and an attitude like that will draw complaints from the parents. The sitter in is very pleased with this result, though I can see the reluctance in the head's eyes. He's a nice guy, with a modicum of understanding of his pupils, if not his staff. He knows the classes work. He's been using me for a while. What he really wants is for me not to do it in front of anybody. But I know there's a line and that I have crossed it. And that I'll cross it again if I don't sort myself out. Now.

"Dinner would be good," I say, finally.

"Great!" says Cath, "only, can we use your kitchen?"

Cath

Wednesday 21st May
Evening
With Alice

With an admirable lack of questioning from Alice, we prepare the meal I invited her to, in Alice's kitchen. We are giggly and excitable, helped by the white wine she opens, hungrily, as soon as we get in. We take it, both the wine and the possibility of an evening away, a few hours release from everything, and we embrace it fervently. We snigger about the rude chopsticks Alice owns and then build our menu around them. Then we abandon the menu and, bent double with laughter over nothing and everything, we slosh red wine, liberally, into a Coq au Vin, which we also snigger about, and which doesn't really go with chopsticks. We are just putting the finishing touches on the mousse, doubling the chocolate content required in the recipe, and then abandoning the recipe altogether, when Patrick comes home. We hear him let himself in, call out for me and then, finally, bemused, locate us here.

"Cath?" he says, confused, then, with an attempt at jocularity, "So you finally worked out the front door then?"

"Window," I reply, and collapse into hysterics. Alice, though she knows nothing of the background to this, joins me.

Patrick. Patrick on the outside. Patrick powerless. And, though something in my heart still pulls at me, reaches instinctive towards him, somewhere inside me I turn a key. And, implicitly, without consultation, Alice and I, casually, lock him out.

"There's probably enough for you," I say. "If you want some."

"Are you sure?" says Alice, peering into the brimming pan. "Actually yeah. There's loads."

And we dissolve, again, into fits of laughter.

Patrick outside. Waiting, patiently, alarm rising in him.

"We could eat in my place," he says, when the giggles subside again, trying, once more to take some sort of control. "I've got better chairs. No offence."

"None taken," says Alice. "I've got better chopsticks."

At some point during dinner, I excuse myself to go to the bathroom. I am already a little warm and swooshy, my vision swinging at the edges again, but pleasantly, like a voyage, like being rocked to sleep. I look at the pale, red rimmed image in the mirror, and then I reach into my makeup bag and apply some lipstick. Just a touch. Better. I add some eye shadow, blusher. When I reappear I have a full face of makeup and feel suddenly self-conscious.

"Cath, did you just go in there and put on makeup?" Patrick. And I see in him the edge of desperation, trying, vainly, to get a hold on the evening. To pull it back within his grasp before it slipped through his clutching fingers. Seriously Cath, you are so –"

"Bloody gorgeous," says Alice, firmly.

I sit up a little taller. And drink a little more wine.

Alice and I begin with the after dinner coffee, which I lace liberally with amaretto. There had been more wine with the meal but it disappeared easily and, as we kept saying to each other, it didn't really seem to make any difference. Then, invigorated, we rise from our respective dining chairs, open another bottle of red wine, and set about composing the most cutting, the most intelligent, biting email of complaint to Brandon Homes that we can possibly create. We go through draft and draft of it, each one a little more outraged than the last. At some point during this process the seething anger gives way to further hysteria and we collapse, frequently, with uncontrollable laughter, repeating each new phrase to each other with ever increasing hilarity. 'Disgusting', we write. 'Appalling'. 'A deplorable lack of customer service'. The word deplorable brings us to new heights of amusement.

Patrick does the washing up.

"Here. Read this," I say to him, when we have finally finished, but he only looks at me oddly, and says he has heard most of it several times anyway. It occurs to me that he hasn't eaten much dinner. Or had much to drink. I offer him a glass of his port but he refuses and says goodnight and there is a strange little moment when he looks at me and I look back and then something happens that I don't quite understand but it ends in Alice saying, "Goodnight," abruptly and Patrick kissing me so suddenly I catch my breath, and there is ice in the kissing.

Later, the evening mellows. I recline on Patrick's new black leather chair. The alcohol I have drunk and the strange deliciousness of being in that chair, (he bought it a few days ago and it is his pride and joy. Naturally, I have avoided it) combine to give me an immense feeling of expansive luxury. I feel strong in this chair. Powerful, somehow. Even, perhaps, a little beautiful.

Alice is curled up, twinkly and elfin, bright against the white sofa. She is curled, as if deliberately, in the dip in the middle, so that she is low against the backrest, making her look even smaller, and somehow more powerful. There is a glass of red wine in her hand, she holds it leisurely, at a slight angle. I note with a tantalising fascination, that the wine is close to the lip of the glass, that it might at any moment spill onto the sofa. I have lit candles around the place, and then, in a moment of defiance, an incense stick. Patrick hates them.

"I love incense," says Alice.

Lazily, I watch the smoke curl up from the incense stick. It's the third or fourth in succession, and the room is filled with a sort of swirling magic. I am a little hypnotised.

Alice isn't looking at me. She is watching the candlelight play on the empty bottles in the corner. The one further away, on the table, is still three quarters full and especially beautiful. The red of the wine gleams richly in the flickering light, and at the bottom of the bottle, through the green tint of the glass and the ruby liquid, looks black and intriguing. I want to tell Alice to look at it too. I want to explain to her how gorgeous it is. But I don't want to break the moment. Instead I sip my wine and feel its warmth spreading through me, reaching its caressing fingers down to the very tips of my limbs. The jazz from the stereo eases its way smoothly into the air, and warms it, blurring the edges of everything.

"Do you ever imagine," she says now, into the pause, "you know, when you wake up in the morning and everything is silent, that maybe you are actually completely alone. Like, nothing exists outside your window and you are the only person left in the world?"

"Sometimes," something leaps in me and I stare fixedly at the wine bottle on the table. "Yeah. Sometimes. I know what you mean."

"Like, some sort of irony – you know. You were so selfish and annoyed with people all the time that God made it true, just to show you, you know that-"

"-you didn't really want it?" I lift my gaze to look at her, but she too, is studiously staring into the corner.

"Yeah. That's what I mean. You wanted the world to revolve around you, and now it does and it turns out to be incredibly depressing." She half smiles, but there's no mirth in it.

"Wow..." I say pensively. I am only half listening. Internally I am trying to count the number of other people I have even seen, from a distance, in the two months.

"And you couldn't say sorry..."

It isn't a high number. I pull myself, with an effort, back to the moment. "You couldn't say sorry," I agree, "because there would be no one left."

"Yes!" Alice is oddly elated. "That's it, isn't it? That's the thing. Because it means you can't even make it right."

"And where would they go?" I say, "All those other people?"

"I don't know."

There is a pause. Then I say, "I think I would kill myself."

She is still looking at the bottles but something in her suddenly freezes. The set of her shoulders has changed. There is a very long pause. Simultaneously the lines of her body are self-conscious and startled, and very far away. "Alice?" I say softly, and the whole sound of the evening changes. "The little girl in the picture you were looking at the other day...who was she?" There is a beat and I realise what I have said. "*Is* she. Who is she?"

There is an even longer pause. I hear the jazz album finish, and the click of the boiler as it turns itself off. I hear the clock ticking in the bedroom. Very, very quietly, Alice says,

"My sister."

Oh." She is still staring into space. I feel wrong suddenly. I feel awful. "Sorry," I say quickly, "none of my business. You know. Just wondered. Anyway..." I take a deep breath. "So are we actually going to send that-?"

"-Tabitha." She lifts her gaze and fixes me with it, so suddenly I find myself, flustered, dropping my own. There is something sharp and hungry in her voice. "Tabitha," she says again. "Tabitha Crayer. Tabby."

I wait, uncertain whether or not she is going to say the name again. When she doesn't I look at her properly and her eyes are huge in the pale of her face.

"Alice," I say gently. "What happened to Tabitha?"

Alice

Wednesday 21st May
Cath's house
And far away

Some things I just knew. Others I could see the effect of, the broken bag, the cut up cardigan. Some things came to me on that anonymous entity the playground grapevine. None of it she ever confided herself. By that stage, I'm not sure she knew how.

They took her books and tore them up or soaked them in puddles or threw them over walls. They held her down while someone found her lunchbox and emptied it out. Once they stamped on her sandwich in the playground and then scraped it up and tried to make her eat it. When she wouldn't open her mouth they smeared it on her face. I think they only did that once, which is lucky because after a while I think she stopped resisting. I think after a while she started to think it was reasonable. She felt she understood them. A human reaction to an odious thing.

They wrote 'Kick Me' on her back. They stole her coat in the winter. They took her bus money and, as the bus approached, they threw it in the road. I was always just a moment too late. She made excuses or she was silent. She never complained.

In class they were more subtle. They wrote raw, cruel little notes about her which 'accidentally' wound up in her pencil case. They stole a key ring or a tennis ball, or some other thing out of her bag and threw it around the classroom until an angry teacher asked who owned it – and then they silently pointed. Later, when she was doing detention, they made faces through the window, from the sun drenched playground.

Silly kid stuff. High spirits.

But they caught her near the bike sheds and they picked her up between them and they dangled her over drains and headfirst into dustbins. They threatened her with lighters. They stuck chewing gum in her hair.

They constantly, relentlessly, cornered her everywhere and tried to make her say words which they had carefully chosen. 'Abacus' or 'Banana', 'Fabulous' or 'Ratatouie'. Or her own name.

It happened to her. It was just that she was easy. They – whoever 'they' were - were animals captured, fighting to survive. We were all in the same prison. All of us were toiling endlessly so that it wouldn't be us.

They passed round her drink flask and individually spat in it. They shrieked with laughter on the increasingly near extinct occasions on which she still spoke.

They hid her homework.

They threw stones at her.

They smashed her artwork.

They were just scared.

Of course, I do not say that. In fact I stop after the first few sentences. I stop when I expect Cath to be hovering between sympathy and shock, interest and tedium. When, even in my own ears, it is all beginning to seem as trite, as commonplace as it really was.

I particularly stop before the last bit. When you are telling a story you have to make it comprehensible. People need black and white.

A beginning, middle and an end.

Cath

Wednesday 21st May
Late Into The Night

"So when did it end?" I ask. "The bullying? When did it end?"

Alice is staring so far into space her eyes are liquid. I don't know, at first, if she's heard me, and I consider getting up, going over to her, comforting her somehow. But I don't. There is something bound up in this moment. Something in the smoky air, something so fragile and suspended so delicately, that a movement, a breath, might shatter it.

Alice stays absolutely still, and then, just as I fear that it has, whatever it was, already splintered, she says,

"I punched Georgie Smales in the mouth."

M.

Thursday 22nd May
1 Hour and 12 Minutes To Go

I decide to do some work. I decide it with rather less conviction than I used to feel when I made decisions. The whole process seems weightier. The word *decision*, now, is closer to *verdict* or *judgement*, than *result*.

If life is like reading through a foreign thesaurus, looking up only one word, pursuing only one of dozens of potential meanings, then each of those we don't choose must be lost forever. We move through life unguided, and we shed definitions with every gesture. Perhaps we shed entire pages. Perhaps the world is filled with scattered paper.

The pages of the living, the pages of the dead.

Every breath that we take is another page turning. But you can't jump ahead. Or find your way back.

Life is a manual we write for the next person.

Alice

Wednesday 21st May
And A Long Time Before

I can still see his face now. Round and pinkish with baby soft skin, pale lips, and beady, mean little eyes. He was flanked by a pair of sniggering imbeciles, as blotched and pasty as he was heavy and he had pushed his chest out and spread his legs and moved right in so he was towering over her, his chest in her face, his soft folds of stomach heaving with his breathing so that the great expanse of it touched her, sickeningly, in and out, in and out. She was standing, frozen, trapped between him and the wall and his lackeys, and she was turning her face away from his breath, mouth closed, eyes flooded, but refusing to beg.

"What, are you scared?" he was saying, and I could hear him wanting it. His armpits were always damp, spreading yellowing circles in his clothing. He panted when he walked up stairs. His shirt was baggy but it was unbuttoned at the bottom, and through it his paunch peeped out and winked, flabby and white, at the outside world.

Of course, the meanness in his eyes was cultivated. He would have been as easy a target as she was. But he turned his weight, calculatedly to his advantage. I had seen him turn up, like a hired body guard, at the side of anyone lofty enough to command him, and back them up in whatever power game they were playing that day.

"You dissin' my friend?" he would say, squaring up to them, the sheer girth of him instantly making them puny. "I'd watch it if I were you."

And then, "Yeah", his friend would say, importantly, "better do as I say. Or do you want Georgie to sit on you?" The whole thing was tragic. But it worked. So now it was him in the driving seat, pushing her, crushing her, into the wall. And she was the one this happened to daily. Who was rapidly beginning to regard it as punitive.

In fact, for me to even see it was some sort of rare and fantastic achievement. She said nothing, told nothing, revealed nothing in words. The situation was obvious. She either didn't need to communicate or she didn't see the point. And for all my continuous stalking of the school grounds, I had never once actually seen it happen. I only knew that it did. I felt it in the air, and in the way people talked about her. It was a diaphanous phantom not solid enough to fight.

The fact is, no one did anything when I was near her. I was respected enough that they knew not to try. The times we were together, I realised later, when we walked home or we walked in, or the odd occasions I managed to meet up with her at break time, they were her few precious moments of peace. Breaks and lunchtimes were staggered, because the facilities were so limited, and the lower part of the school had their breaks while we were in lessons. When they were summoned back in for afternoon teaching, we had the run of the grounds and canteen.

Every now and then, just to see if I could do it, I bunked off my lessons and joined her for her break time. She looked at me then, just like she did as a baby. Thirteen years on, and I was still Tabby's favourite. And nobody ever bothered her those times.

She had endured a lot worse already. This was probably one of the lesser offences, but even so, it was an unexpected moment of brilliance. In the midst of this campaign of sneaky, careful persecution which had been, until now, so impossible to witness, I had simply rounded the corner one day between lessons. There he was stupidly, blatant and blundering and full in the act.

She registered me first. I saw surprise and relief on her face, and the imprint of the bricks on her cheek. His lackeys looked up, half grinning, half uncertain, and then stepped back to abandon him as I moved towards them. I felt the wind lifting my hair behind me, the drum roll in my rib cage, the sharp taste of adrenaline rise in my mouth. I could hear the pulse of my blood in my ears and then, finally, he noticed me. I saw myself in his tiny, piggy, little eyes and then I was in front of him and I drew my fist back and I frowned with concentration. I willed all my strength into my whitening knuckles, into every muscle and sinew of my cocked arm and there was a split second of electric silence. And then I felt the collective intake of breath and I released my fist and I let it fly, a fevered, heat seeking missile into the pale, half open, wet of his mouth.

I knocked four of his teeth out. I'd caught a bit of his nose as well and there was blood everywhere and of course there was hell to pay from all associated adults. I think the sheer force of it had knocked him over, perhaps combined with the shock, or maybe he was simply perpetually unbalanced. Whatever it was, the jarring impact did something to his neck, as well. He was walking around like a gap toothed, wonky meerkat for weeks afterwards.

I had little bloodied tooth marks on top of the bruises on my knuckles. I showed them to everybody with grinning pride. Or to adults, with an attempt at pitiful simpering. That didn't really work. That kind of thing only worked if you were Tabby. I had defied the regimented pathways of far too many school rules by that time. I had written a few too many swear words on blackboards. Arrived home trailing too many screwed up detention notices. Anyway, my heart wasn't in it.

The fact was of course that I was punished, hauled up to the headmaster's office, grounded at home. I was threatened, briefly, with legal action by the somewhat hysterical Mother of Georgie Smales, though that died down, wisely, in the wake of my own accounts of his intimidation of a child. Tabby looked, to all intents and purposes, about eight to his fourteen years – the implication wasn't good. And Tabby's stuttering, unintelligible statement spoke, for once in her life, for itself. They backed off. Our Mother didn't, nor the various uncles and aunts who gathered, as always, full of advice on what to do with this problem offspring. The teachers viewed me with new suspicion and I was informed by a vitriolic deputy head-teacher, that I had sunk to new depths and was destined for nothing, the way I was going, but trouble. My defence, that I was protecting my sister, worked only to the extent that when I mentioned her name, their faces softened, but the usual adult idiot mantra, that Tabby should 'just ignore them and they will go away', that 'two wrongs never make a right' and that the best thing I could have done would be to 'go away and tell a teacher' immediately kicked in. It is a private battlefield, the school arena, perhaps created by adults, but a war, nonetheless, that they cannot easily fight in. I informed the headmaster that if he could prove that a teacher could have thumped Georgie Smales as effectively, then I would be willing, next time, to call a teacher. I would, I told him, very much like to see that.

I came very close to being expelled.

But, as always, it was her face, the plain adoration on my sister's face that made it OK. All the time that I was Tabby's protector, her guardian, if I was beloved of Tabby, everything would be fine.

It was OK that she was cooed and cuddled and fussed over, and I was sent upstairs to my room in disgrace. That the aunts and uncles and friends of the family listened with frozen encouragement on their faces, while, she, forced to speak, struggled her way through a sentence, while, I, eavesdropping at the top of the stairs, longed to rush down and tell them my own account.

It was OK that I overheard my Father saying jokily, "Well I will say one thing, confining Alice to her room – certainly makes it a whole lot quieter!"

"Perhaps you should do it more often." An Aunt.

As for Georgie Smales, well of course he was now afraid of me. In reality I knew well that the fear was not new to him. I could see it on his face long before I approached him. An endless, aching yearn for safety. I think the mental spectacle of anticipated cruelty, the crucial need for a large persona to match his uncomfortably large physique, was in him daily. I think *Georgie Porgie, pudding and pie* was strung on a loop in the back of his mind.

He left Tabby alone after that. But I expect, in the wake of being floored by a girl, he had to work a lot harder to save his reputation. Either he, or several other of his victims, suffered harder in the wake of it.

So that was that. That was Georgie Smales scared to touch her. It wasn't where the rest of it stopped. It should have been. It should have been that simple. One punch, an example, and a scared little boy ceases his campaign of terror, followed, almost instantly, by all the others. But it doesn't, it never works like that. Perhaps at the beginning it could have been salvaged that way. Before it had gone on so long and run so deep. She had reached, perhaps now even passed that point, the psychological barrier where she would stop, even internally, protesting, and begin to agree with them. She could almost, at this stage, actively seek out the persecution. And as for the others, out of the initial mindless scape-goating, genuine hate had been cultivated.

But it should have been the finish. That would have been so much neater. So many, many things would have been different. And perhaps then I would be able to look, without pain, at her picture. I would not find it so hard to say her name.

Stories should have a beginning, a middle and an end.

Cath

Wednesday 21st May
Even Later

"So that stopped it then?"

I desperately want an answer. Something in me, hugely, hungrily, needs to see a resolution. A conclusion. An ending. Scrawled on the walls in the long congealed blood of Georgie Smales.

She doesn't reply. I continue, growing more vehement, trying in my vigour, somehow to draw her out, "That put paid to it. Well done you." Alice's face is unreadable.

"No," she says. "Yes, well...no. No, not really."

She stands up abruptly and everything, every door that had opened seems to slam shut in her features. I can almost feel the draught of it.

"I should go. It's really late. Thanks." And with that staccato little finish she totters slightly, regains her bag and her composure, and she is gone.

I stand in the silence and a chill passes through me.

Tabitha. Tabitha Crayer.

I think she might be dead.

I stand for a while, swaying slightly, in the wake of Alice's sudden departure. Then I stagger to the computer. It glows blue in the semi darkness. The email we have crafted with so much giddy humour greets me, like a remembered holiday, still there on the screen.

Dear David Brandean Marstin,

We hope we have spelled your name right. We did not have a note of who you were, and simply had to decipher it from your signature, which we are afraid, is not entirely clear. Luckily we could deduce it from the list of your generous pension provisions detailed within the Annual Report and Accounts which were kindly provided to us by Brandon Homes.

We are writing to thank you for your lovely letter, and the bountiful provisions which Brandon Homes has seen fit to make for us, on the occasion of our homes being flooded and entirely ruined within weeks of moving in.

In particular we would like to thank you for your utter neglect to reply to any of our collective or individual letters, phone calls, messages and emails. We would like to applaud you for your deplorable lack of customer service in finally replying after months of ignorance (we mean this in both possible senses of the word) with a pre-fabricated letter and an electronic signature. Have you, in fact, even seen the letter which you apparently sent to us? We attach a scanned copy in case you have not.

Furthermore, we are thrilled and delighted with your frankly disgusting behaviour in failing to warn us at any point in the purchase of our Brandon residence, (or at least, in plain English written in a font which has not been designed by and for the average household flea) that we were in fact purchasing in a known flood zone.

We are overjoyed to inform you that we can recommend Brandon Homes as being the most appalling and immoral extortion racket we have ever had the joy of dealing with, and that we will not hesitate to make this recommendation whenever we may have the chance to do so.

Thanks to you, we have parted with pleasure with so many of our most treasured possessions and pawned the rest to pay for the extensive reconstruction and redecoration work required in the wake of the (entirely unheard of) natural disaster of being flooded in an area which, we now are elated to discover, has been flooded several times before, though never mentioned to us by your helpful estate agents, the lawyers you recommended or any of the drive-by surveys you helpfully provided.

We remain, (in all possible senses of the term) forever indebted.

Yours sincerely,

Your Residents

David Brandon Marsden. David Bloody Brandon Marsden. I save the email carefully. Then I email it to every single one of the various email addresses I have collated in my hunt through the web and the Annual Report for Brandon Homes. It goes to the sales team, the legal department, and reception. It goes to the surveyor they recommended, the building contractors and to the woman who did nothing more than hand Patrick the keys on completion. It goes to Mr. David Brandon Marsden's secretary.

I click 'Send' with a flourish.

Then I zigzag, alarmingly, through the hallway, stumble through the bedroom door, and fall into bed.

Alice

Thursday 22nd May

7am

I wake up and waves of last night's memories sweep in across the white swirl of the ceiling and engulf me. At the front of my head, just above my eyes, I can feel something pulsing. If somebody were to come into the room now, I am sure they would be able to see it. It would be a huge throbbing growth across my forehead, blue with veins and stretched, protesting skin. But only that part can be attributed solely to a hangover.

I feel opened up. I feel as though surgeons and amateur cameramen have dissected me in the night for entertainment. Have rummaged about in me, picking up pieces to find things I had so carefully hidden under them, poking the quivering gelatinous masses which constitute my organs, my kidneys, and my heart. Somewhere inside me a child's voice says, *"You did it. You started it."*

And I did. I know I did. For months now, I have been leaving a trail for Cath to follow, with the knowledge that she would ask the questions I have worked all my life to encourage people not to ask. Because she's a good listener? That doesn't explain it. There have been plenty of good listeners. I never wanted to talk.

No. With an effort I heave myself up onto my elbows and fight an immediate wave of nausea. It isn't Cath's listening skills. It's Cath herself. That thing in her eyes that I try not to read. A secret pain, stubbornly unspoken, and from which I have consciously turned away. Cath's life, still so unknown to me, has become somehow inexplicably mingled with Tabby's, sending distant ghosts spinning out of the walls.

I groan. I feel desperately exposed. I want to reach back into the murky depths of last night's ramblings, and seize handfuls of words and pull them all back. Through the gentle, kohl smudged eyes of Cath, the whole world has been watching my dissection. I swing my legs over the side of the bed and heave myself up. The room swims slightly and then re adjusts.

"Shut up," I say violently, to no one in particular. An unexplained sob, like a bubble of oxygen bobs up and sticks at the back of my throat. I never cry. I swallow with vehemence, but my eyes are not listening and I can feel them prickling, hot and pink. I slam my hand into the side of my cabinet, angry at something, but I punish only myself. Pain fills my hand and I curse. Whatever I am angry at watches me from a distance, smugly. I plunge my throbbing hand between my thighs and bend over it, feeling the water in my eyes escaping cleanly, watching it glitter as it falls to the floor. I stay there until I am certain there will be no more.

Shut up.
Shut up.
Shut up.
Shut up

Cath

Thursday 22nd May
9.30 Until 11.45am

I wake up oddly disorientated. The ceiling looks cracked and unfamiliar. I can't immediately move, so I gaze at it for a while, letting it focus. The realisation of where I am dawns on me and my first instinct is to stiffen and to locate Patrick. But the bed is empty beside me. Sunlight pokes and prods itself through the blinds at the window, like a breezy, overly cheery nurse, brisk and unsympathetic. He must have gone to work. It must be late.

I struggle onto my side, propping myself heavily up on my elbow and reaching for my watch. Half past nine. I am impassive at this news. An academic does no work, Patrick has always told me. Nowadays it's true. I should probably be researching. But I don't do that anymore. And I don't think anyone has noticed.

The house seems unnaturally silent. I sit up. As if waiting for me to show movement, several realisations crash over me at once, like freezing waves, making me gasp for air. I have a sense of horrible embarrassment. What did I do last night to Alice? Why push her like that? Probing and poking at her, peeling away at her most difficult secrets? Who did I think I was, some kind of therapist? I recall myself from Alice's perspective, sitting, smug and heavy in Patrick's chair *(Patrick's chair! I have to check if I broke it)* and asking questions in a stupid, patronisingly gentle voice, like an amateur doctor or a child playing a role. No wonder Alice left. I will have to apologise.

Also, there is an insistent swollen feeling in my abdomen, and a faint nausea at the back of my throat. The nausea will pass. But I really need to pee.

Sighing, I heave myself up like an arthritic ninety year old, and plod, carrying with me a weighty sense of general depression, to the bathroom. I push the door. It doesn't open.

Patrick.

I swear, once, under my breath. Then, because it feels good, I do it again. I reach for the most vicious, nastiest swear words I know, and I spit them out into the stale air. The bedroom windows are all closed, which is unusual. Patrick usually leaves at least one of them open. Just a crack. To get rid of the damp. I limp towards one. If I am going to have to search for a key, I may as well have some air.

It doesn't open. The keys, usually hung behind the curtains at the side of the window they belong to – are not there. I check. This goes for every window in the room. I go to check the lounge and kitchen, the spare room, even the utility cupboard. I can't get in. The doors are all locked.

Patrick has given this morning some thought.

My bladder sends a little shooting pain, just a subtle reminder. The alcohol with which I drowned myself last night needs to exit. He has done this, though not quite so drastically, before. One of these rooms will contain the keys to the others. I have to find one and then the rest will follow. I only hope the first one happens to be to the bathroom. Swearing again, I start to search. I storm back into the bedroom and pick up cushions, open boxes, rifle through drawers, pull back curtains, feel on top of cupboards. I don't take care. I drop things on the floor, toss soft furnishings over my shoulder, leave contents of cupboards and drawers and boxes scattered around them, in spectacular disarray.

Nothing.

The air in here is hot and sharp, tinged with alcohol and sweat, and the heavy scent of sleep. I go back to the windows and tug at them in frustration. They won't open. Why has everything, *everything,* got locks on? Why, if not intended to be a place of imprisonment? If not designed as a sort of spider's torture chamber, cocooning us like struggling, unwary flies.

"David *Bloody* Brandon Marsden." This time it makes it out of my mouth, and the word 'bloody' is a howl, explosive and enraged. It echoes around the silent house. I listen to it, shocked. Perhaps I am truly going insane.

A sob escapes me.

I search the rest of the bits of the flat I can get to. I find nothing. It's nearly midday.

The flat is increasingly stuffy and hot, the air stale, as if with our collective misery. I feel as though something died in here. As though I am searching through the rib cages of skeletons, the corpses of lost ideals and love and hope long since starved and beaten. My abdomen is cramped and deeply painful. When I walk now, I have to double over. My bladder feels hard and raw and swollen.

I really, really need to go to the toilet.

"Patrick?" I say to his carefully rehearsed answerphone, "Patrick, please call me back. *Please.*" My voice breaks and for a moment I can't say anything else. I stand there, phone to ear, panting and gasping, mouth opening and closing like a live, half gutted fish.

"Message time closing in ten seconds," says a smooth, pre-recorded female voice. I try again, but choke. I am cut off.

I sit, folded over, head in hands, rocking to soothe the pain and to clear my head. Inside me long fingers of dark liquid seem to seep from my bladder, reaching out around my intestines like poisonous claws. Grabbing. Squeezing. All I can think about is the pain in my stomach.

Alice.

I am not sure if she will want to see me, but she has a bathroom. With a toilet.

Newly energised, I get up and hobble to the front door.

It's locked.

He's done the double lock thing.

Alice

Thursday 22nd May
Still Morning

Eventually I pull myself, at least to some extent, together. I walk into the kitchen and pick up the phone.

"Good morning, Pickersfield Community School." The sing song voice on the other end sounds distracted. I can hear the muted murmur of people and the odd harsh plosive. Somebody cursing at the photocopier.

"Hello, it's Alice Crayer, I do the PPS sessions...I – I'm afraid I won't be able to make it in today."

I have only one session today, nothing tomorrow and then it's half term. They have only one session they'll have to find cover for. But still. This is something I have never done before. My voice sounds wobbly and hoarse. It sounds stupid and phoney. In education, you never call in sick. It's an unwritten rule. It's a cardinal sin. I allow myself to explain that I have a stomach bug. I just about manage to stop myself from going into far too much detail, from over compensating with made up medical jargon. A voice tells me to get well soon. It sounds disgruntled. In the background there is a sudden bang. Somebody is kicking the photocopier. In every school I have worked at, kicking the photocopier has been a well-known remedy to force it to work. Nine times out of ten it does. And it's tremendously satisfying. When you are a teacher, you are forbidden to show any anger. The happy morning ritual of abusing the photocopier is the only genuine outlet you get. I hang up with relief. Somehow the churning sharp edges of my insides settle. I curl up on the sofa and stare into space. I can relax now. I can spend the day sitting in my own warm misery. The prospect feels luxurious. I pad about in my pyjama bottoms for a while, listening to simple, inconsequential noises. Together they form a kind of silence. The clatter of heels in the car park. The sonorous ticking of the clock. I do everything very, very slowly, like an invalid only now being nursed back to health.

A far away aeroplane. The gurgle of the pipes.

Small features, cocked habitually onto one side like a tiny, alert little bird. Hazel eyes, flecked with green. High cheekbones, pale skin. A slight nose, faintly freckled, turned up at the end. Ruffled, faded, hazel hair.

Her face is so clear to me.

I look in the mirror and transpose it onto mine.

Cath

Thursday 22nd May
12.30pm

In the end I can't. I just can't any more. I walk around dizzy with pain, without any idea any more of what I am doing or what I am looking for. I feel half delirious with the cramping in my abdomen. I have stopped expecting Patrick to return my phone messages. Inside me, my organs have clenched and entwined themselves, choking each other, grabbing fleshy, bloody parts of me - and squeezing. I have an enraged creature trapped inside me, fighting its way through my skin. I will explode in a mass of red spatters and slimy white tubing.

I am drowning.

Blindly, I stumble back into the bedroom and I pull from the bottom shelf of the bedroom bookshelves the biscuit tin I have had since I was a child. My 'sweet tin'. It has yellow daisies around the base. Lambs and ponies skipping through them. It's the only thing I can think of that's still definitely mine. Now it holds loose change, as rejected as its container. I have already poured most of it over the floor in my search for the key. Now I tip out the rest, flinching slightly as it lands on Patrick's new carpet. He only got the bedroom re-carpeted last week. Now the whole room looks as though there's been some sort of explosion. Later, I will have to clear it up.

I pick up the tin, shame already colouring my cheeks. The hallway is laminated and it would be more practical to use my erstwhile sweet tin in there, but, if I am going to do this, the bedroom seems more private somehow, though I know in this flat there is no real escape. This too silent structure, with its locked windows and its frowning mortices, will watch and judge me. I apologise mutely to the tin, reminding myself that it has not, for some time, held anything edible. Then I close the bedroom door.

Carefully, I squat down, positioning the narrow opening of the empty tin beneath me. My bladder is screaming. Heat rushes through my lower abdomen and I have barely enough time to grab my jeans and wrench them down. But I have already unbuckled, and then unzipped them to accommodate the swollen protuberance that is my belly, and so it takes only seconds, precious seconds and then I release and I let out an involuntary noise, half groan, half sigh, and squat there, on the bedroom floor, a shameful, swollen carving of a fat girl all alone. Emptying her bladder into the tin that once held a little bit of her childhood.

And I am so focused on my still aching organs, on the great and terrible relief, coursing through me, on the rattle of urine into that pale yellow tin, trickling in behind those innocent, prancing lambs, that I don't hear his footsteps in the lobby outside. Or his keys in the lock. I don't hear him drop his bag in the hallway, casually, as though everything is normal. I don't hear anything until he opens the door and walks into the bedroom.

"*Cath!*"

I jump.

Violently.

A little bit of wee squirts over the edge of the tin and begins to dribble slowly down the outside of it, approaching the floor, and Patrick's new carpet.

"Cath! What the hell are you doing?"

He is frozen in utter disbelief. I look up at him, his face, a mask of disgust and incredulity. I cannot move, for a moment. I cannot speak. Urine, unstoppable now the flood gates are opened, continues to splash and rattle towards the rim of the tin. It's the only movement in the room. There is a long, long second. I feel like an exhibit in a Victorian circus. A deformity for visitors to look at and thrill over. To relish that horrible fascination. And then cover it up to make sure they can still get some sleep.

I jerk myself into action. And in doing so I lose my balance. There is urine on the carpet. There is urine on my leg, soaked into my sock. I stink of it. Trousers down, pale white bottom like a distasteful moon, hastily resurrecting its position, wobbling over a narrow tin. Snot and tears and a desperate attempt to finish, to get rid of the last, shameful trickle and simultaneously, to pull up my clothing. Like some kind of animal. On the floor of the bedroom.

"Cath!"

I am snivelling. I am yanking up my jeans and not caring that it still hurts, buckling them viciously. My bladder protests, sore and angry, though now, at least now, it is empty.

"Patrick...I'm sorry. But you hid the key," my hoarse voice turns angry, it conquers the tears and the crack and the full, choking feeling at the back of my throat. "You hid the key and I couldn't get into the toilet."

He is shaking his head in revulsion.

"Cath. What are you talking about? The bathroom is open. Look."

He strides tensely to the bathroom door and pushes it. Hard. It sticks a little. And then it swings open.

I feel hot and dark and damp all over. The scent of ammonia is already strong. Sharp and tangy on my clothes, on my skin. I bury my face in my hands. I try, very hard, to disappear into them. To climb, like a fat jellyfish into my own chubby palms, and dissolve. There are shuddering sobs in me, shaking my whole body. They are angry and dry, as though I have no more need of water. As though I have squeezed out, along with my urine, my daily allowance of tears. I make a small noise, high pitched and keening. When I speak, my voice is wild and muffled,

"Bloody David...Brandon...Bloody..."

"What?" says Patrick, his voice full of disdain, and with an undertone of fear. He is back in the doorway, but he's made no attempt to come closer. The way you might treat wounded vermin. You want it out of your sight, but if you touch it you might catch something. And you're afraid in its madness it might turn rabid and bite you.

"What are you...what-CATH!!"

I have staggered backwards. Into my sweet tin.

It falls.

It rolls. It leaves an arc of fresh urine. Seeping, silently, into the carpet.

Alice

Thursday 22nd May
1 p.m.

I have been telling myself I do not want to see anyone. I want to curl up quietly reabsorbing my secrets, breathing back in the words still in the air from last night. I tell myself this. But I leave my door ajar.

When she comes it is sudden and it is at a run. I have been sitting on my sofa, staring into space but the staring, this time, is no longer a wallowing, but a kind of waiting. It is as though, last night, Cath and I sealed some sort of unspoken pact, and neither of us have considered the terms of it. When she appears I look up without surprise, because of course we both knew there is something more we need to do here. Something unfinished. We need to finish it. We need to talk. *I* need to talk. I opened a furious dam last night and then I tried to pause the raging river mid flow. But these waters feel trapped and restless and heavy. And I don't think I can keep them contained for long.

The, odd, inappropriate, grin of greeting that has sprung to my face fades.

Cath has burst through my door at a run, skidding wildly to a halt at the end of the sofa. She is breathless and shuddering, her jeans done up awkwardly, the belt pulled across viciously tight and straining at the buckle, and her T-shirt is rucked up at the front, and half in, half out of the top of her jeans. There is a vague smell about her that I can't quite place, and her face is a deep, painful red. As though just beneath her skin she is bleeding, horribly, from some terrible wound.

She doesn't wait for me to speak. She doesn't wait for me to respond to her. She rushes in and immediately starts speaking,

"David Brandon Marsden." I don't immediately recognise the name. I am transfixed by the speaker. She is practically shouting, like an intoxicated teenager, unable to regulate her decibels. For a moment I am checking her pupils, wondering if she might, somehow, have taken something.

"This is where the CEO of bloody *Brandon Homes* lives. This is it! This is his address."

Vaguely I register a crumpled bit of paper. She is waving it in the air and then she slams it on the desk and I can see in her face something grim and something so dark it's impenetrable, but there is also an unnatural sort of cruelty - something angrily excited and they are all crowding up, jostling for space on her face. If she has taken something, it isn't something you'd ever want to take.

She is talking fast, urgently, willing me to understand, wanting me to know all the details. But she keeps glancing back over her shoulder, at her silent and so hastily exited flat.

"He put his home address on public record so you can find it. You can *find* it, just like that on the website, well, you have to pay a pound on Companies House.."

"On what?"

I am a little confused but mostly I know I am only playing for time. The something excited in her face is reflecting dimly, dancing back across mine. Because I think I know where this might be going. And nothing in me is wise enough to stop it from arriving.

"The CEO. Well the real one – I think they've got an acting CEO in place now – but it's the real one we supposedly got the letter from – and he's got his address on the Companies House website. The law changed so they're allowed to just put up their office address or something but he's obviously a bit slow and he hasn't changed it."

"Oh..."

"You *know.*" She is glancing over her shoulder at increasingly short intervals. She needs me to catch up quickly. She needs a comrade in arms.

She needs a good fight.

"I emailed our letter to him last night."

I am surprised she managed that. I didn't think either of us were fit to press a button by the end of last night.

I sit, dour and stale, on my replacement sofa. I survey, behind her, my new flat. Which I have paid for twice. And which somehow was never the same the second time. I think of the spiralling depths I seem to be caught in. And the fact that I was doing OK before. And I wonder, just maybe, if this ridiculous idea that Cath has, apparently for weeks now, been nurturing in herself, is actually true. If everything really dates back to that flood. I wonder if somehow, the people we were, the previous Cath and

Alice, were drowned that day, in the five inches of mud water that invaded our lives.

I look up at her glassily. She is still willing me to understand.

"Of course I didn't get any reply yet. Did *you* get a reply from him yet?"

I have not. Neither have I looked. I am not quite alert enough to point out that, until just now, I didn't even know our email had been sent to him. But something in me is stirring. I like it. I like the idea that I hate the CEO. I like the suggestion that my life is his fault.

"So let's *get* one. I mean, he hasn't bothered to read any of our messages, except to send us a standard letter. He earns bloody *fucking* eight times our salaries – he can afford to listen."

Cath never swears. Cath is, at least in this fevered incarnation, standing quivering in front of me, not in her right mind. She needs something. But is it this? My mind is moving very fast. It looks like the countryside out of the window of a fast train. The situation has, I tell myself, been extremely frustrating. It would only have been a matter of courtesy. The man could have engaged with us. He could have replied.

"Alice?"

I am aware of myself suddenly. I think something cruel and exotic is pulling at my mouth. Across the room, in the mirror, like a stranger, I see a look in my eyes that I know I don't want to examine too closely.

I say, "Cath. Calm down. It's OK. Are you alright?" and then, unable to leave it, unable to leave it alone, now it's there in my mind, I say, innocently, "I'm not sure I know what you're getting at."

"Yes you do." She doesn't sit down. She can't. But she isn't stupid. The flint spark, so unfamiliar in her eyes, has pleading in it. "It's not that bad. I'm not suggesting we burn down his mansion. But just.... we have his address. We can *go* there. We can demand an explanation in person."

There is a pause. Then, furiously,

"He's *ruined* our lives."

I should have known at that statement. I should have stopped it immediately. Even she knew it. I watched her face react to itself, watched her hear her own voice and wonder how it had got there. I try for levity.

"Well, I think mostly just ruined our bank balances. So you want to go there and sit in his lounge and teach him how to spell our surnames?"

I have a silly half smile on my lips. They are not saying yes.

They are not saying no.

"No, but...Alice, you *know*...it would be just to make our point. Just to tell him. Ask again for compensation. It's a trip to Manchester. It's an interesting city and...well...what *else* are we doing?"

And that, with another of those nervous glances behind her, tells me all I need to know. She doesn't just need to go there. She needs to get out of *here*. But what am *I* doing, exactly, I ask myself as I reach for my coat, for my wash bag. Looking after Cath, maybe? I stuff a few of my larger tops in a holdall, and an extra pair of pyjamas. She has nothing with her.

Hazel eyes. Lumpy ballet shoes. She curtseys out at me.

I yank the zip shut on my bag and shoulder it. In the same movement, I stride over and I turn that picture firmly face down. Then I stand it back up again.

Am I looking after Cath? Or looking after me?

Cath

Thursday 22 May
2.15 pm

I stare directly in front, eyes forward. Eyes and mind on the road. On nothing but the road. I concentrate. I pour all of my energy into concentrating. And inside, I shut a door on everything else. It protests and surges and scratches at the door but I am grim and determined. I am driving. That is all I am doing. Just driving.

It was hard to convince Alice to let me drive her. Originally, we were going in her car, she was firm about that and I didn't argue. I just didn't want to waste any more time. But when she started the engine, the battery was flat. She was distracted last night, she said. She must have left the lights on. And I remembered then, meeting her out in the car park, climbing out of the window because I couldn't open the front door. Waiting for her. Waiting while she sat, for what seemed like a decade, in her car. And then knocking on the window and inviting her for dinner. And then she got out quickly and we went into her flat. Her headlights shining out across the tarmac behind us.

Even when we knew her car was out of action, she didn't want to let me drive. Looking at me across the roof of her car, concern in her eyes. She didn't think I was in the right frame of mind to be in charge of a car, wasn't sure it was safe for us. I see her point. I'm not entirely sure either.

But the other options, to go nowhere, or to ask Patrick for jump leads, were more dangerous still.

It started raining as soon as we got on the motorway. Big falling sheets of it, so heavy it feels as though it is made up, not of separate droplets, but a constant, heavy flow, as though we are moving beneath a mighty waterfall, as though the roof were being gradually battered in. I fix my eyes on the long grey mass of road in front of me, the thing I see in snatches between swipes of the windscreen wipers, like some surreal stop motion animated film. I change gears, move my feet on the brake and the accelerator. I avoid other vehicles. I drive.

I really, really want a shower. Between my legs it feels damp and itchy. I feel, though when I glance down at them they look disturbingly normal, that my jeans must be dark and patchy, sopping and stinking. I haven't even washed my hands yet. They seem dried stiff, encrusted with urine. I feel as though Alice knows, somehow. As though everyone can see. But Alice doesn't seem to know. Alice hasn't asked. She gives me sideways glances every now and then, curiosity mixed with a kind of dread. I have no intention of talking. I have no intention of thinking. I have no idea what we are doing here.

I watch the road, I change gears. We are driving.

We have sat in silence most of the way. Wrapped in our own thoughts. But I am not thinking. I am driving. I am a cold, hard ball. I don't care. And I don't think. I just signal, turn, accelerate, and brake.

Alice is navigating. She has her phone on her lap. She checked the train times before she finally gave in. But this is England. The trains take hours. And we knew, both of us, that if we didn't do this now, we were going to think better of it.

Don't think. Just drive.

The rain falls. I imagine we are driving between sheets of it. Sharp sheets, like guillotines, or plates of broken glass. I imagine it is an old fashioned computer game. I dodge the rain to progress to the next level. I drive.

Alice suggested we stop, take a break, have a coffee, buy petrol. But we have enough petrol. Alice suggested I pick up toiletries perhaps, a toothbrush. *Clean underwear.* I think about it. But if I stop I might just stop forever. I might stop and find I cannot possibly carry on. I might stop and anywhere that I stop I am certain I will find Patrick, my abandoned book publication, the endless whirl of things that once were, and things that could still have been. I might collapse in the garage forecourt, blind with it. I might catch sight of myself in the wing mirror.

I really, really need a shower.

I grit my teeth so hard it makes my head hurt. To my left the speedometer creeps up dangerously. A lorry beeps angrily at us and I jump a little, startled by the sheer size of it, a wall of lead and metal rising up to the side of us. The roof of the car barely clears one of its wheel arches. As I stare, shocked for a moment, unable to think, it begins to creep in front of us. A large, pink thing emerges from the driver's window. An arm. It feels odd to see something so human emerge from this creature of weight and metal. It doesn't look as though it could be controlling this beast. It looks more as though the machine is half way through consuming it. The human arm raises its middle finger and thrusts upwards, jerkily. He has been trying to overtake. I take a breath. Let him pull in front. Alice's eyes are wide. Fixed dead centre. We trawl in his wake. I feel trembly, as though this monster has dented the fragile wall I have built to protect myself. The cage which is already bulging, full of so many other monsters, longing to escape and commence their inevitable torture.

What is he doing, anyway? Lorries are supposed to drive slowly.

Mentally, I re-form myself back into that ball, that cold hard ball of concentration. I check mirrors, signal, accelerate, move. I cross into the fast lane and speed up. I'm not supposed to. But I stay in the fast lane. It seems safer somehow. I concentrate. I watch the lights blur in the wet of the rear windscreen, leave those other cars, that other life far behind. My eyes grow hot, for a moment, and prickly. I blink hard.

Don't think.

Don't think.

Just drive.

M.

Thursday 22 May
42 minutes to go

I am sitting, business like, at the lounge table, my lap top spilling a blue, screen shaped oblong of light onto the desk in the dark. I look, I imagine, like a picture of a person doing some work. I remember that when I actually did work, when it was commonplace, I never thought about what I looked like. Now I have to carefully stage it, like a pantomime.

I open the forwarded email of complaint. I have printed it to too, and it lies, innocuously, next to me, on the table. It was sent at 2.37 this morning. Drunk and giggly? Or tortured and sleepless? I re read it and smile. Drunk and giggly. It is quite a good letter.

'The most appalling and immoral extortion racket...'

Probably I should be outraged, on behalf of my company. But I am not sure what the company is now. When I probe it, it scatters like sand and reforms into something I'm not sure of. It was easier when I began. It was easier when it was smaller.

Outside the cars are dashing through rain. I can hear the aggressive swish of the water. I can hear each droplet rising up, and splashing back down. Each one, individually,

243

landing on the rough black tarmac of the pavement. If I listen very carefully I think I can hear the tiny, secondary bounce and split of each liquid particle. I can hear my own senses, fizzing, tingling.

Life is so beautiful. There is just too much of it.

'...ignorance, in both possible senses of the word...'

I rather like these people. Maybe that's why Claudia sent this one through to me, as part of my carefully packaged little parcels of work. Easing me back in. Perhaps she knew I'd enjoy it. I open a new screen.

I am sorry to hear of your experience and would like to write to you personally to convey my deep regret...

Office speak is so comforting. And so utterly meaningless.

We can't take responsibility of course, but perhaps we can offer a small gift as compensation for your difficulties, which may be put towards the cost of your refurbishments...

The legal department will go crazy.

Purely as a gesture of goodwill...

The finance department will go crazy too.

There never used to be 'departments'. There was just a couple of people I had to go and persuade. Old Edith, with her stern half lenses and her soft centre, spouting legal jargon and the plight of women in the workplace. And Tom, fingers on his calculator, easy grin on his face, "show me what you want then...let's see what we can do". But he held those purse strings so tightly you'd have to wrestle it away. Which was the whole point of course. It was why I employed him.

Now the finance department has fifty people in it. And the lawyer I'm meant to speak to wears short skirts and high heels and a sense of entitlement.

Before, we all called each other by nicknames, jokey and taunting, except for Edith – and I was just a guy who had a crazy idea.

Now I'm the CEO. But I am also a delicately avoided problem. I am the one they have been clearing up after these past six months.

I thought your letter was clever. But I'm sorry you felt that way in the first place. Here's a cheque?

I sigh.

I look around the room. In the minimal light, slicing in through the blinds from outside, it looks faded somehow. The flowers on the table are drooping.

I have to go out.

Alice

Thursday 22nd May
2.50 p.m.

When we check in to a hotel, a dingy affair overpriced at £50 a night, but just around the corner from that Holy Grail, the house of the infamous Mr D B Marsden, we are giggly and excitable. Which is an odd switch of mood because we've driven most of the way here in tense silence. Relief, perhaps. Frankly I am amazed we are still alive. We are not getting back in that car, I promise myself, until Cath is cured. Of whatever it is. Patrick, probably. He of the blundering insecurity and the half hidden snipery. And as we are led to our twin room by the surliest receptionist ever invented, I am a little pleased by the concept. It's half term next week. I like the idea that Cath and I might just check out of our lives for a bit, Wrap everything up neatly and then come home in time for tea.

That won't happen of course. But it's OK to daydream. And still, I glance back at Cath, walking tensely behind me, just a break would be useful. Even that would achieve something. *And who appointed you Chief Counsellor Alice Crayer? Do you actually think you're qualified?*

Silent hazel eyes, so huge in that pale face. When I meet their gaze they fill up with salty resentment.

We get into the room. I put my things in the bathroom. Then we stand by our respective beds, looking awkward.

"Do you mind if I have a shower?" asks Cath, tightly. Then she laughs a little, hollowly, "I *really* want a shower!" And that is funny....why? In the last few minutes I have suddenly lost patience with us both.

"Yes that's fine. No problem. I'll wait here," I say shortly. She disappears. I feel guilty. "Feel free to use my shampoo and wash stuff," I call to her.

"Thanks."

I sit on the bed. I listen to the sound of the shower. Then I drift off. I am resigned to it. I don't even try to stop myself anymore.

They are in the park again. And I've stopped going, mostly, but I have to today. I have to go to the shop to buy eggs because Mum's making a cake. And I don't know how I'll get them back again without getting them broken. I walk fast, hoping I can be strong but purposeful but it doesn't work and they see me.

"Ooooh, Twiglet! All alone today? No big sister? No friends?"

"Ahhhhh, bless. Poor ickle Twiggy."

"Looking sexy though, isn't she?"

There is a roar of laughter. They are boys, older than me, and bigger. They have sisters and girlfriends in my year. That's how they know that I am useless. That I am fair game. I'm Twiglet.

"Oh yes, very sexy, especially in those tights, all those wrinkles at the bottom"

I am still in my school uniform. And nothing ever fits.

They move, in a pack, away from the swings and they stand in a line across the path. Across my path. These are the boys who said, "We'll be back."

"No one around, is there?" one of them says, conversationally.

"Nope."

"No one at all. We could do anything we wanted."

They are theatrical, these boys, more than the others. They do it like it's a film. I wish it was one. In a film I would do something.

"So what shall we do?"

"Shall we rape her?"

"Nah, too ugly."

They burst into fits of uncontrollable laughter, scattering and holding onto each other in mirth.

"Nah, too ugly!" they keep repeating to each other and collapsing again into further hysterics.

I continue to walk, numbly, along the path they have vacated because they are so amused that I am not even worth raping. Though of course, something that big, it was never a real threat. Nothing ever is.

Shall we rape her?

Yes.

Please.

Do it.

In a film they would do something. Something undeniable and awful. And then it would all be so clear. And so simple.

I jerk back to reality and realise that the shower has finally stopped. I hear the sounds of Cath stepping out of it, the towel pulled clumsily from the rusting rail, the bolt squeaking as she unlocks the bathroom door. I check my watch. It's been over forty minutes.

"Alright?" I say, automatically, as she appears.

She has the towel wrapped around her, inexpertly, precarious. Beneath it her skin is red and raw, as though she has been scrubbing it viciously in very hot water. She is shaking a little.

"I'm sorry," she says, "I think I used all your shower gel."

And then she bursts into tears.

They are violent sobs, wracking her body and squeezing her ribcage, so that she gasps and pants for air. I guide her, gently, to sit on the bed and I sit beside her and hold her shoulders, at first awkwardly, then tightly, as if I can somehow, by doing so, hold us both together. Between sobs she apologises, constantly and incoherently and I, in turn, make small soothing noises which cannot even begin to approach the problem. She rubs the tears away roughly with her fingers, so roughly that I take both of her hands forcibly in mine, and wipe her face for her with the edge of the quilt. Her skin is burning hot, and she flinches when I touch it. But that alarming red colour has faded, at least, to a purpley pink. I don't think she's done herself lasting damage. This time.

"Cath," I say, when the sobs become more infrequent, and her breathing more regular. "It's Patrick, isn't it? What's he done, Cath, what's happened?" But the sobs only redouble in number and vigour, and the reply is disjointed and lost in the gap between her chin and the floor.

"Cath?"

She grows calmer, lastingly so now, and there is a defeat, a weariness in it.

"Nothing," she says flatly, "that's the thing. Nothing happened. Nothing *ever* happens. There's no story."

And I understand what she means. We're adults now. We don't cry for no reason. There must be an event.

Sticks and stones may break my bones, but names will never hurt me.

Apparently.

But people don't just steal your dinner money any more.

They never did.

M

Thursday 22nd May
12 Minutes, 30 Seconds To Go

I put the printed version of the letter of complaint down very carefully on the table. It is white and crisp, pleasing with its black type and its sharp straight edges against the lacquered brown of the wood. Very carefully I move it, gently, with the tips of my fingers, until it lines up exactly with the corner of the table. I survey it for a moment without touching it further, just to make sure I get it right, and then, concentration furrowing my forehead, I fold it precisely into three. The ends are perfectly parallel. The first sentence lines up faultlessly with the first fold of the paper. For a moment I consider folding it further. Echoing the little computer icon with the envelope on it which is its electronic alter ego. I used to be very good at origami. I gaze, in indecision, at the letter. It meets my gaze undaunted, supremely confident.

'We hope we have spelled your name right,' it says, *'we didn't have a note of who you were'.*

I think I know how it feels.

Carefully, I place the letter inside the briefcase. Then, equally carefully, I shut down the computer. I pick up the other papers on the desk and I slide them back into their folders, their clear pockets, their envelopes. I return them exactly, to the way they looked when they arrived. Cleanly,

I snap the catch down on the briefcase. Everything inside is perfectly ordered.

And I think, if only the world could do this. The vast extremes, the scattered, chaotic moments. The heaving, breathing life of it. It could all be kept tidily. Everything in its place.

My wife will be home soon.

I will go out.

Now.

I will get her some milk so that I can make a cup of tea. That much I can handle. I can handle that.

One word of the thesaurus, one page at a time.

Cath

Thursday 22nd May
4.01pm

We don't say much to each other after that. There is not much we can say. We don't really have any suitable vocabulary. Alice lends me a baggy t shirt and a pair of tracksuit bottoms which I suspect she intended as a pair of pyjamas. But when I ask to borrow them she doesn't question me. I have scrubbed my underwear in the shower and now it is damp against my skin, but it's clean. My whole body feels tingly and sore, but it's cleaner, I've felt cleaner ever since I cried.

We sit in silence and then Alice, helpless, says, "David Marsden then? Shall we pay him a visit?" and I nod, and we walk out of that room and I am saying, *David Marsden. David Brandon Marsden. David Bloody Brandon Marsden* in my head but it seems suddenly unsatisfying.

We leave the hotel. I feel weak but new somehow, cleansed. Alice reaches for my hand. My head feels empty.

We come out of the hotel and we cross the road and turn right, Alice navigating in silence. It seems a long walk down the street that leads to the street that he lives on. It seems quite a long street. All along it are little lampposts and on the lampposts are hanging baskets. Birds sing in the aftermath of the rain and the pavement gleams, wetly. The houses are clean and freshly painted, quaint in different shades of pastel. This is the kind of neighbourhood where people meet up, they get together and form committees and talk about co-ordinating their decor. I think about it, trying to find a kind of anger inside me but I know, at the same time, that I too, want to live here. It is that kind of neighbourhood.

Eventually we near the end of this road, where there is a perfect cross junction with another. We turn. And we walk down the street that he lives on. David Brandon Marsden. There is a small shop halfway down it. Other than that it is almost exactly the same as the one we have just walked down. Alice points across the road. Number 42. We keep walking, but slower.

I stare at the house that he lives in.

Name: David Brandon Marsden
Address: 42 Canterbury Drive, Manchester, MA12 3PW
Occupation: CEO

I have no idea at all what we are going to say.

M.

Thursday 22 May
1 Minute 47 Seconds To Go

I count the money so that there is exactly enough for a pint of milk. I put the coins in my pocket and walk through the hallway and stand at the door. I breathe deeply, once, and then I lift the latch.

I keep myself focused. I repeat to myself, carefully, each moment's instructions. I try to make everything one thing only. All of it – only a step at a time. Fleetingly I remember there was an era when I didn't mind the entangled mess of the world. When everything seemed possible – and I could hold it in my mind all at once. All together. It was perfectly natural. I must have been very young. It must have been very long ago.

I step outside. Then I turn back to face the door and breathe once. I turn the key, check the door handle, turn again to face the road. I look across it and focus. Focus only on the shop. I imagine the milk I will buy there.
I take a step. One foot in front of the other.

I keep myself focused.

Alice

Thursday 22 May
4.07 pm

We are nearly at the shop. It is a small building with murky windows, incongruous in this neighbourhood. It is almost directly opposite his house. We prepare, hearts thumping ridiculously, to cross over. And then we stop, very still, very suddenly. A man emerges from the door of the house.

I fight a childish impulse to run, to turn and bolt like a sullen teenager, surprised into betraying fear.

He looks for a moment, in our direction, without registering us, and then he turns back and carefully relocks the door, tries the handle, turns back to face us – and steps out into the road.

There is a car – out of nowhere – a thud – and then silence.

M.

Thursday 22 May
1 Minute To Go

Oddly I know what is going to happen. I see the man in the car, just a flash but enough. A man with his hand on his chest and a look of something terrified and resigned on his face. I see it, quite literally, in the whites of his eyes.

But I don't try to stop it. I actually pause. I stop for a moment, a tiny, immeasurable moment, just watching, mesmerised by the man behind the wheel. The man who is about to kill me. I have milliseconds, just that, a tiny window, but they are milliseconds which feel like some kind of eternity. But I don't try to jump back, to shout, or to step sideways.

Perhaps, after all, this is simply the next step.

It is the next word, the next page, in my half written thesaurus.

Alice

Thursday 22 May
And A Long Time Ago

I remember.

I remember the first time I found her with the pain killers. She was sat at the kitchen table with little mounds of them in front of her. Several, careful little mountains of white tablets, arranged symmetrically over the table, as though, for some time, she had been sitting there, arranging them. It never occurred to me that she might have been stalling, might have hoped for an interruption, or been too nervous to begin. I knew her too well for that. She was simply preparing it thoroughly. Ensuring her last deed was done, just so. When everyone else was supposed to be out.

I remember first walking in, and looking at her, and seeing it. She seemed, that day, even smaller than usual and the pills were huge, they were like tombstones in front of her. She was there, pale as always, jumping in shock as I walked through the door. Knocking the table violently with a skinny, grazed knee.

I wondered why my mouth was open when I wasn't surprised. I wondered how long she would have sat there, just contemplating, before she reached out and touched them. Before she put out her hand and she took the first one. I wondered whether she would have swallowed them one by one or in fistfuls. With water or with orange juice. Or in hard little gulps on their own.

These were the things I wondered.

I sat with her then. With a kind of solemnity only achieved in those who are not yet adults and are no longer children. We sat together and I held her hand and all the time I was there the pills stayed on the table. All the time I was there she didn't take them. Neither of us said a word to each other. There was no persuasion, no power play, no emotional speeches. We just sat there together and we looked at the tablets, and in my hand I felt hers slowly stop shaking. I don't know how long it was that we sat there. Time seemed to lengthen itself like a malevolent shadow. Afternoon sunlight winked and played across the white plastic crisscross on the kitchen windows. The light seemed to have got restless in our stillness. I watched the digital display on the oven and the microwave. The microwave was one minute faster. I remember thinking it sort of didn't matter, if time was circular anyway and that meant the microwave would hit midnight before the oven, they would reverse roles and the oven would, at least numerically, be later. Then the microwave would be behind it by a whole lap. I thought about saying this but I didn't.

Tabby's hand was cold in mine. Cold like it might have been if she had taken the tablets. If I had come home a few hours later.

If I squinted I could see the ghosts of digits in the digital faces. I could see it there like a wraith. 88:88. I watched the minutes pass and measured them in lines of neon. When I remember it now I think of us as frozen, like statues. As though we didn't move at all. As though neither of us even really breathed. But in reality, at some point, I at least must have done, because the table got knocked again, accidentally and one of the little mounds of tablets wobbled and then collapsed, clattering. One of them veered off, rolling, upended, across the table, before spinning itself loudly to a rest. The sound of it echoed like gunshots around the silent kitchen.

"Sorry," I said to Tabby, in a hushed sort of whisper, as though the most important thing here was the arrangement of the pills. As though it was all just another meticulous art project. Another of Tabby's exquisite creations that I had accidentally stepped on, or spilled something on, or smudged.

We sat. And I looked at the digital displays and held her hand firmly, damply in mine. It was the first time in my life that I had ever been so utterly unsure what my sister was thinking.

Had she planned it, for weeks? Or was it on impulse? Would she have regretted it later - *too* late? And how would it have been, what exactly would have happened? Would it have been violent and bloody and thrashing or more like a sedative, a drift into sleepy eternity? When would we have found her? Would she have been dead already? Would her body be cold, her hands gone rigid? Or would we all have arrived home, perhaps together, to find her convulsing, foaming, eyes glazing, gasping out our names through lips blue tinged and bloodied, with her final, whistling, agonised breaths?

The sound of the car drawing up the drive. It was a slow building rather than a sudden noise but it still made me jump. And then I heard the muted voices of our parents, climbing out of the car, closing doors, rattling keys. It occurred to me that this must have been what we were waiting for. The arrival of adults. Authorised personnel.

"It'll be OK," I said to Tabby, somehow finding my voice now, "Dad will put the pills away."

Of course she was silent. And I suppose I was missing the point.

We waited, quietly as they came through the front door, locked it behind them, and removed their shoes. I think in that time I could hear my heart thumping. And then they opened the kitchen door and walked into the room, casually.

There was a moment of even greater silence. Their open mouths, taking it in, as though they were offering silently, to open them even wider and swallow and take the whole table in and make it all right. I suppose there might have been some part of them that hoped it wasn't quite the way it looked, but by that point something had finally released in me. There were tears in my throat and my nose and my eyes and I didn't know where they had come from or why there were there, because, after all, it wasn't me. It wasn't me who had been planning to make myself die. And through the water in my nose and the wet on my cheeks and the sweet, salt taste on my mouth, I poured it out. I told it all in the words that Tabby would not use, and I told it fast, gulping, feeling strange little convulsions which might have begun life as tiny, smothered sobs.

"I found her. She was here and there were all these tablets. And I sat with her and we have been here for hours and she hasn't taken any, she hasn't taken them now because I was here but she might have been going to, well she definitely was and it was lucky, wasn't it that I came home early because I skived that detention but that doesn't matter now does it because if I hadn't been here she would...she would...all dead maybe or nearly died - and she was going to take them. They were here. All here ready – but she knows now, don't you Tabby? She won't really take them – "

My Father's voice, urgent, commanding. "Shush Alice"

I stopped abruptly.

I remember that. As though he had reached down inside me and flicked a switch I didn't know how to operate.

They sort of scooped her up, amid a lot of fuss and Mum crying and dabbing her eyes and Dad pale, and his face all set like plastic. They took her outside for a walk in our little strip of garden.

I stood in the lounge, watching them through the back door. I watched their backs as they retreated, the three of them, walking, like bodyguards with their protégée, away.

"Alice, give us some time now. Give Tabitha some space."

M.

Thursday 22 May
56 Seconds To Go

There is a noise. A sudden noise, sharp and yet also soft and muted. Like a fist hitting a cushion. A bird flying, thoughtless, into curtains. I hear this noise as if from very far away, and I am not sure where it might have come from.

There is a rushing sensation under the soles of my feet, and an odd lack of tension in my toes. My ankles feel loose and lost somehow, and my heels are disconnected, numb.

And then I look.

I look and I realise it's because my feet have left the ground.

There is a strange, slow moment. The final page in my inconclusive and fraying thesaurus.

And I am floating upwards, I am driftwood between them.

The bright, bright blue that is the sky.

And the glitter in the tarmac, like a promise of stars.

Cath

Thursday 22 May
4.07 p.m.

The car was going very fast, too fast and it came out of nowhere and it went in a perfectly straight line, too straight. For a tiny, fleeting, split second moment I had a glimpse of a man inside and he seemed somehow oddly shaped. There was something wrong with the shape of him and at first I couldn't quite put it together. Later, when the car is a spire of black smoke in the distance, I will retrieve the disjointed pieces of my memory and put the picture together and realise, with hindsight, that the man at the wheel was clutching his chest. That the strange spike in him, – that this was his elbow, his fist bunching his clothes. His eyes wide and panicked. I do not know that I see this at the time that I see it. It is a vision which I will be haunted with later.

And the car, speeding so sudden, so straight, it slammed into David Brandon Marsden. Who I recognise, sickeningly, from the glossy posed pictures in the Annual Report. It slammed into this man, this David Marsden, who was just – only just stepping out into the road.

And now I watch as he is lifted high into the air and then it seems he glides for a moment, leisurely, aboard the evening breeze, while the car below him speeds up, and disappears into nothing but a sickening schedule of sounds.

Crash. Splinter. Scream. Thud.

Katie Hall-May

M.

Thursday 22 May
48 Seconds To Go

Beneath me, I can feel air. It holds me gently. I lie down on it and look upwards, and I feel the tiny, fizzing, heat points that are the individual shifts of light. I watch tiny organisms and dust particles floating upward as I sink down, playing on my fingers, dancing with me. Catching fire in the sun. Above me, the clouds are moving, slowly. They morph into birds. They become rays, they are sky.

The tarmac, when it greets me, is softer than I remember. I had always thought of it as a hard, smooth substance, but now that I am testing it, I see that it is actually rather fuzzy at the edges. It catches me, like a child's trampoline in slow motion, tossing me gently, enveloping me again as I land. I feel the fibres of it, soft and insistent, reaching out to reclaim me.

I lie back and allow myself to be absorbed.

Cath

Thursday 22 May

4.07 pm

The man lands on the glinting tarmac and somebody, one of us, Alice or Cath, screams. What I will never be able to figure out later, is whether his descent really was so ambling. If he really did actually float down to earth. It seemed like ten minutes – it seemed like an hour - between the car hitting and him landing, during which we all watched. It seemed as though there were hundreds of us, all watching, hypnotised, by his casual, meandering descent, unhurried as a newspaper on a summer breeze.

Thud.

Everyone has frozen. I am dimly aware of Alice standing next to me. Somewhere, much further down the road, a thin spire of smoke begins spiralling, lazily, tracing its signature into the sky. I do not turn to look at it. We do not go to investigate. We know that the mystery car has stopped.

We have stopped. The car has stopped. And the man lying now in the road, the man who earns £400 thousand pounds a year base salary, plus £500,000 in bonuses and benefits, and whose ear we have come to pour our complaints into – has stopped.

M.

Thursday 22 May
7 Seconds To Go

I lay my head back on to tarmac and take a last, luxurious breath.

Life is like reading through a foreign thesaurus. When you look up one word, you find another twenty. If you look up even one of those twenty, you are already forty meanings away from the first one.

And there's a good chance one of those brings you back to the start.

Alice

Thursday 22 May
And A Long Time Ago

And I remember the second time we found her.

The second attempt was more successful.

M.

Thursday 22 May
Time

When life comes to an end there is always a last word. A final thought for your personal thesaurus. Perhaps death is simply a passing on of that half-finished manuscript, a casting of it into the wind, in the hope that somebody, someone, somewhere might pick up the loose pages and put them together.

And as the light gradually shrinks in my vision, until I am no longer lying looking up at the sky but at a gentle light far away, like a steady burning candle, I gather the pages of my dog-eared thesaurus, and release them, gently, into the wind.

Muffled voices fade out around me.

The last thing I hear is the sound of scattered paper.

Cath

Thursday 22 May
4.25 p.m.

There is police tape and panic and there are people looking out of windows. There are officials and professionals and paramedics. There are stretchers and head shakers and subdued, murmuring voices. For some reason there is an abundance of thick, crimson blankets which they insist that Alice and I are wrapped in. They do not immediately wrap the man up in them. There is a huddling around him, a kneeling of paramedics, a testing of pulse, a respectful bowing of heads. And then, only then is there a light, respectful spreading out of the blanket. Over his feet and his body and then over his head.

There is a tent erected around him. In case it rains, I think, and then realise it's to stop people looking. I am looking. I am staring. I am doing nothing except stare, open mouthed, as though I can make sense of it if I can only study it carefully, like a book or a particularly complicated formula.

There are white forms for witness statements and an efficient policewoman. Her tabard says *Manchester Traffic Police* and she looks jaded and impatient, as though she's seen it all before. We sit on the roadside and one of the neighbours provides us with tea and I feel guilty for being there and for feeling snide about the neighbourhood. The policewoman instructs us to take all the time that we need. I am not sure precisely what it is we should take our time doing. The black type on the statements swims about on the page. The box we should write in seems alternately too large and too small. There is a biro with *Manchester Metropolitan Police* on it. It shakes a little in my hand.

Someone, a paramedic or a doctor, arrives and inspects us with an air of the expert. We are poked, and shone lights at, our temperatures taken and we are tucked into our blankets like children. We are, we are told, in a natural state of shock and we should keep ourselves warm and breathe deeply and slowly so that our adrenaline levels will normalise.

All around me I can see curious pairs of eyes peering out, from houses, through windows, walking by. But we are the only ones who saw the accident. The *Manchester Metropolitan Police* biro keeps running out. It is replaced with another one, which only says *Biro.*

We are understandably traumatised, we are informed, delicately, but our witness statements will be crucial.

"It's easier for the families," says our policewoman, "if it's clear and settled. It allows them to mourn."

There is red tape in abundance, to match the red blankets. There seem, now, to be hundreds of bustling people, swarming all over the scene like officious, fat bees. I am trying to force words out of the end of the new pen.

All I can think of is that there isn't much blood. You expect some in these moments. Perhaps we watch too much TV. I expected pools of it, spreading, glutinous and sticky. I dreaded and feared it, but in fact, the pale face of him, bright against the tarmac, the whole, perfect body of him, it doesn't seem real. I wonder suddenly if they are sure he is dead now. Perhaps he was only concussed. Perhaps the blanket is smothering him.

Maybe the blood is there after all. Perhaps it hides, sensitive to our emotional delicacy, concealing itself quietly beneath the weight of his torso. Gushing out later when it is darker, and quiet.

Alice

Thursday 22 May
5.40 pm.

After what feels like an inexorably long time we have completed our statements, recorded our contact details and we are released.

"Did you know him?" says the policewoman, when he goes over my statement.

"No," I say quietly.

I realise with surprise that it is actually true.

I glance at Cath but she tells me nothing. She is pale and concentrated. And I realise as I look at her that this person, this Cath, who will cry on me, but who has never even begun to confide in me, who looks at me with something akin to admiration, but doesn't try any more to conceal the cracks behind it, this Cath is a mysterious force outside of my control. Things I say to her barely ripple the surface, things I guess at remain, at her will, just a guess. This Cath person, she reveals to me nothing. She walks next to me in a bubble made of a glass I can't penetrate. And it feels lonely. It awakes in me a loneliness I haven't felt since childhood. Since the last time I walked beside somebody else I couldn't get through to. Somebody else who told me nothing.

Like furtive animals, seeking cover, we begin, instinctively, to move back towards the hotel. To take a shower perhaps. To lick our non-existent wounds. We walk slowly, as though everything is a terrible effort. Neither of us really says much. My hair is a mass around my face, as if it flew up in outrage, blood red and indignant, protesting at this subterfuge in which we pretend to be bystanders. We were his ill wishers. We came here, drove for hours to knock on the door of his home – and do what? And give him a piece of our minds? Steal a vengeance for a couple of months' worth of 'musty'?

Cath

Thursday 22 May
5.55 pm.

I think the driver was having a heart attack.

Later, I will know this for certain. Later I will scour the online newspapers and search for a report of an accident on Canterbury Drive. A *fatality*. And I will still catch my breath at that word, though it is no surprise to me. Later I will become obsessed with looking up the report on that accident.

But I know even now. I saw the driver clutching his chest. For a moment, I think I might have seen the fear in his eyes, although the memory is already eroding, bright and sharp and painful, but losing details around the edges. I heard the police talking about it. They found him in the crashed car. They found heart pills in his dashboard and his doctor's card in his wallet. I imagine him dead, still clutching his stopped heart. The car oozing smoke like the blood that there wasn't. He was probably dead, or close to it, at the moment of impact.

Nothing malicious. Nothing punishable. He just happened to be having a heart attack at that moment. Just happened to be driving his car at the time. And he just happened, in his final death journey, to take somebody else along with him. It was an accident, unfortunate, but a simple coincidence.

They have taken our statements, our details, our signatures. Perhaps, I keep thinking, they know somehow, from my face, from my handwriting, that I am the sort of person who hasn't been into the office for months, who abandons her research. Who wees into biscuit tins and spills urine onto the floor. Who drives for two hours in the rain to confront a man about two inches of floodwater. Who is not even, at this moment, wearing her own clothes. Perhaps they know I am not just some innocent bystander. After all, this is a world where people die accidentally, without intent, without reason, without warning or ceremony. Life is a fragile, insignificant pastime. In this kind of world the small details matter.

I have to remind myself, often, that Alice and I are not actually culpable. That the fact we were there, that we knew who he was, that we came to complain to him is not the same as actively killing him. Not the same as anything but a petty shamefulness, a childish petulance. But each time I tell myself it sounds more like a lie. As though the truth is that somewhere, in some parallel universe, we absolutely caused the whole thing.

"Stupid," says Alice, suddenly.

I wonder which of my thoughts she is reading.

"We haven't eaten," she says, "we need to go and eat. That was a horrible experience but there was nothing we could do. Nothing we can do now. For either of them."

I look at her face. I would be impressed by her pragmatism. By the fact that she is right. Except that her eyes are far away. Her face is even paler than usual and as I look at her she presses her lips them together in a gesture I have somehow become familiar with. A movement of her muscles, half defiant, half unconscious. I look away again.

We go to eat.

The process of finding the restaurant, asking directions to the town centre, walking round it, looking at menus, selecting a table seems dim to me, it seemed dim even as we were doing it. Until finally, I seem to be opening my eyes and the world slides, bumpily, back into focus and I find we are sitting, facing each other diagonally across a cool, spotless table. I am in the corner seat of the corner table of a quiet Chinese restaurant. Smells of spices and lemongrass swoop through the air, wafting under my nose and filling my senses with a renewed, and insatiable lust to eat. My mouth waters simultaneously with saliva and acid and I swallow awkwardly. Alice's face seems jaundiced beneath the warm lighting, and she's half in shadow, but her eyes have been recently sharpened. She looks up, she speaks to the impeccable waitress, we study menus in silence. We speak again to the waitress, who bows to us. We order.

For a little while we converse only in platitudes. We reflect that it couldn't be helped, that it had been terribly sad, that these things happen. We speak in soft, respectful voices, different to our own, as though our lips, on autopilot, have not enough energy to produce greater volume. After a while we both sense the futility of this and fall silent. Alice is staring into middle distance. Blood is still pumping in my ears, so loud I think other people might hear it, the blood that is mine, his blood that there wasn't.

I am seized by a huge and violent hunger.

We have seen a man killed. Two men. Killed in front of us, outright. I suppose it could have been worse. I suppose they could have been writhing, screaming, in agony for hours. Limbs twisted impossibly, bodies knotted, entwined with bits of melting metal. My stomach lurches and I taste liquid again in my mouth. The skin around my eyes feels dry and brittle, like dried sweat or tears, though I don't think there have been either. I am callously, cruelly, hungry. The waitress arrives with Alice's meal and my plate, and I help myself urgently to unlimited buffet, feeling horribly crass for doing so. I try not to pile my plate too high. I return to my table and attack my food with the chopsticks in the hope they will force me, through my own blundering ineptitude to eat slowly and tactfully. To eat the way Alice does, chopsticks poised, the food on her plate moved around, congealing, not much of it making its way to her mouth. My mouth is an immense and bottomless need. It gleams wetly, the oils from the food shining greasily on my lips, maybe even my chin. With every mouthful I feel more like some cartoon beast, shovelling scraps, but even so I give up on the chopsticks and pick up a fork and then I give myself up to eating, urgent and tasteless. Alice moves a piece of tofu listlessly around her plate. I curse my hunger, clear my own, and help myself to more buffet. I will not, I promise myself desperately, have dessert. Instead I sit there, second plate cleared away. Trying to look compassionate, to look subdued, to look shocked, to look any of the things that I actually feel but all I can do is to sit there and stare like a starving cat at the uneaten food on Alice's plate.

And then somehow, for some unacceptable reason, I absolutely have to know. I have to know the rest of the story. I have to know more about these strangers, this Alice and this Tabby, with whom I am occupying my mind in the hope, perhaps, that they will crowd out everything else. I have to understand this person, opposite me, whose body has sat or walked beside me on our journey to the death of Mr David Brandon Marsden. I don't know what it is that makes me want to know so very desperately. For an instant, I imagine Alice's fist, swinging round, connecting with a small fat schoolboy with Patrick's face. I shake my head, clear the image immediately. Patrick is not Georgie Smales.

And we are not children.

But still. I have an urge to know *something*, to know anything other than that body lying motionless in the middle of the road. Either that or we just have unfinished business. Alice, Tabitha, and I.

"Alice," I say, and the room swims in the horror of it. "Um...your sister...the stuff at school - did it...I mean, did she resolve it...?"

There is a long pause. Alice's eyes are shafts of pain beneath which I am writhing. Now I begin to sweat.

"I'm sorry. I didn't mean to...I just wondered." Another pause. But I just cannot leave it. I can't stop it at this stage. "Alice – did it...did she..." I can't bring myself to say the words. Mentally I test out different phrases, a hundred different possible euphemisms. "Um...did it drive her to....?"I trail off.

Alice is glaring past me at nothing. Her lips move and when she speaks it is wonderingly, as if she is only just remembering.

"Drive her..." she stops for a moment, and there is silence, and then it seems that she snaps back into focus and she speaks again but her voice now is clipped and uncompromisingly bitter.

"Drive her. No. She walked."

Alice

Thursday 22 May
Inside A Chinese Restaurant in Manchester
And A Long Time Ago

The second time it isn't me who finds her. It is my Mother. She is walking through the front door, carrying shopping bags in the crook of one arm. My Father is behind her, a box in his arms full of bottles and tins. He puts it down on the step to unlock the door and my Mother is talking, not breaking her step as she moves through the door and into the hallway. She puts down the shopping bags to take off her coat. She opens the coat cupboard talking, talking. I have been 'irresponsible, not to mention stupid'. I should never have been caught skiving that nice Mr Lucas' lessons. (She doesn't say 'caught'. She doesn't say 'skiving'.) I should 'know better by now'. My life 'depends' on my GCSEs. She hangs up her coat, holds her hand out for mine. I need to 'pull my socks up'. It's time I 'stopped playing around' and I settled down. In real life 'no one is going to want to employ someone who can't even be bothered to turn up for geography lessons'. She hangs up her coat. She looks at my Father for a response and he agrees, distractedly, watching next door who is waxing his car. We have been to the supermarket – I was dragged out with them both to be lectured. I have been listening only to parts of it, and mostly watching Damian Cuttles who left school last year, and works in Sainsbury's and is gorgeous. She closes the coat cupboard. Talking, talking. She calls me 'Alice Lucy Crayer'. She picks up the shopping bags again.

Then she opens the kitchen door and she screams.

My Father is pushing, pushing past her and his eyes are wild and my Mother falls against the cupboard but she doesn't cry out. She is silent, mouth open, like a fish, she is gasping at air. I try to budge past her too but she has righted herself and frozen and she is blocking the way. I peer around her, and my Father is kneeling, kneeling down over something stretched out on the floor. And then my Mother is still standing there, but now she is making a noise which I cannot find a name for - and I cannot see what it is they are looking at. It takes a few seconds and at the end of it I am still at the back of what seems like a crowd of unmoving bodies, and all the while, there is the terrible sound from my Mother. And I *know*. I *know* what it is. What it will be. Something boils up in my windpipe and I try again, more violently, to push my way past and just as I do so my Mother, sprung somehow into action, whirls round and lunges for the hallway telephone. And then I stop. I stop moving. I stop trying to get past.

I am only very small at the back of a large crowd because my Mother is saying, "Yes. It's my daughter. Please. Yes. She's unconscious. I think she's taken a lot of painkillers."

There is a pause on the phone. I can hear my Father saying something, cradling something there on the floor. I can hear my Mother's ragged breathing, listening intently to a strange, remote sounding voice on the other end of the phone. I can hear my teeth, chattering slightly. I realise it must mean that I am shaking. And I wonder, what I will be like without a sister. Not what *it* will be like. What *I* will be like.

And the hallway spins.

My Mother says, "No. No. It must have been an accident. I don't know how many…I'm sure she wouldn't."

I hear the voice on the other end turning conciliatory and for a moment I imagine it, reading its instructions for how to deal with distressed relations, for how to get past their infernal stupidity, their utter blindness and then, to my alarm, the voice is shouting, it is screaming and crying and it fills the hallway and only at the last minute do I realise it is me. It is my voice. I am screaming.

"It's NOT! It's NOT an accident. She wanted to do it before and we wouldn't LET her. It's not an ACCIDENT!"

And then, already overcome by hoarseness, my throat tightening, but all the while powering it, forcing it out so that the words pour like a tidal wave, the weight of it crushing the breath out of us, drowning us all;

"It's because of school. Of COURSE she meant to do it! She MEANT it!"

There is a hiss, like a horrified pantomime audience, and my Mother makes a sort of involuntary, sudden movement towards me, but she is held by the curling wire of the telephone and the tinny, careful, professional voice still murmuring to her on the other end of it. My Father says, in a voice of terrible tiredness,

"Alice, be quiet."

And I look up at my Mother from the bottom of an immense ocean and I can see it, feel it looking at me there in her eyes, a terrible broken sort of rage.

The tears come then, loudly, finally. And I wonder, not for the first time, why, when it is Tabby who has the speech disorder, it is me who is always being told to be quiet.

Cath

Thursday 22 May
9.40 p.m.

We sit and stare at each other for a little while. Alice has stopped talking without really concluding and I assume this means that this is the finish. A crumpled heap on a kitchen floor. This is where Tabby finishes. Where, by the look in her eyes, Alice does too.

We sit and stare for a moment and then I say, "I'm so sorry." I say, "Your poor sister," and, "must have been so hard for you – all of you, so hard for your parents. It must have been so hard..."I fumble and stumble and spill meaningless platitudes out of my mouth like excess spittle. I say, "Anything I can do," and, "Any time you want to talk," and, "I'm here for you." I say, "It's awful, schools these days, or in those days...not that it was – not that you're...but anyway..." I say, "She had a brilliant sister," and I try to smile sadly but I have got the tone wrong. I say, "Life can be so hard," and, "It's so important isn't it...to have help...for children." I say, "Such a shame," and, "Such a waste," and, "I'm sorry."

What I want to say is, "*Fuck*." But even that word is not harsh enough, not terrible enough for the way that the world is this evening.

I say, "I guess I just don't know what to say."

Then I realise that I have been talking at her constantly for close to five minutes.

I stop. Her face is full of anger and I don't know who it is aimed at. She opened her mouth at one point, as if to stop me, but now she has closed it. Closed her mouth and her face and, for a moment, her eyes. Then she opens them again, puts down her chopsticks very firmly, drops some money beside them, stands up, and walks out.

I think of the little girl in the tutu. With the hazel hair and shy eyes and the dainty half courtesy.

I feel sick in more ways than I could possibly describe. But I am not sick. Instead I pick up one of Alice's chopsticks and I stab a piece of her tofu and then I start to cry.

Katie Hall-May

Alice

Thursday 22 May
And A Long Time Ago

I am standing in the playground. I am standing by the fence watching the water ripple across the huge, brown puddle which has collected, right in the middle. On my skin I can feel it prickling, stinging. The gaze of them. Glancing, calculating, looking at me – and at the water. Everybody has unconsciously formed a ring around it, crackles of excitement like electricity charging the crossed diamond wires of the fence behind me. I can feel them looking. I can feel their waiting. Their planning of it.
One way or another, I will end up in that puddle.
I feel very, very weary. Not afraid. Only tired. I can't be bothered with it any more.
They are only hesitating because of her. She is out with her class at the edge of the playing field, doing some sort of biology or geography experiment. She is tense and watchful. Her eyes do not leave us. Alice Crayer has drawn blood on my behalf before. They will not risk it outright. But it is a matter of time. They will seize their moment, it will happen today or it will happen tomorrow. Does it honestly matter?
Suddenly, something snaps in me, a sort of explosion of weariness and I can't stand the waiting and I just want it over. I push myself off the railings and through the crowd

and I walk right into it, into the middle of the puddle and I can feel the cold shock of it, and the soaking of my socks and the water, flooding into the spaces between my toes. I walk through the growing chorus of whispering, murmuring, excited half laughter. I walk to the very centre of the puddle and then I stop and, slowly and firmly, I sit down. I sit down in the puddle and I stretch out my legs so that as much of me as possible is thoroughly sodden. And I ignore their noise, rising now to a crescendo, ignore it and the teacher who is hurrying, hurrying over, and I feel the cold against my goose pimpled, indignant skin. And I save them further effort for later by removing my coat and spreading it out in the water next to me, just for good measure.

And I try very hard to ignore the unbearable look of disappointment on the face of my sister. My erstwhile protector.

I am sorry. I am really, very sorry, I tell her silently.

The teacher arrives, the students scatter and I begin to get to my feet, head down, teeth chattering.

I am sorry Alice, but we were never going to win.

Who knows, if that was why. If that was what she was thinking.

It doesn't matter.

Either way.

I don't accept her apology.

Cath

Thursday 22 May
11.45 p.m.

It is nearly midnight when she arrives back at the hotel. I have paid the restaurant staff and left, escaping the confused, sympathetic looks on their faces, the taste of tofu in my throat, lodged with mucus and salt. It felt strange, paying them, the lights in the restaurant suddenly too bright, the faces, for a moment, hostile. I wondered what it is and then identified it as simply being alone. It has been a long time since I have been alone outside of the house. A long time since I did, for myself, something basic. Like paying a restaurant and walking back to a hotel. It is an unnerving feeling, like the moment, halfway up a steep set of stairs or a hill, when you become aware, sharply, of exactly where you are. How precarious your grip is and how perilous the fall. It has been so long since I have done this, that I moved, somehow, past the drop in my stomach, and I walked a little taller. I smiled at the staff, which was hopelessly misplaced given that they had just watched me finish dinner alone and in tears. But they smiled back, and I recognised it, just for a moment, that brightness in people's faces that means you managed to connect. I used to love that. I used to watch it happen.

Often.

And then even as I was realising it, I was growing self-conscious and I fumbled about in my purse and dropped coins on the floor.

A cafetiere. A slow arc of urine. A dip in the sofa. A hole in the wall.

"Oops a daisy," said the Thai waitress, proud of her idiom. She bobbed down daintily to pick them up.

"I'm really sorry," I said.

"Why sorry?" she asked, confused. "Is fine."

Behind her a row of waiters and bar staff nodded emphatically.

Is fine.

Now I sit, somewhat sheepishly, on my bed. I have turned Alice's shower gel upside down in the hope there might be some left for her shower. I have washed my clothes with the cheap bar of hotel soap and dried them with the hair dryer, scenting the room with acid chemicals and burnt dust. I have alternated wildly in indecision. I have considered going back out, in the rain, to find her. But then I have thought about the look on her face when she left me. Blood and chalk dust. The missing teeth of Georgie Smales. Even so, I keep opening the door and glancing down the hall. My shoes have been on and off several times.

When she arrives, she is pale and set. Her face is a mask but there is something I don't quite expect there. A bitterness, a sort of feverish anger. An odd and illogical kind of emotion, like a chemical reaction, dried on her face.

"Hi," I say.

She says, "Hello."

Both of us sound exhausted. Each syllable falls out like wet concrete onto the sickly red and orange swirl of the carpet between us.

"I'm really sorry," I say. "I didn't mean to be presumptuous. I just..."

I just felt as though it was something she needed to talk about. It had been there since I first met her. It was breathed, since the moment she first met me in the lobby, took me into her flat and bathed my arm, into all those things she *hadn't* said. It was in the pauses, the hesitations, the looks, the abrupt exits.

"That's OK."

There is a pause. I want so much to make amends. I want to move past the whole miserable subject, to bury it tactfully and let her pretend it unsaid. But somehow I can't quite walk away from it. And it's not all because I want to help. I'm like a child on the roadside, encountering road kill. It's become a morbid fascination, something I cannot stop myself from prodding.

"I just-"

"-I think-"

We both stop abruptly. I say, "Sorry."

She says, "You first."

"No, you."

There is another pause. It goes on so long I think it may not end and that we will be discovered, centuries later, a pair of shrivelled stringy skeletons, melting untraceably into a red and orange carpet. We both open our mouths and draw breath. But she remains silent, looking at me expectantly. Facing me through air heavy with things unsaid and things which ought to have been undone. I want to reach out and slash through it the way she did with those nettles.

"Alice, I'm sorry. I mean... what I'm trying to say is that I'm sorry about what happened to Tabby and...this evening and the accident and all the rest – and I think we should probably just settle down now, just settle down gently and get some–"

"She's not dead."

My mouth forms a word which is stillborn. I close it again.

"She isn't dead, she's perfectly happy. She lives in New Zealand and I don't write to her."

The venom spits out in her words and spikes through the thick air of the room and I draw back, physically, in surprise at the intensity of it. Alice's face is flushed, her fists clenched. She is suddenly suffused with rage.

"Wha...bu..." I sound ridiculous. My mind is reeling, the fabric of my assumptions frayed and bleeding. The things I think I know are unravelling. I have cried for Tabby. I have cried for the loss of her. I have witnessed the sudden demise of two relative strangers, and now everywhere I look I am imagining death.

But there had always been hints of it, there were so many little suggestions. It was there in the gaps, the evasions. In her eyes, in the set of her shoulders.

There was always something in her face when she talked about her sister. But I never identified it as hatred.

Katie Hall-May

Alice

Thursday 22 May
A Dingy Hotel Room
And A Long Time Ago

For four of the days they keep Tabby in hospital I am not allowed to visit her. She is too ill, apparently. It would upset her. My Mother and Father are there at the hospital almost 100 percent of the time. I am at home, old enough by now to fend for myself. I wander around and eat junk food and I skip school and I watch the sympathy cards and the little gifts and the condolences and the kindnesses pouring in through the letterbox, the telephone, the door. Every now and then either my Mother or my Father come home and look at me carefully, as if checking for lice. They ask me gently, how I am feeling and if I am all right and assure me I don't have to go back to school if I don't want to and they ask me if I want to talk. My replies are hollow and dutiful. Their enquiries are similar. I skip school. I watch morning TV. I use the phone to vote on chat-lines and enter competitions. One day I don't get dressed all day. I miss her. And sometimes I really don't.

Eventually I am taken to see her. I arrive at the ward and everything and everyone in it is clean and white and smells of chemical bleaches. I find her bed easily because I have to fight through what seems to be a mass of flowers and teddy bears and worried relatives in twin sets and cardigans. Scuttling around the outskirts of it, a nurse tries desperately to persuade people to make space, to go home, to keep the noise down. My sister, she tells me sternly, is tired. Finally I shove my way through it all to her. She is small in the bed when I get there. Small and exactly the same. The smile, the timid, self-effacing glances downwards, as if life were an undeserved and wonderful gift, every visitor a beautiful moment. As if she hadn't tried to abruptly end it all five days previously. She looks at me and she smiles and says, "Alice," but only because it is a name she has learned how to say without stuttering.

"Apparently you puked green sick."

"Alice!" says my Mother, sharply.

A thousand relatives simultaneously suck in their breath.

I look at them. I look at her. I realise that they also are looking at her. Only Aunt May is still regarding me disgustedly, a frown on her wrinkled, freeze-dried forehead. I hate Aunt May. I hate all of them. And I know, even as I think this, that they feel quite the same. Only possibly a little less intensely. They are saving their emotional reserves. They are going to need them all for Tabby.

Cath

Friday 23 May
The Very Early Hours of the Morning

I realise that I am standing. I stood to greet her, I suppose. And then, in the whirl of things, as we seemed to spin and cartwheel, above the spin and cartwheel of the red and orange carpet below us, I didn't think to sit down. I am a numb recipient, wordless, swaying beneath the barrage of information that I suddenly recognise that I don't want to hear.

She is talking compulsively now, her mouth a red slash in her face, her tongue spitting, hating even the words as she says them. Her face works furiously as I watch and I know she is living it, she is not only retelling it. But, though she barely pauses for breath, she speaks very clearly. As though it is important that I know this.

And I stand there, and I try to focus on what she is saying, but my mind, in the background, is struggling frantically to unreel and disentangle and let them all go. All those other images that make up the story I thought I was hearing, that make up the story that I, in turn, had made up.

It was there. It was all there in so many perfectly orchestrated moments, unravelling at just the right pace, each episode revealed in a potent mixture of looks, omissions, words and walkouts. Alice. The fierce protector, the heroic almost adult, grieving the untimely death of her sister, blaming herself because she didn't spill quite enough of Georgie Smales' teeth to prevent it. It was there. It was a story. It was an Alice.

An Alice I wanted for myself. But this is not school. And I am not seven. And, anyway, it seems now, that this is not Alice.

I stand very stiffly and I don't reach out and touch her. There is rage on her face but I don't think it's for Tabby. Not all of it. I recognise it all too well. And I know that years will pass, decades will quietly disappear and all the while she will clutch that rage to her like a child with a comfort blanket, and it will be eating her. Slowly. And with intense concentration.

I would like to reach out. I would like to steal it away. I would like to face the wild cat, fighting and spitting, wipe away its tears and release it from its prey.

She sees it in my face, but only part of it, and her eyes flash in their red rims and she pulls herself up to her full height and faces me, angrily, miserably.

"Oh it's all right," she says with deep and bitter sarcasm. "It turned out OK in the end. It was OK for Tabby. She came out of it fine."

I would like to face the wild cat. But I am afraid.

And as I feel myself drawing back, as I feel that familiar sensation, as though everything inside me, every wet, pulsing organ, is shrinking back to protect itself, backing away, I think, disgustedly, that I am always afraid.

Alice

Friday 23 May
The Early Hours Of The Morning
And A Long Time Ago

Eventually they let her out of the hospital.

"She's a brave girl, your daughter," says the nurse approvingly, to my Mother. Brave for what, I want to ask. For putting up with the disappointment of not succeeding? For doing it in the first place? For being forcibly resuscitated? But I don't say it. Nowadays I have learned how to say nothing.

The relatives are always here now.

"Close to death," they whisper to each other, when Tabby and I are in our rooms or in bed. I don't know why they are surprised. After all, it was what she was aiming for.

But I stand there, sometimes, at her door while she is sleeping, and I watch her and I feel the panic rise up inside me. Because I can't find the tenderness. I can't find it now – that grain of goodness that was there in me. That made me OK. That made me Tabby's guardian angel.

There is something cold growing in its place and I worried that it will become a stone and then I will find it is my heart and I will pluck it out and throw it at her.

"Alice is being very troublesome," says my second aunt, clearly audible from downstairs.

"She's always been that way," says my Mother, "different to Tabby. I mean Tabby has her problems, bless her, but Alice is – I don't know – different. She's sly. Tabby was never sly."

A small, hazel haired little girl, in a tutu, half curtseying, perpetually nodding. A small beauty, with a gawky sister. An older, taller, sullen figure, like a blot on the landscape, red haired and wild tempered.

She got her first proper ballet shoes shortly after that photo was taken – and I got thrown out of the class for misbehaving.

Cath

Friday 23 May
The Early Hours of The Morning

What would this new Alice think of a person who urinated in biscuit tins? Who threw up into toilet bowls? Who walked back, every time, into the rooms she was locked out of?

This Alice gave up on the last person who was weak.

I look at Alice's face as if for the first time, and I realise, coldly, how twisted it is, how warped by the story she's telling. There is catch and spit in her voice, and the tears in her eyes, wiped away violently, are warm and stale, the skin reddened beneath them. Her words are her punishment, a riot of unsympathetic onlookers, trampling her and each other to reach the front.

But I can't help it, as I adjust my mind, as I try hard to focus on what it is she's saying now. I can't help but smell it. The stench of school in the room.

The dust.

The glue.

The shifts of power.

Alice

Friday 23 May
**The Early Hours of The Morning
And A Long Time Ago**

My Mother, approaches me on Sunday,

"I think it might be time to go back to school now, Alice."

The firmness in her tone. The edge in her voice.

"What about Tabby?"

I feel the eyes of my aunt, suspicious. I see how every emotion that flits across my face will be noted, registered. She continues to watch me. When I catch her eye she does not look away and for a moment I almost forget why we have not been to school. Forget that it was something Tabby had done, and not just another of 'Alice's misdemeanours'. I wonder if my aunt remembers.

"Tabby will go back on Thursday." My Mother's voice sounds too smooth, too patient. I wonder how often she practised this conversation before having it for real. I wonder if my aunt advised her.

There have been numerous meetings with the school. With teachers and head-teachers and counsellors and child psychologists and nurses. Tabby is going to have a special contact, a counsellor in school who will meet with her weekly. The headmaster has addressed the primary perpetrators and assured my Mother that the situation will not recur. It has been dealt with severely and there will be no repeat performance, and the situation was explained to the whole school 'very delicately'. Which means he has told them just enough. Just enough for rumours to be circulating wildly. For theories and speculation and opinions and dramatic, wholly fictional back stories to add depth to the plot.

So Tabby won't be back until Thursday and the urge to find out the real details, the thirst for the genuine juice, will just be peaking.

I have three days.

I am only barely aware of Cath now. I can remember it all so clearly. Standing there, in the grey gravel carpark at the entrance to the school gates, my aunt's gaze on my back, my bra strap, new and stifling, digging into the skin at the back of my rib cage.

I have rehearsed this moment, this return, so often. It has taken so many different forms, so many genres in my mind, that it feels now, as I stand, hesitating in front of it, like another rehearsal, or some kind of film set. As though there is not only the gaze of my aunt, but a whole audience, out there, unseen and unknowing.

Of course, in a way there always has been. I have replayed this scene so many times in my memory, so many years, so many future Alices all returning, hopelessly to this one little drama, travelling back constantly to this moment. Insisting, mercilessly, on reliving the action, making over and over, the same childish errors. An audience of Alices, compelled and reluctant, spectators from ever increasing years, ever changing locations. Perhaps I knew it at the time.

I watch myself hesitating. Staring up at the rough slabs of concrete which, together, create 'A' block. A slight breeze moves my hair around, blows my skirt just a little, against the back of my thighs.

It is surprisingly easy to say it. To stand in a hotel room on a swirling orange carpet, telling the whole stupid story out loud, very clearly. Pouring narrative out like noxious gases, into the air, into the incredulous ears of a woman with confused grey green eyes and with whom I recently watched two men die.

I join the crowd of regretful, watching Alices. This time I have brought a guest with me. We stand here together and watch it all unfold.

I hesitate for a minute, a surprisingly small figure, there in the carpark. There is a slight breeze and my skirt blows gently and then I move. Onwards. Away from my aunt, who has only given me a lift to make sure I go in, and I walk across the concrete and past the row of teachers' cars, sunlight glinting off windscreens into my eyes. I walk past the tutor room but I don't go in yet. I pass the staff-room and there is a rustle of heads turning towards me, alarmed teachers, caught off guard in their few moments of sanctuary, before their clamorous clients pour in.

My form tutor extricates herself and hurries to greet me.

"Hello Alice. Are you OK? How is your sister?"

"Fine thanks, Miss," my tone is measured and polite and immediately puts her on edge because the last time we exchanged words I was either skipping detention or being told off for doodling in the new biology text books.

I move on. I go into the canteen to buy a sausage roll and Doreen is in there and she says, "Hi love"

And I say, "Hi," and wait for her to ask, but she only says, "Ninety pee, sweetheart. You're in bright and early." And I remember she doesn't really know my name and I am relieved and I am disappointed.

I walk out of the canteen and towards the playground and then I lounge in the corner eating my sausage roll, the crisscross lines of the metal fencing making faint grey lines in the white of my school shirt. I wait.

In approximately five minutes they will begin to trickle in from all corners of the compound. Straggling at first, the odd one or two figures, identical in uniform and forbidden yellow trainers. Ties clumsily knotted, or rejected, or lost. Luminous sports bags, silver handbags, fraying khaki rucksacks, and, very rarely, the odd satchel, ironic or misguided. They will come slowly at first, then a rush, and then finally, when the school buses creak into the layby, they will all be here, a laughing, shrieking mass, an animated wall of sound.

The first rumble of approaching voices. I hear them and I feel the frisson of excitement, fear, anticipation beating in my chest. And the new thing, the new hard cold thing in there, the solid thing growing where there used to be my heart.

They come to me gradually at first, then pick up speed. It begins with the students in my year, or in Tabby's. The ones who know me. They drift into the playground and hang around in little groups, looking at me, pointing me out to each other. The look on their faces is strangely similar to the one on my Mother's, or my aunt's when they talk to me, except in this case it is tinged with a delicious curiosity, an interest which in adults is largely absent. They look over, meet my eyes, look back quickly, look again. They discuss strategy in excited, urgent whispers. Who will move first, who is going to ask? I cultivate a look of indifference. I try to convey an impression of infinite secrets. I have no idea if it is working. But I know it doesn't matter anyway. They will come. They will hesitate at first and then throng to me.

Rachel Blackthorne and Karen Pickering. They are the front runners. Hardly surprising. Karen just has to be first to know things and Rachel has some kind of medical need to be the centre of attention so they stick together like glue – and the situation suits them. I watch them approach and I am carefully casual.

"Hi Karen. Hi Rach."

"Hi Alice," says Rachel, "Good to see you back." She has practised it clearly, the clipped, adult tone, the business-like greeting.

"How's Tabby?" asks Karen. They look at me intently.

"I'm OK," I say deliberately, pausing long enough for others to straggle casually over, emboldened now that somebody else has asked it. I see Ben and Steve and Janine, who are my friends, join the crowd, shooting sympathetic glances at me. Not saying anything, just waiting, listening, supporting. I try to communicate to them silently that they don't need to feel sorry. That I am fine, that I wanted this, that this is the plan, but I have an audience to satisfy, and I intend to do it just right.

"Well I'm OK. I mean...obviously...Tabitha..." I let the phrase trail off because there are still people joining, drifting into the playground, noticing, listening, but this time I don't need to pause because the waiting is over and they are asking things quicker than I could answer them anyway.

"Is she coming back?"

"Did she really try to kill herself?"

"Excuse me, is your sister in a coma?" That from one of the younger ones in Tabby's year. Probably only learned the word 'coma' last week.

"So was it you that found her?"

"What did your Mum say?"

"Is her name really Tabby...or Tabitha?" Lisa Weeks, irrelevant and dim as usual, though I suppose since half of my present audience only knew my sister as "Twiglet", the question might be reasonable. She is twirling her hair in her fingers. She tried to perm it recently but the perm didn't take so she just twirls it constantly, like that's going to do it. It doesn't matter anyway because all the boys thought she was hot before, and now with the hair twirling thing, they actually think it's some cute, sort of shy thing. Typical. Ben and Steve are two of my best friends, but honestly, boys can be really stupid.

"So when did she get out of hospital?"

"Is it true it's because of getting, like, bullied and stuff?"

"Did she really nearly die?"

Even Georgie Smales is here now, hanging around carefully on the edge of the crowds. He's still a bit scared of me, so he doesn't get too close. I guess his nose tingles every time he sees me. But he's here anyway. They are all here. It is that terrible, aching need to know, that desire to be the chief of something, chief news bringer, chief questioner, the person I trust, the person I told first, the person everyone else has to go to if they want to find out more. People who spent days devising increasingly nasty ways to get at my sister, are braving my infamous wrath to find out about her. People who are my friends, people who have never met either one of us. Everybody wants to be the comforter, the listener. Everybody, right now, wants to be near *me*.

I open my mouth and they fall silent. I have my audience. I am ready to be heard.

And all those watching future Alices who return, almost daily, to this moment, cringe in unison, and turn away.

I begin with the green sick. The smell of it. The projectile nature of it. It was on, I tell them, the *kitchen ceiling* for fuck's sake, swearing deliberately because, here, it is currency. It was green, I tell them, like a fluorescent highlighter is green. Like radioactive substances in children's cartoons are green. Like snot is green.

Then I move on to the tablets themselves. The empty packets of Rennies we found along with the painkillers, that she had taken just to make sure when the paracetamol ran out.

"I mean, when we looked further there were empty *vitamin* boxes – like she was trying to overdose on vitamin E or something!"

I talk about the matted sweat and sick in her hair, the incoherent sentences she mumbled when the paramedics tried to move her, how she thrashed and kicked when they manoeuvred her onto the stretcher. I talk about the kidney shaped polystyrene sick bowl by her bed when I visited the hospital, about the drip in her arm and how they pumped out her stomach.

I do impressions of her finally waking up in the hospital, a high pathetic voice and an exaggerated stutter. I mime my aunt trying ineptly, fussily, to place a blanket over her and I relate how she nearly pulled the drip out while doing it and how Tabby just sat there and let her do it, not even having the gumption to just come out and tell her that she didn't need a blanket, she didn't actually need anything right now and, if the original plan had gone right, she wouldn't ever need anything ever again.

I put my head on one side and I nod so violently my vision blurs and my throat is sore from making my voice so high pitched and I say, "Oh...th...th...*thank you* for vi...visiting me...I...I'm sh...sho...egg...eggcited..."

I lisp horribly, sickeningly, forcing saccharine into every last little crevice of my voice to counteract the bitterness. Even so, my voice which is rising now, loud in the stunned silence.

I talk about a suicide note, although there wasn't one. I wonder, aloud, at how it is that a person already so skinny could possibly have managed to get even skinnier.

I keep on talking and talking and only the tortured future Alices see it in time. The open mouths, the shocked little gasp from Lisa, the surprise turning gradually into disgust, the moral outrage. Even Georgie Smales looks disapproving, though he is pleased too. There is pleasure in his face.

Actually, I notice suddenly, he has lost quite a bit of weight.

At last I pause for breath, or for a laughter which I finally realise hasn't come. There is a silence. And then,

"*Seriously?*" breathes Sally Hammond, her voice actually hoarse with moral indignation.

"Yeah..." but I falter now. It is beginning to dawn on me. It is beginning to become clear that I am not a celebrity. I am a stupid child standing in a corner bad mouthing her sick sister. My back against the fencing, and a crowd seven or eight people deep all around me.

"Yeah. Seriously."

My voice is small and defensive.

I stand in a hotel room with an orange swirly carpet and a woman whose face now echoes the expressions of my schoolmates. With the woman who has somehow compelled me to try to explain a thing which I have not, for over a decade, been able to begin to explain to myself. How she's done that I'm not really sure. Only that sometimes, in the twitch of her mouth, the hesitation in her voice, the nod of her head, I look back through years of comparative adulthood, and see a child with hazel eyes. I saw it in the way she apologised to me the first time she met me for somehow causing the flood in our flats, and I saw it tonight, when she used the contents of my wash bag to scrub herself raw.

Somehow, when I spend time with Cath I can't help but look down some wormhole and see - a child with hazel eyes and little faded ballet shoes. And standing alongside her clumsy big sister, who grins with none of that delicate subtlety, and who, though there is nothing much wrong with her speech, hurts with a much less expressible pain.

We stand together, Cath and I, and we watch myself, so much younger and stupider, burst into flames in a school yard, crash and burn.

Cath

Friday 23 May
2.20am

In the end it is amazing how little I actually say. How little, after this tirade of words, either of us actually say when she's finished. There is a silence, so long that I think we will expire here, we will shrivel and die on this orange carpet, unable to breathe in a room so filled up with old pain. And then she sits down, suddenly, on the bed, as though her legs are not capable, any more, of supporting her. And I look at her and she looks dog tired. As though there is nothing left in her except the urgency of sleep.

She doesn't fight it when I say I might leave. We both know at this stage that we can't just settle down in twin beds next to each other, as though nothing has happened. And we can't finish this conversation, if it could be described as one, because neither of us actually knows what we think.

I am angry, I think. But I couldn't be sure of it. Or, if I am, in whose defence.

"Will you be OK?" I ask, with treacherous hesitation, because we both know that I am going anyway. "It's just I need to...well...we could maybe talk in the morning..."

Neither of us wants to talk any more for some time.

"I mean if I take the car, are you OK to get the train? I think they run pretty..."

"I'll be fine." She says it fiercely at first and then, with that gesture, a sort of wave of her hand which somehow encompasses both a plea and a dismissal, "I'll be fine. I'm always fine."

And it's back, that defiance, that resignation.

She knows there is nothing we can say tonight.

I open the door. And just in that moment, she says, wearily, "Just do it, Cath. Please. Just do what you need to."

And then I walk out of the room and I leave her.

I drive. I drive through wet and shiny motorways, lights bouncing and imploding into the tarmac, and a parade of images, mixed up and unbelievable, bouncing and refracting through my mind.

Locked doors, lost laptops, library books, urine. A man in the road and a child in the playground. Vomit and death and the smell of petrol. My Mother, full of love and gentleness, handing me a yellow biscuit tin with lambs on. For me to use to keep my sweets in. An exaggerated stutter, a dip in the sofa. Blood on the nose of Georgie Smales. A bar of chocolate on the table, a cafetiere on the floor. *"Trust you Cath, trust you..."* A ghostly Patrick.

I grip the steering wheel hard and I drive right through all of them. Alarmed, they scatter.

I drive over them.

Thud.

Alice

Friday 23 May
A Silent Hotel Room
And A Long Time Ago

Of course it's a kind of exquisite hypocrisy. An honour among thieves. You can drive another child to near suicide, but once the deed is done, once the game is played out and the loser identified, once there are no more questions about how or what that child will do next – then you relax, your morbid curiosity satisfied, and you offer that loser nothing but your comfort, your support, your olive branch. To continue the persecution at this point feels like nothing short of attempted murder.

And if you are that child's sister, her established protector, her flesh and blood, it is an unpardonable display of callousness.

"Alice Crayer, you know the one with the red hair, do you know what she did..?"

"Did you know that her sister...?"

"And then she..."

"And then Alice came back in, right, and started saying all this stuff..."

"Her own sister..."

"No way?! *Seriously?*"

I was regarded with the sort of sickened curiosity roughly equal to that with which you might look at a criminal. A murderer. Or a psychopath.

Tabby arrived back to find herself surrounded with her erstwhile tormentors, now eager to make amends, to be friends, to be *best* friends. Confidants. And, unsurprisingly, she welcomed the sudden change of events, listened with alarm and quite probably genuine heartbreak to the many eagerly offered recounts of my actions, my dissemblance, my treacherous speech on the morning of my return. My change of attitude, the two faces of the terrible Alice Crayer. We never discussed it. We didn't fight or shout or communicate. She simply withdrew from me. We quietly ceased speaking.

And of course it was not long. It was not long for me before the first wet sticky lump of chewing gum, glistening with saliva and gluing my coat to the back of the chair. The first globule of inky spittle shooting, cruelly accurate, into my hair from the hollowed out end of a biro.

"You girls are so careless," my Mother said mildly, pleased because both of us were still breathing, I suppose.

The thing that adults never realise about children, is the extent of their cruelty. The extent to which they will use a tool which they don't understand. And this is different. That's the other thing people don't realise. The only thing worse than being an innocent victim, is being a guilty one. The one who deserves it.

They whispered in corners for weeks. We were older now so the tactics were more subtle. All of us by then were growing older and the last of that amoral aptitude which adults dreamingly call 'innocence' was leaving us. We needed a reason now, a genuine transgression. It was no longer enough for a person to be small, or fat, or wear glasses. The cause suddenly mattered. It was not persecution but punishment.

They warned off new boyfriends. They wrote notes in the toilets. They spread rumours, hid homework, falsified timetables, circulated faked photos. I knew this was it. The school had its own sixth form. There was no escaping to college. This would be my experience all the way through until we left. I had earned it.

These, said adults with unpardonable stupidity, so pleased to see Tabby progressing so well now, these were the best days of our lives.

I close my eyes which feel dry and used and discarded. I fall into sleep like a brick from a skyscraper. Asleep in my clothes in a shitty hotel room.

Cath

Friday 23 May
4 am.

I am seated in the middle of a brightly lit service station, and the noise, even at this hour, seems to reach out and hold me, enfolding me in syrupy armfuls of sound. Coffee machines hiss and grind and clatter. Tills spring into jangly action. People order their coffee. Breakfast sizzles. There is excited conversation. There are children, sleepy and sullen, or hyperactive. There is the clatter of cutlery and, right above me, the perceptible buzzing of a blinking strip light. I cup my hands around my coffee and I sink back into it.

I like it here. The sheer, glorious, colourful chaos of it. I like its eye watering, electric brightness and the fact that there can be no shadows, no blurring. Everything is a primary colour, every corner, every edge is sharp and simple. There can be no hidden places, no shadows. I have been here an hour. And my thoughts are only just, like long abandoned model soldiers, twisted and melted and stepped on and chewed at, beginning to form themselves into some sort of order.

A child rushes past me holding a bag of Doritos. She trips, falling on top of them, gets up and continues, the contents crushed to powder in her unknowing, fast gripping, miniature hands.

In the past twenty-four hours I have urinated into a tin, pursued a man, seen him die at my feet, and heard Alice, the protector, turn tormentor and finally learn to hate her victim. In the past four years, I realise, I have watched Patrick do the same.

"I'll have a latte," calls someone. "Actually no. Make that a hot chocolate."

Who are any of us anyway?

Somebody orders a soy cappuccino. The barista is flustered because she can't find the soy milk. I watch impassively. I can see it behind her.

And who am I? That confident university tutor doing a hapless student a favour in the library, or the clumsy idiot who lives in Patrick's flat? Corporate vengeance seeker? Good with people?

The child with the Doritos is eating their powdery remains enthusiastically, painting her mouth an unnatural orange. I watch her and remember a previous me.

The biscuit tin was for the sweets I would buy on a Friday evening, after swimming, with my pocket money. The lambs on it cavorted happily beneath white clouds, which matched their fluffy white tails. There were sunflowers in the grass they played on, a splash of colour amongst the paler yellow and the white. It was a tall tin with a narrow opening. As I grew older it got harder to fit my hand into.

"Blimey," says a man behind me, "that took long enough."

"Sorry," says his partner, "there was a queue."

I never tipped the sweets out though. Which would have been easier. I got my hand stuck quite often. To get it out I would trap the tin between the door and the doorframe and pull, jerking and scattering sweets across the kitchen linoleum. I could have found other ways. But this way made me giggle.

"Cath," said my Mother mildly, "that's not what it's meant for."

The tin is dented all round the edges. In places it is still marked with the paint from that old, battered kitchen door.

There is a scar on my elbow, and another on the bottom of my foot where I scratched at the nettle stings. My hands are pinker than they really should be, and there is still a slight scratch on my palm. Ice from the freezer is sharper than you think.

That's not what it's meant for, Cath.

"Have you got a light?"

"It's no smoking, Jamie, read the sign."

"Yeah I know. I know. I'm gonna take it outside..."

Just do what you need to.

"Come on. I'll bring it right back."

"Oh bloody hell. Five minutes then. All right? I'll have one with you. Then we have to go."

I look around at the swirl of people. Everyone here is going somewhere. Even me.

"Sat nav's driving me crazy."

"I'll meet you at the car."

I knew, really. I knew before I came in where I was going. I knew before I ordered my first coffee why I'm here, beneath these striplights. In this glorious cacophony.

Behind me a baby is crying. Its Father hands it to a weary looking woman cradling a hot chocolate.

"I think he needs his Mummy," he says.

"He *always* needs his Mummy," she replies with weary irritation. But she takes the child carefully, replacing her drink with her baby.

I look at my watch. He'll still be at home. Timing now, will be everything. And it's still much too early.

There is a quivering in me as I order another coffee.

It's going to be a long wait.

Alice

Friday 23 May
8.45 am.
A Dingy Hotel Room

Sometime during the night I have taken my clothes off, though not bothered to put on pyjamas. When light starts to creep around the edges of the browning blinds at the windows, I am still lying here, naked. I don't feel anything in particular, other than numb and exhausted. Somewhere inside me there is even something which feels just the tiniest little bit better. So I have unburdened myself, have I? I have halved a problem by sharing it? Brilliant. I am a walking cliché, giving truth to all the smug tales all the smug old wives have been smugly telling their bored grandchildren for all these smug years of human existence. The part of me that feels a bit better is being laughed out of town by everything else in me, but mostly I am lying here ignoring all of it, just listening dispassionately to cars and footsteps and all the busybody sounds of the morning.

There is a sudden sort of generalised crashing sound at the door and I realise I am about to be besieged by the cleaning staff. I leap out of bed and grab a sheet and then shuffle, swaddled, across the room to hold the door closed and ask them, in a hoarse sort of whisper, if they would mind coming back later.

"Well you should put out your notice if you don't want disturbing – that's what it's for." She is disgruntled and wheeling an enormous trolley full of weak looking bleaches and paper thin toilet roll. I watch her leave, my eye to the keyhole, muttering to herself and shaking her head.

Then I turn and survey the situation I have put myself in.

The room is brown. Last night it seemed mostly to be orange but now, in the day, I see that somehow its very essence is brown – brown seeps through the cracks, the corners, the window, the crevices. It emerges, stealthy into the white lines between the tiles in the bathroom.

I shower. I try not to touch the walls.

Katie Hall-May

Cath

Friday 23 May
Patrick's Flat
9.30 a.m.

I don't feel upset as I do it, or tearful. I don't feel any all-consuming rage or elation. I don't even feel afraid or excited. I just feel flat. I feel flat and stolid and practical. Placid and efficient.

I park around the corner and watch him leave for work.

Then I drive in, past the bald patch of faded green that once was a nettle patch. I get out, turn my key, walk in. Everything is the same apart from a note on the table from Patrick, and the keys, ostentatiously inserted into every internal keyhole. I ignore the note. I know what it will say and it is not going to help if I read it.

I pack shoes and hats and bags. I consider the best way to transport what is mine. I make a dozen phone calls, trapping the phone between my shoulder and my ear. I take a room near the university without viewing it. I call my bank and my doctor, my dentist and my work. I inform them of the change. I leave nothing undone. There is no stone unturned.

There is a kind of remembering in me. As though I am returning to a vacated body, or the same skin but re-inserting a previous mind. As though Patrick, and everything about him and in him, was part of another person, fading out into space. I don't feel anything about this feeling. It doesn't unsettle me. But after a while it seems callous, so I try to remember him, to remind myself. I sit an internal exam on Patrick studies.

He is broad, with blue eyes. He used to have a habit of blinking very quickly, three times in a row, when he was tired. He did that the first day I met him. He likes to buy things but he forgets about them very quickly after. He is fastidious, even so, about keeping things in exactly the same condition he bought them. He doesn't like to break the spines of his books. Sometimes this means he doesn't read them.

I pull out every bag I own, and two suitcases. I pack other things into boxes. I wrap up all my breakables. I look in the fridge and there isn't much there. I take the tofu and the rye bread because they are mine.

He likes his meat very rare but he can't stand the smell of it raw. He goes through periodic health kicks but he loathes obvious health food. He goes to the gym regularly. He drives when he should walk. The hairs on his arms are almost blond.

I wonder, should I leave him something? There are some vegetables, going off, and some meat in the freezer. I could do a casserole perhaps. A pie. Or a soup.

He is witty and bright in groups of people. The bigger the audience, the bigger the laughs. He tells people I am an academic. Perhaps because he is big, when he says it, it seems small.

I think of my friends, back then. Of their response when they met him. Their incredulous voices, increasingly concerned and outraged at my weakness. Their advice, so many times over, to get out and get rid.

He used to ask me in those insecure moments, late into the evening. Did I think he was worth it? Did I think he was a bad person? Every few weeks he had some sort of worry about his work. Every month he was convinced that they would or should sack him.

I am nearly finished. I can still do it. I move into the kitchen, open the fridge, pull out vegetables, open the cupboards for spice. I will do it. I will leave him a pie.

He used to go on about the softness of my skin. When we made love, the very first time, he was shaking. He used to thank me, afterwards, with a sort of sycophantic fervour. Now when he kisses me, he doesn't close his eyes.

I braise the meat in red wine. I use the ready roll of pastry, but I add something to it. A sprig of fresh rosemary, pressed into the dough. A pinch of mixed peppercorns. I brush it carefully, so that every inch of both sides is covered in a salty golden layer of melted butter.

Then I bake it into the largest ceramic pot Patrick owns, and I pour in the meat and the vegetables and with them, I pour in every bit of that hot, pulsating emotion which still fills the hole in my heart that is Patrick.

He used to eat things I cooked with unbridled amazement. How could I produce something that tasted like heaven? He used those sorts of phrases self-consciously, carefully, the smile on his face half apologising for it. He used to reach round to hug me from behind when I was cooking. He liked to do it when my hands were messy or occupied. He liked spontaneous affection, but it had to be his.

I taste the sauce carefully. I give it just a little bit too much seasoning so it will hold its flavour when reheated. I put the oven timer on, so that the pastry will not lose its freshness but the pie will be ready just half an hour after he gets in from work. So that it will greet him. The scent of it, wafting into the lobby. It will say goodbye to him on my behalf.

I have worked in a sort of reverent intensity. I have worked amid visions of Patrick's face, when he eats it. Every mouthful a gift, every morsel a message. I have become so excited about leaving him this gift that for a moment I want to hide here somehow, to watch him receive it. I want to stand there and hold it and give it to him myself.

When I close the oven door I no longer feel this.

I wash up. I dry up. I put everything away. There is a new cafetiere on the table half filled with cold coffee. I hesitate and then leave it there.

Trust you, Cath. Trust you.

I move around the house, gathering the last of my things, and placing them in bags. Little visions of him present themselves everywhere. Patrick cooking lasagne. Fresh in a towel from the shower. Watching girls in the carpark. Talking back to the radio. I reach across them for plasters, cosmetics, umbrellas.

Until finally, it is half past one. And I realise, with a sort of sudden shock, that I have finished.

My rucksack stands in the hallway, groaning already under the weight of its contents, the two more hardwearing cases glowering over it, snobbish and superior – and equally crammed. They will travel, somehow in the front passenger seat. My car, ancient and tired from its earlier excursions, is already crammed full of boxes, bin liners and clothing and it regards me in alarm out of the corner of its headlights. I am doing it, I tell it. I am doing it. I have done it.

I have shoes and books, folders and CDs and coat hangers. Everything necessary to leave somebody who once loved you.

I stand in the doorway, and I look at the flat.

I look at the chrome door handles and the lights and the laminate flooring. The black and white print on the wall. I look at the little pile of rubbish which I will take out with me. The two suitcases. And the rucksack. I look at the shadows they cast on the wood. I listen, for the last time, to the muted hum of the refrigerator, the whispered tick of the clock. I pull my coat on. I pause.

He used to point out my blemishes. Pinch an inch on my stomach. When I tripped up I would catch him rolling his eyes. If I called him at work he would be dismissive, taunting. He would play to an audience I couldn't see. I would hear them though, laughing. After a while I laughed too. And I didn't call him. Unless there was some kind of emergency. A fire, perhaps. Or a flood.

I stand, suspended, tingling, and staring at the front door keys in my hand.

There is time.

There is time.

For one last message.

I think of it, and my heart beats faster, throwing itself against the constraints of my rib cage. I go a little cold in my stomach. And then I make my move. I leave my rucksack where it is for the moment, and I move now and I act. I act on that thought, so delicious and shameful, before I have time to think better of it. Before I have time to think about it at all.

It takes two minutes to betray him.

And then, when it is done, and the evidence hidden, so cold and bright against the skin which my heart is trying to pound its way out of, I heave my rucksack onto my shoulders, pull my hair out from under the straps and pause only to pick up my bags.

Then I open the door and I am doing it, I have done it.

I step out of his flat.

And out of his story.

Alice

Friday 23 May
1.35 p.m.

Fresh off the train I bump into her in the lobby. She has a rucksack on her back and two bulging suitcases. *Finally*, I think, and something inside me wants to jump up and down and cheer and something else wants to cry.

I smother all of it. I am tired. Tired of emotion, with all its cloying subtleties.

"So," I say, mildly, and inadequately, "you're off."

She puts down the cases. She is flushed with something. Fear, excitement, adrenaline. She looks elated and terrified, and something else. Something guilty. She keeps glancing down at her cleavage. It occurs to me suddenly that she doesn't remind me of Tabby any more.

"Um yes," she says, the words delivered too quickly.

"Um good!" I say flippantly, and then, "I mean, not that you're…"

But she is laughing. Through all the flitting, fighting emotions, she is laughing.

"I knew what you meant," she says, reassuringly and she looks at me with that familiar hint of apology, but there is something else now, something suspiciously like pity. My stomach goes cold for a second. Have we somehow changed places?

And then, there is a noise from outside, just a bird or a cat or something, and she starts, her whole body jerking in such panic she looks like she's ducking from gunfire. No. We haven't changed places. No yet, anyway.

"Bloody cats," I say quickly, and then, "He'll still be at work now."

"Yes," she laughs a little, but there is tension in it, her hand fluttering, distractedly, up to her cleavage. Everything in her is poised now. She picks up a suitcase.

"So where will you go?" I ask.

"I have a room for a few nights. After that I don't know."

Something in me is desperate to somehow detain her. To put off the moment when she will walk into a new life and I will be left behind stuck in the old one.

I gesture, impulsively, to the closed door behind which my flat lurks, waiting. "You could always stay with…"

I trail off.

She smiles. But she doesn't respond.

Of course not.

"Too much water," I say, "you know, under the bridge."

It's pathetic. But she laughs anyway, properly this time.

"A bit," she admits, and laughs again.

Then she picks up the other suitcase.

"Good luck," I say.

"Thanks." There is a pause. And then she says again, "Thanks Alice."

I hold the door open for her. I help her squeeze in the cases.

She starts the engine.

And she's gone.

I stand there, in the lobby, watching the exhaust from her car swirl and dissipate. Listening to the sound of the engine fade out into nothing.

Afterwards, it's very quiet.

Perhaps it is the quiet which makes me so aware of Patrick when he finally comes home. I like to think it is that, and not that I am, despite myself, listening out for him. Have been listening out for him since the moment she left. Either way, as soon as I hear the slam of his door in the carpark, I become frozen with listening. I hear his feet in the lobby. Is there a new hesitancy in his steps? I am probably imagining it. I hear his key in the door. Hear him step inside. Silence.

There is a scent in the hallway, something meaty with herbs.

Silence.

Shaking myself physically out of my stupor I march myself into the kitchen to make a coffee, more as a distraction than to satisfy a need. And it is only as the roaring of the electric kettle dies away that I hear anything more at all from his flat.

A dull sort of thunking sound.

I pause. Hold the teaspoon. Listen. Silence.

And then, just as I begin to move around again in the kitchen, it starts up again, increasing in fervour, and then stopping, abruptly.

Silence.

After a while I lose interest. I give up pretending to be out. I survey the contents of my fridge without interest, then wander into the lounge again and put on a film.

The opening credits have barely finished rolling before there is a high pitched weening, accompanied by a strong smell of burning.

Patrick's smoke alarm.

Followed swiftly by a series of violent crashes, and then several loud cracks and a splintering.

That is it. And then silence. I don't hear anything else at all. I don't know what the hell has been going on in there this evening.

"I don't know," I say aloud to the small figure in the photo frame, "what the hell has been going on in there this evening."

But she doesn't reply. Because she's only a child. And anyway, she's too far away.

Cath

Wednesday 4 June
And the last 13 days

From the moment I leave I feel utterly and completely gone. I look back at it all from what seems like an impossible distance. I never once think about turning back. There, on the road, numb in my car, rattling and coercing it along roads and side streets, persuading it to start again after pausing at traffic lights, heaving it along with all its weight of bags and memories. I never have to force my hand back to stop myself putting everything into reverse. Perhaps it just seems impractical, after all that time I spent packing. Perhaps I am afraid that if I go back there now, he will be home already, will be, even now, discovering my duplicity, my last mean little action which, somehow, shamefully, I know will be the spur of strength that I can dig into myself when I am flagging, and urge myself on. A little metal object, tucked inside my bra. Cold and delicious against my skin.

I keep it there, my little evidence of power, all through the awkward introductions with the officious landlord, and the frozen few hours just after I walked into the empty room in the shared house which will be mine, all mine, for as long as I want it, and instead of excitement I feel only fear. That is the moment when I nearly turn back, in that room, with the door closed and my belongings piled hopelessly on the bed and the floor, so that I can hardly move anywhere except back out of the door. In the end I just ram the rusting bolt across on the inside. I shut the world out and me in. And I touch my hand to my cleavage and find that little shaft of silver, cooling my skin, and beneath it, the hot wild pumping of my heart.

I work up the courage to go back to work and, faced with the mild concern of my colleagues, who assume I have been overtired or ill, I find myself simply carrying on. I don't explain, don't change anything, I just get on. I pick up my research where I left it. And when the publishers email again, just a routine courtesy because I remain on their mailing list, I allow a tiny glimmer of possibility to wink at me from a long way off.

I change my phone number. And remember with relief that Patrick never took enough interest to find out my work number. I am very diligent about closing the old life off. Packaging it up and sealing it and storing it somewhere in the locked compartments in the shadows of my head.

I go to a letting agency, stand at the window and look at adverts for flats to let. The agent catches my eye and beams at me. I mutter some excuse, crack a brittle and unconvincing smile, and flee. The next day I go back again and this time I manage to get through the door. I blink like a mole in the face of the strip lights and the glossy pictures and the talk about 'aspect'. And then I flee.

I have no trouble closing off the old life. It's the new one that strikes abject terror through me.

A thin sliver of metal, secure and glinting between lace and breast. It is my guilty secret. It is my talisman.

The third time I dress up, put on makeup and high heels, stride in to a different agency and request full brochures on properties for sale. If I am going to live this life, to walk into this world full of cavernous possibilities and assume my place in it, I may as well stand up straight and face it properly. The agent is delighted. I view a couple of flats. I discuss surveys and mortgages. I have a meeting with my bank.

It takes me a day to prepare for each step and a day to recover.

In the meantime, I make friends with my housemates, each as transient as I am. It is a house for the lost. The 'passers through'. I buy food and use the kitchen and I cook for everybody, friend or stranger, who happens, for however short a period, to share my new found living space. They love it. I accept their flattery.

When I talk to them my knees tremble so violently I think they will buckle.

But they don't.

And gradually, in what is really barely two weeks, I grow able to assemble a sort of cosmetic confidence. I can mock up a shadow of a certainty which I imagine others are born with, and which maybe, at the edges, I am starting to feel.

And that cold shape in my cleavage has grown warm with my skin.

Sometimes, I barely know it's there.

Alice

Wednesday 4 June
And the Last 13 Days

I just get on with it of course. That's what I do. I clean. I sort cupboards. I shuffle the bits of dog eared paper that I have been told to 'keep safe', from one box file to another, and relabel it. I contact the school and arrange to go in and replace the sessions I missed. The head understands. After all, it's important. We can't have year ten bouncing around catching babies and STDs in the long summer holidays, can we? Not with their mocks coming up.

The second half of the summer term is always quiet. I have no real bookings. There are too many exams and sports days and college days and options days and presentations and career talks to fit in to the already bursting timetables. I do one off sessions here and there. I teach an evening course for parents who are worried about how to break the terrible truth of sex to their children. They are always a certain type, and they are always dressed in cardigans and have nice, neat hairdos. They never miss a session and they never turn up late. Not a single one of them ever actually follows my advice.

I make plans and phone calls and confirm my bookings. I review the lesson plans I make that I will never follow. I review the sanitised versions that I give to the head-teacher and never, for a moment, intend to follow.

Frankly, getting on with it is all there is *to* do.

That and the studious avoidance of Patrick.

It's been very quiet in that flat since whatever it was that was going on in there that very first evening.

He never came near me. He still hasn't. In fact, since the initial cacophony, I have heard so little movement that I find myself, sometimes, listening out for it, a little panicked, visions of various acts of desperation filling my mind with that morbid mixture of excitement and dread. But I always hear something. A sniff or a cough. He's in there all right. He's definitely still breathing.

And then I make myself move, back, away from the doorframe. Resist the urge to drop by full of cheery false sunshine and ask, all bright innocence, how Cath is today,

"It's just, it occurred to me. I haven't seen her for a while…"

Curiosity is so often cruelty in disguise.

"Excuse me, is your sister in a coma?"

It's been a strange couple of weeks. I have rattled around in it. The most important thing seems to be to try not to think. I have thought and talked and remembered and retracted and talked again quite enough in the last few months.

In the last few decades.

"Alice, settle down. Let your sister talk."

But she has nothing to say, this child in her photo frame. With her hazel eyes and her ballet shoes and her perpetual nod. This faded figure who smiles at me, and who used to be my sister.

Tabitha Crayer.
Tabitha.
Tabby.

Since I got back from Manchester she has seemed younger somehow, trapped in time in her picture. Looking out through the glass. I notice that she still has a few strands of fire in that amber, a spark amongst the flecks in the hazel of her eyes. And she's smaller than I remember. When I really look at that picture. Tiny, in fact, as though viewed from a great distance.

Tabby, a tiny speck in a whole world full of time.

It all seems so much longer ago.

And then one day, I receive a text from a number that I don't recognise.

There's a funeral next Thursday. Want to go to it?
Cath.

I wasn't sure if I'd hear from her, and then at the same time I was. Because Cath is one of the last surviving members of that breed who spend more time thinking about others than themselves. She was never going to walk out and leave me to stew in it. To wallow in whatever oily soup we had brewed together, above a disgusting orange and red swirled carpet in a ratty hotel room in Manchester. Cath won't walk away even from the people she needs to.

There's a funeral next Thursday.

She can't even walk away from a dead man she never knew.

But she managed to walk away from Patrick.

Cath

Thursday 12 June
Church of the Living Word, Trufield Road, Manchester
The funeral of David Brandon Marsden

My feet are flat and silent, carefully motionless inside their newly polished black shoes and their newly purchased black tights. The heels of the shoes make a loud clicking noise on the stone floor of the church and I am self-conscious. Once I am seated I plant them carefully, so that I won't have to move them again when we stand up for the vicar, or to sing.

Having obediently filed in ahead of the coffin, we have stood up when told to, and knelt when told to, and now sit, buttocks aching, on the hard polished wood of the pews. On the floor, by my feet, I have a prayer mat. On it, pixelated in tiny cross stitch, an unidentified saint reaches out to bless me. The halo around his head is picked out solidly in gold thread and if I angle my head a certain way it glints in the light. I have been doing this more frequently than seems appropriate.

There is an order of service but it doesn't seem to happen in order and three separate books which I must juggle and shuffle, panic rising in me as I try to find in time, the right page for the prayer or the psalm or the hymn. I worry about being the last to stand up, or to sit down, or to turn and face the altar, or to turn and face the choir. I keep

Alice, always, at the periphery of my gaze, so that I can do whatever she does, with the exact same timing, because she, as always, knows what to do.

There is a roof so far above me I feel dizzy when I look at it. It is ostentatiously beautiful. At the places where the beams meet there are heavy round stones which are delicately carved and delicately painted. I am afraid one will fall on me. There is an organ with pipes so large I could crawl into them. There are cold stone angels suspended above the altar and the pulpit is carved with a stern bird of prey.

I feel lost here. But then, since the day I walked out of that flat I have felt just a little bit lost everywhere. It is weightless, this freedom. It is hard for my feet. They are never certain if they have quite found the ground.

I intone the text that is marked *'congregational responses'*, speaking slowly, carefully, timing my voice to match the vicar's.

"Let us pray," says the vicar and, just like that, we are praying. I bow my head at the angle which makes my saint glitter back at me, and note with relief that it doesn't seem compulsory for me to kneel on him.

I am not lost, I tell myself and the saint. In this new world of gaping spaces and alarmingly open possibilities, I am not entirely lost. I am simply surveying it, carefully.
And little by little, I am going to map it.

The prayer is over, and it seems we are standing again, though I am not entirely sure what for. I slip a sidelong glance at Alice. Her profile is made paler by the light from the window. She looks brittle and delicate. There are a hundred things I want to say to her, elbowing each other, jostling frantically for position, but now is really not the time.

Through the shoulders and collars, ponytails and hats I can see the coffin, a tight collection of cedar wood slices between the people. It sits on a small trestle table, dark respectful young men in dark suits wait at the outer edge of the congregation, ready to convey it to its last destination.

I shudder, and briefly close my eyes, trying not to recall those last few moments, the sound of the impact, the sudden sharp rush, the sight of him, airborne, falling back down again towards the leftover exhaust in the wake of his unfortunate, coincidental killer. I try not to think about what his plans were. What he was going out for, what he would have done if he had only managed to gain passage to the other side of the road. I try not to imagine the way his evening might then have unfolded, caught by a pair of vengeful homeowners, coerced into a pathetic, verbal confrontation, achieving nothing, wasting time. I try not to think but I just can't help it. I wonder what he would have done when he returned to his house, when we had left him alone, what small household rituals would he have gone through, what inconsequential domestic tasks. His unscheduled exit from consciousness witnessed by two people who had looked him up on the internet, who didn't even really know who he was.

And now we are about to find out. A woman is climbing the steps to the pulpit, climbing carefully, holding herself together, clutching a piece of handwritten paper, and breathing deeply, steadying her nerves and her voice. The front of my order of service is plain white, with simple, tactful black font. It says *'David Marsden will be remembered with love and affection by many'*.

I close my eyes again as the woman begins speaking, I want to remember him with love and affection. I want her voice to drown out the endless replay of the only auditory impression I have of David Brandon Marsden.

Screech, clatter, scream.

Thud.

Alice

Thursday 12th June
The Funeral

We are unnaturally quiet, all of us, sitting here, stiffly in rows, feet shuffling, men coughing. We are a sea of heads, bobbing and jerking in unison as we are invited to sit. We are clad in black, in brown, in grey. We are uncomfortable in ties, in shirts, in blouses. We are hushed and obedient.

We are the dearly beloved. Except that some of us had never met him. The first time we set eyes on him was the day of his death. I supress a shudder, focus on the tiny figure of his wife, listen hard. And try to learn.

David Brandon Marsden was born in Barnsley, Yorkshire, in a poor estate with little access to books and a perfunctory experience of education. Cocky and disruptive in lessons, he secretly worked hard, and eventually some young, idealistic teacher spotted his talent, and entered him for a scholarship at a posh grammar school in the next town. Clearly the odd one out among his peers, he nevertheless managed to remain ever popular with both students and teachers and graduated with straight A grades and an offer from Oxford University. The rest, apparently, is history, everyone knows about David Marsden, how he pulled himself up from the gutter with sheer talent and uncompromising determination to become the CEO of a successful housing company. He had, (and this is revealed a little furtively), recently spent time on extended leave of absence, due to illness but all the same, the point was, it seems, that he was the walking example of social mobility, and an inspiration to many.

Only according to Mary Marsden, beloved wife and Mother of his twenty-two year old daughter, this is actually not the point. Everybody talks, she says, about David Marsden, the self-made man, the successful businessman. But not of his gentleness, his patient, open attitude as a Father, his never failing sense of humour, his interests in literature, in art and dance. He was a philosopher, she tells us, he thought about life. He had opinions and values, ideals and curiosity. He had an energy, even during his period of illness, which was almost entirely intellectual, a spirit of reflection, a seeking of peace.

Like most other funeral subjects, David Marsden was godlike to the extent that you began, if you weren't careful, to wonder how on earth he wasn't also immortal. The dead, being dead, have never annoyed, never once spoken with their mouths full, or left their socks on the floor, or interrupted somebody, or thrown up when they were drunk. But even so, despite all the parts of me that want to pick at it, to dishevel, to surround everything with the spiky cloak of the cynic, the fact is, now I *know* something about David Marsden. Suddenly, somehow, the airborne body, the crumpled form in the road, is only a shadow, a form taken briefly in the grand finale, and the real David Marsden is the perfect being, the endless source of talent and virtue that his wife is describing. And I know him now.

I am the dearly beloved.

Cath

Thursday 12 June
The Funeral

There is some more standing and some sitting and potentially some praying, though at least on one occasion I missed the cue for that. My mind keeps drifting off on tangents so that by the time I realise, by the stir of hushed chatter, that the service is over, I am overwhelmed with guilt that, after everything that led us here, I haven't been able to afford David Marsden the luxury of an hour of my full attention. I stand, with Alice, compelled by the movements of the people either side of us, and dazedly collect up bags and cardigans and dignity. I am concentrating on silencing the clip of my heels on the floor and for a sudden moment I wonder, stomach droppingly, whether the dead can read our thoughts.

Alice

Thursday 12 June
The Funeral

"So that's what it looks like," I say, "the funeral of a millionaire. Just like any other funeral really."

A lame statement, limping out of my mouth like a child trying to get out of doing PE, but we needed to say something. You have to say *something* as you sneak out at the end of a funeral for somebody you never met. Someone you nevertheless deliberately and avidly hated. We are studiously avoiding the line of well-wishers telling poor Mary Marsden what a great man her husband used to be, and what a terrible loss it will be to mankind. Who knows? Perhaps it really is.

"Mmmmm," agrees Cath, pensively, squinting in the sunlight which seems suddenly blinding after the sombre interior, "I guess life is not just about money, is it?"

There is a pause. We watch the mourners leaving the church, a line of solemn black silhouettes. We watch as Mrs Mary Marsden pauses mid polite conversation, to avert her face briefly, and wipe at her eyes.

I think of her words in the church, all the things about David Brandon Marsden that not even the people who knew him, knew. I wonder about the things that even Mary Marsden didn't know. I remember us, sitting in Patrick's flat, warm with wine, looking up the remuneration section of the annual report, tracing our fingers from his name to his pension entitlement, carefully fuelling our moral indignation. Money he never got to draw.

"No," I say. "I guess it's not about money."

"I guess not."

There is another pause, and then I say,

"So that just leaves the sex and booze."

For a moment we both just stand there, stunned. For once, even I am taken aback by my own outrageous flippancy, standing there surrounded by tolling bells and ancient gravestones and hushed voices and bereaved relatives.

And then suddenly we are laughing, snorting, covering our mouths like drunken teenagers, and retreating, hastily away from the churchyard, away from the curious gaze of onlookers. I am praying that the collection of darkly suited gentlemen and their sombre, ironed ladies will assume we have been overcome with grief, or a touch of sunstroke, or an asthma attack. That poor, dignified, eloquent Mrs Marsden will not have seen us, that her daughter is too distracted to notice. And in reality it is OK because we were already standing well back from the church door, well into the shadows, but even so I am acutely aware of our crassness, and the more aware I am of it, the more the need to scream, to shriek with laughter builds up in my throat until my tonsils are raw and my eyes red. I look at Cath and she, too, is flushed, eyes streaming and I think, *at least we look the part now*, and that thought is even more vulgar and horrible.

We keep walking and convulsing until, finally, we stop. We pause a couple of streets away from the church and we look at each other and then Cath says, weakly,

"Oh my...what are we like? It's a *funeral*."

"I know," I say, but even so, I can't help enjoying it. I like being whatever it is we are like. It's more fun than not being. And anyway, we've had plenty of heavy moments. Life owes us a bit of light relief. Even if it does happen to be somebody's death. The thought sobers me a little, though not enough, and we stand for a while in silence. Every now and then little bubbles of our waning laughter erupt again and disperse themselves gently into the air.

"I mean honestly," she says "all I can think about, is even if we'd caught up with him, what on earth were we actually going to *say*?"

"Hi Sir...er...our flats are a bit damp..."

We dissolve again and then we carry on walking. No particular direction, just companionable movement.

"So what now?" she asks after a while and then there is another eruption because all I can say is, "Sex and booze?"

Cath

Thursday 12 June
After the Funeral

I have suggested orange juice and chastity belts and then been surprised by my own wit, and by Alice's giggles. In the end we have compromised and searched around for a friendly looking pub. We sit opposite each other in the sunny courtyard, and Alice orders wine and I revert to the old days and order a pint of Guinness. This amuses Alice immensely.

"I never knew you were a beer drinker," she says, raising her glass in a kind of salute to me. "Guinness of all things. You surprise me."

My stomach drops briefly, and then I mentally reach and grab hold of it and settle it back where it belongs. It is OK, I remind myself, to cause surprise.

I never drank beer with Patrick. He thought it didn't suit me. I guess he didn't know it was what I always drank. Until I met him. With him I drank cocktails and spirits with slimline mixers. It gave me wretched, acidic, head spinning hangovers. It made my stomach churn. I guess it just didn't suit me.

Alice is waiting for me to say something and I can tell by her face that she has been waiting ever so slightly too long.

"Well, you know me," I say lightly, "with my beer drinking and my burping competitions..."

It comes out smoothly, cleverly even, and I can see that she is surprised again. I smother a sudden memory of a comment about my beer paunch, and my hand goes automatically to my stomach.

"You're looking well," says Alice quickly and firmly, and I know, somehow, despite myself that I am.

"Thanks," I say, "you too."

There is a pause.

There are things I want to say and I don't know how to start them. There are things, I know that she wants to ask. But she doesn't know how to phrase it.

"So, you're staying on then?" she says. "In Manchester?"

"Yes," I tell her, "for a few days. Thought I should stick around a bit. See the city. You know. If a thing's worth doing..."

She nods. But I know that wasn't the question she wanted to ask. She already knew that. We talked about it. When we agreed we would, each of us, get the train. I don't think we wanted to do that drive again.

There is another pause. I am sorting through words in my head, ordering them ready to assemble and present them to her, but as I open my mouth to deliver them, she laughs, and points out to me that I drink my pint with my little finger held out.

"You see," she says, "I always knew you were cultured. You've probably got roots in royal lineage."

"Royal lineage?"

"Oh you know, some aunt of some cousin's daughter's dog was related to some maid who was the secret lovechild of the gardener of the uncle of a woman who slept with Henry V or something." She wags her finger at me, "I know your game. You were probably keeping it quiet in case I was only hanging out with you for the money."

"Didn't basically everyone sleep with Henry V? *You're* probably related if you look back far enough."

"Henry V was a lovely chap. He was sadly misrepresented by evil historians."

"You're right," I say. "I am being mean and unfair to him. He was a delicate flower. Poor old King Henry."

There is a pause. Alice's face is working, feverishly, as if fighting with itself to get the words out. Eventually she says, "Cath, I'm really sorry about the other week. You know, in the hotel..."

I am so relieved that we have finally got to this. "No, *I'm* sorry," I say earnestly, "running out like that, it's just I..."

"No not that, the other...what I told you. What I..." for a moment her voice box defies her and she drops her head, flushing furiously and, although I have never met her, I see a tiny hint of Tabby, "...what I did."

I can see her trying to explain things to me, trying desperately to tell me that she feels better for telling it, but that she is deeply ashamed. To tell me that she revisits that moment in the playground every day, every hour, that she has done so for years. I can see her trying to explain things that I already know.

And I know that I need to give her the time for it, but it isn't coming out right and she stammers and scratches about and blurts out half sentences. Then she stops, suddenly and finally says,

"Oh bloody hell. Forget it. Let's talk about sex again, it's my specialist subject."

"Alice?"

"Yes?"

I take her hand in both of mine, and I need, I crucially need her attention, and so I do it not gently, but hard, squeezing her fingers so that she catches her breath and looks up and meets my eyes in surprise.

"It's fine."

"What?"

"It's *always* been fine. Alice. You were a child. You were fourteen. You were just fourteen. Nobody when they are fourteen knows what they are doing."

"I..."

But I don't let her finish. I don't even let her start. I continue talking, firmly, insistently, with a voice of authority that I have never used before. That I didn't know that I had but that I know, somehow, that I have to use now.

"What about those kids you teach sex to?" She smiles, with some difficulty, but I press on. "Do you blame them, when they mess it up? When they get it all wrong?"

"No, of course not, but they're just kids, they don't know yet, they..."

She trails off.

"OK," I say, "I absolve you. Is that what you need? For someone to tell you that you can stop constantly punishing yourself? Didn't they do that? Already? Didn't they punish you in school?"

There is a pause.

"Alice. Come on. It's over."

She is still moving her mouth, desperately, but she can't get the words out. When she does, it is bluster.

"Wow you're good, aren't you? Who made you psychiatrist of the century?"

"Alice, seriously."

She looks at me.

"You were a kid. A silly kid yes, but come on, some of us are silly kids *now*." For a moment, my head swims with thoughts of Patrick. I think of him. I think of me. I think of my wee on the carpet. I take a breath, which shakes only the tiniest bit right at the edges. And then I carry on. "And all those other kids, including your sister, they were all silly kids too. So what makes you think you were sillier than any of the rest of them? It wasn't all that unusual. OK? The whole same thing probably happened to two-thirds of all school kids all over the world. So..."

I pause. I feel dizzy suddenly, faint with the effort of it, and the pub seems unnaturally silent. I laugh a little, release my pressure on her hands, which are shaking.

"I absolve you, Alice. It's fine."

"Well thanks. That's very good of you."

Neither the sarcasm nor the joviality works. Her voice is too low and her eyes won't meet mine. They concentrate into middle distance because she cannot, will not, let the water that is in them spill over. I want to relent but this isn't quite finished and this new Cath is ruthless.

"There's one condition..." and now I allow myself to smile, and it takes my breath away, it is such a relief. "Alice," I say, "either leave that photo up, once and for all, or even better – get a new one."

Alice

Thursday 12 June
The Pub

There is a pause. The pub courtyard seems to be rapidly emptying, as though on some pre-arranged signal, and she's obviously rehearsed all this so very carefully, I wouldn't be surprised if it was Cath who had done the arranging.

I am staring at nothing, the way you stare out of a car window when you think you are going to throw up all over the inside of it.

"Alice?"

There are a hundred emotions churning about in my stomach, and the strongest one, unbelievably, is a kind of excitement. There is actually hope in there. Even so, the tears are swelling in my eyes and I won't cry now, I never cry, I simply refuse to, so I pick up my barely touched glass of wine and I stand up and stagger a little, because my world hasn't entirely managed to stop spinning.

"Fancy another drink?" I ask her, and then I have turned and gone inside before she can respond because, thankfully, even this new, astonishingly confident Cath is still actually Cath and her reactions to everything are still slightly delayed.

I fall through the toilet door like a desperate drunk and I drop my bag on the floor and stare in the mirror and then I ignore everything else and I concentrate, ruthlessly, on breathing. I breathe slowly, and deeply. Then I pour the rest of my wine down the sink and I stand there and hold two fingers up to my eyes to catch the tear drops. I do this, unmoving, for a very long time, just to make quite sure that there are no more coming.

Then I spend a while with my hair, patting and smoothing and straightening and gripping with a care I have not shown it in all the time I have been growing it. My hands, as they busy themselves, are shaking slightly but by the time I finally give my reflection one last, long, defiant, glance, they are still by my side, and I walk to the bar with a high head, and, inconceivably, a lighter heart.

As I approach with the drinks I can see her, shifting, uneasily, on the bench, and when I appear she looks immensely relieved that I haven't run out on her completely. I can see the questions, the creeping self-doubt in her eyes, held at bay for a heroic length of time for our Cath. I am really rather proud of her. I provide her with her second Guinness with a little bow and a flourish. She smiles, tentatively, and raises it and I raise my own glass to meet it, and look her, carefully, right in the eyes.

"I have decided," I announce, with a mock ceremony which convinces neither of us that the moment is not important, "to choose to accept your absolution."

There is a perceptible sigh of relief which starts in her core and pervades her whole body.

"Good," she says.

We drink. We both take quite a few gulps, larger ones than are strictly polite, and we are each holding glasses that retain only half of their original contents. A child in the beer garden is screaming blue murder because, in a failed bid for freedom, it fell out of its chair. The noise drowns us out, which is good, because I am struggling to gain control of my voice box long enough to say 'Thank you', but instead I am watching the child's parents and thinking, inexplicably about Mothers. The Mothers you see in films or read about, with apron strings and floury hands and soft, gentle bodies, designed for running to, for the burying of small sticky, tear stained faces. Arms wide, held out in welcome, or comfort, or simply the reassurance that they are there. I don't remember that much with my own Mother. But I saw it, I think, from a distance, with Tabby.

Perhaps I was too prickly to be comforted? Too spiky to hold close?

The child stops crying, bribed with a sweet. And the garden is quiet. But I don't say thank you. It just doesn't make it out somehow.

Cath waits until we are leaving. We have drunk and chatted and laughed and talked nonsense and generally assuaged our over powered emotions with trivia, and I am literally standing there, my hand on the pub door handle, when she does it.

"Actually," she says, very casually, as though we'd been discussing it all the time, "you should probably return this."

And she reaches up suddenly, and scrabbles around in her cleavage for just long enough for me to have to turn round and glare at the grinning barman, pulls out something which glints in the sunlight, looks at it for a moment and then closes her fist around it briefly, before offering it to me.

I look at her.

I look at it.

It is a small silver key.

"You can take it." she says, "I don't need it anymore."

Katie Hall-May

Cath

Thursday 12 June
And The Day That I Left

I poured everything I had for him into that pie and then there wasn't anything left except anger. And I stood there a long time, looking back into the flat. It seemed to me that in every corner there were shadows and memories, pulled together and crafted from all of the scraps of humiliation and fearfulness which littered the floor. I hated that place passionately and I clung to it in dread because I didn't know what I would find outside it, with only myself for company. And I wasn't sure what there was in myself except for a sort of crumpled mess.

The most appropriate thing, it seemed to me, would be to smash the place up with me inside it. I imagined the walls, creaking and falling, the clouds of wood dust and concrete and that black foam stuff they put around pipes. I thought of the doors, cracking and splintering and tumbling heavily downwards, on and through and around my body, until eventually all that was left would be a neat pile of wreckage, synthetic and human, ceramic and metal and blood and wood.

But I didn't do that.

Because somewhere in the middle of my imagining of it, a part of me stopped. My eyes refocused. And I found myself staring at the little keys in the doors.

Just time.

Just time for one last message.

I thought of it, and my heart beat faster, threw itself against the constraints of my rib cage. The very idea of it spread cold in the pit of my stomach.

But the longer I hesitated the more right it seemed.

I locked the door to the bedroom.

I locked the door to the toilet.

I locked the door to the kitchen.

Each time I heard the bolt click home it seemed unnaturally violent. Each time I did it, even though I was expecting it, the sound of it always made me jump.

And then I was there in the hallway, doors closed around me, and three little silver keys in my hand. I opened the utility cupboard door, and stood, looking in. Two mops and a hoover. Some pipes and the boiler. And a cluster of little bits and pieces we had forgotten the use for, collecting dust and carpet hair and predatory spiders.

I hesitated for just one minute, heart thumping painfully through my shirt, and then I threw the little silver keys as hard as I could, into that cupboard. I threw them so hard I felt the air leave me explosively, so that as they were clattering down in the darkness, each finding their own little place of obscurity, I was suddenly fighting for oxygen. For a moment my vision blurred, briefly, and I waited just in case I might decide to undo this. But the water that there was had been shallow and perfunctory, and the tears dried coldly, before they fell.

So I closed the utility cupboard door and then I locked it. I locked it and then I picked up my bags and I found I had the strength, after all, to walk out of the flat.

I didn't bother to lock the front door. I left my door key on the mat.

But I kept that utility cupboard key, which had once been so very, very important. I kept it hidden where I could feel it, cold and hard against my skin. And gradually, I let it warm me.

Alice

Thursday 12 June
Leaving Manchester
Again

So that is what happened. A stupid game with locks and keys, set up by Patrick and finally, devastatingly, won by Cath. I suppose the fire alarm was set off by the pie in the oven. Characteristically, she hadn't thought of that detail. Or maybe she had. He must have camped out in the hallway, hoping she might still come home. And then broken the kitchen door down to turn off the oven.

I shouldn't have much sympathy really. What is he, but a little boy, playing at pulling the legs off spiders and then wondering why they no longer run. There is innocence in it, somewhere, but it's the innocence of a child. And we all know what children are capable of.

I stand on the pavement and wave her off, watching her retreating back, set hard and determined, exploring Manchester.

I have a little silver key in my hand.

I could still see, right at the very last minute, as she turned to depart, that fleeting panic in her face. A sudden quailing, stubbornly quashed. This is how Cath will face the world now. A heady mixture of excitement and fear.

I stand on the pavement and watch her.

I bid her bon voyage.

Patrick

Friday 13 June
The Flat

Alice comes round, today. Out of nowhere. I assumed she wasn't ever going to. And if she hadn't, I wasn't going to blame her.

Her hair is redder than I remember. But her eyes are steely when I let her in. I feel afraid, which is ridiculous, but I accept it. I have accepted a lot of things in recent days. I watch her scanning the flat, watch her take it all in. She's not that surprised but she is a bit shocked.

I suppose it is a bit of a mess, really.

The doors are splintered, and they have holes where the lock should be. The holes are jagged and a bit vicious, and the sawdust and wood and the old metal lock cases are still on the floor by the doors where they fell. The kitchen door hangs, drunkenly, from half its hinges, and the fire alarm is dangling from the ceiling by a wire, from when I tried to disable it so I could hear myself think. There are large flakes of paint on the floor from the door frames, which also have holes gouged out of them, and there is a lot of black stuff on the kitchen ceiling and worktops from when the oven caught fire. It smells of smoke and acid. The black bits of whatever it was in the oven are still there in their cracked ceramic bowl on the table, where they have burned a perfectly oval scar into the wood. There is that hole in the plaster. And the sofa broke the other day but I haven't bothered to fix it.

I suppose I should have cleaned it up. Or something. Called a locksmith. I don't know. It just seemed fitting.

"Um...Hi," I say, and then I stutter a bit trying to say something polite, but it's all a bit useless and inconsequential. Her eyes travel furtively to the utility cupboard door, which got the worst of the treatment because it was the last one I broke into, and I had really got into the smashing things up part by then.

"Sorry," I say, not knowing exactly what for, and not especially caring.

"Hi," she says, carefully, eyeing me as though I am an animal that might run for it, "are you...have you...are you OK?"

It hurts her a bit, I can tell, just to say it.

"I'm fine," I say.

I didn't leave the house after that first evening. At first I was just tired and I suppose I was upset. But then it just became something I did. A sort of recuperative penance. Pottering around in my ruined building, wearing my dressing gown and my boxers and that sort of warm mustiness that you get when you haven't really bothered to wash. Sleeping into the afternoon. Eating things out of tins. Sitting on the non-broken end of the sofa.

Work called after a while and I remembered I should have phoned them so I said I was ill and I suppose they accepted it, and then I just took holiday when I was bored of excuses.

I'll have to go back eventually. I'll have to go back quite soon. And I'll have to fix things and cook things and have some kind of a shave.

I'll do all that. I'll do it later.

Alice

Tuesday 25 June
School

I stand in the grey gravel drive, just inside the school gates. The buildings loom above me, but somehow, everything is smaller. Even so, as I stand there I feel the gaze of a hundred past Alices looking at me curiously. I feel the suspicious eyes of my aunt, my bra strap digging into my rib cage. Empty of children, the place is silent, considering. It is a ghost school and when I move I will walk through the corridors, I will clear paths through a hundred milling ghosts. I will scatter the drifting thirteen year old forms of Rachel Blackthorne and Karen Pickering, Ben and Steve and Georgie Smales. Excitement churns inside me, but it is mixed with something else, a sort of acidic fear in the back of my throat, a shivering in my limbs that I have not felt for years.

I would turn back. But it's too late now.

I stand there hesitating. Staring up at the rough slabs of concrete which together, create "A" block. A slight breeze moves my hair around, blows my skirt just a little, against the back of my thighs.

And then I pull myself together, adjust my bag on my shoulder, and walk in.

"Would you like a drink Mrs Crayer?" says a slight woman in a yellow skirt who doesn't know me.

"Just water please. And it's...um...Miss," I say, and she shrugs a little defensively, and turns back to her desk to pick up the phone.

Reception has changed. There are potted plants now, several of them, which, combined with the large white floor tiles and lemon coloured walls, give the impression of a sort of large plant bathroom. The receptionist invites me to sit down with little more than a vague wave and a swish of her yellow skirt. There are two lemon coloured chairs now, something between an armchair and a box. There is a little coffee table.

"Your water, Mrs Crayer. The headmistress, Mrs Gladstone, will be with you shortly."

Mrs Gladstone. I saw her name on the letter but I hadn't realised she was headmistress. She was head of my year. I suppose it has been a while. It has been sixteen years.

My mouth is suddenly dry. I nod feebly at a retreating yellow skirt. A small drip of water makes its way down the outside of my glass and spreads, insidiously on the perfect surface of the new coffee table.

Reception has changed. It is spotless and airy, artificially cheerful. It smells of efficiency and adults. It is a place where there are no children. Where the impression of order and calm can insinuate itself, subtly, into the minds of visiting parents, carefully removed from the deafening, rushing, exuberant reality.

But even so, I can still see it. I can see the old place hovering behind the décor, crouching behind the furniture like an ill-fitting shadow. I can see the fraying cushioned seats of the old wooden chairs. I can see where the noticeboard used to be, hanging always at a slight angle, official notices and school rules and staff photographs fighting a continuous battle against persistent postings of cartoon depictions of bloated, wart ridden teachers, lewd diagrams and scrawled obscenities. There was a desk just there, where the palm tree is standing. We used to take turns to do shifts there in year ten, completing worksheets and textbooks and greeting conspicuously absent visitors. Well most people did. I wasn't allowed. And anyway by then I guess I wasn't presentable. There always seemed to be chewing gum on my shirt, spit balls in my hair.

I longed for a shift on reception.

There used to be an entrance mat, a grey one, on the floor at the doorway. There was a fire bucket in the corner. There was a plaque on the wall.

"Well, well. Mrs Alice Crayer!"

I am standing, glass in hand. When she comes up behind me I jump violently, sloshing water on my hand and down the front of my blouse.

"*Miss*," I croak.

I am led into an office which, thankfully, I don't recognise. It says *'Mrs Gladstone, Head Teacher'* in gold letters on the door. We are seated and I place my water, with some relief, on the desk between us.

"Well I bet this is a bit of a step back in time for you, eh Alice? A blast from the past!"

She still looks at me the same way, suspiciously weighing things, narrowing her eyes behind her glasses. "And a teacher yourself now I see... of sorts."

She still speaks to me the same way, the note of warning in her voice, the phrases so inhumanly calm, so measured. The way you might speak to some kind of wild animal, or a mad person. There is a letter on her desk marked, 'Mrs Gladys Gladstone'.

Gladys Gladstone'. Oh my word. We could have had some fun with that one. If we'd only known.

Something in me rallies.

"I don't like to think of myself as a teacher. Not, of course, that I don't absolutely respect the work that teachers do," I make my voice as polite and as poisonous as hers, "it's more that I think of myself as someone who really *engages,* really *interacts* with the reality of life for a fifteen year old. Well, for any age, really." I laugh condescendingly, meeting her eyes as though I am inviting a confidence. "After all, sex is with us for the rest of our lives, isn't it?"

She colours, drops her eyes for the first time and I rejoice. *Ha. Bet it isn't with you is it, you old hag.*

There is a pause. She takes a breath and I feel a little rush of power, and then a little rush of contrition. We both take a moment to collect ourselves. I remember, with slight surprise, that I am now an adult.

She says, "Well Alice, Mrs Crayer, I am very grateful to you for approaching us and offering to visit our school, especially as it must be a little out of the way for you now, living as you do in ..." she consults my letter, "East Grinstead."

"That's no problem," I say quickly," I travel a lot actually. I've been to schools all over the UK. I think schools find that it's often easier to have somebody from outside to talk about this sort of thing. I think the kids find it easier."

She bridles a little at the word 'kids'. She probably calls them 'children'. But she says nothing. I continue,

"In a lot of places I do a whole course, for half a term or a term each year group, and then other places I do the sort of thing I'm doing today, just a one off introduction, a workshop on sexual responsibility or relationship issues." There is a pause. "An open and positive discussion," I say, "on the benefits of safe sex."

The magic words. She visibly relaxes.

"Well I think that will be what they need. I've got you in on the eleven o'clock slot, just before lunch as you requested. This must be quite a trip down memory lane for you. I doubt you normally think about us much. But you certainly made an impression. Several impressions in fact, as I remember. Generally on other people's faces."

For a few seconds, my heart races. I swallow carefully. It passes. I smile at her politely, with just a little hint of boredom. She waits. I continue smiling. Her curiosity is not satisfied.

"So what made you approach us out of the blue? Are you visiting your parents, perhaps?"

I left them just after I dropped out of sixth form. I left them the address of a friend, an older man named Dave whom I had had a brief affair with. I had no intention of living with him, but he'd promised to pass on any post to me.

To this day I tell Dave of every move that I make. Every new address I faithfully notify him, he just as faithfully notes it down. He is under strict instructions never to reveal my whereabouts to anyone.

Tabby sent me something when she moved to New Zealand. It was a standard notelet with her new address on it. I told Dave to destroy it.

My parents never tried to contact me.

This is so hard. This is harder than I thought. I don't know if I can do it.

"Not really," I say vaguely. My voice is hoarse.

I went back there five years ago. To our old house. Just to see. It was all boarded up and construction workers were milling about and winking at me outside. They were working, they said, for a Mr Davison, who was doing the house up before he sold it on. My parents must have moved away years before that.

I waited until dusk and returned to the house and sat there. It was a bitterly cold day at the end of October and the street was silent. I sat on a wall for an hour and just watched it. A silent shell of a house with rubble littering the garden.

A silent shell of a daughter.

A little girl lost.

"You all right darling? Looking for something?" an old man, ragged at the edges, stumbled past me with a bottle of gin and some crisps. He offered them to me enthusiastically before wheeling round to be sick into somebody's bin.

"Just some people," I said quietly, to the sound of his retching, "who didn't leave a forwarding address."

"Just old times sake?" Mrs Gladstone says to me, nodding knowingly. She is utterly clueless.

"Of course," I say brightly. "Old times' sake."

She rises to show me to the room, in which I will meet my subjects. To my surprise, when we get there, they are already gathered, shouting to each other and laughing and milling around. At the sight of her they start, deliberately slowly, to bring the chatter down to a more acceptable level, to slouch, sullenly back into plastic seats.

"Well good luck, Mrs Crayer," she says disparagingly, surveying the human clutter before her. "If you need anything call me. Oh-" it is as if she only just thought of it, "and pass my regards to your sister. How is she doing now?"

I catch my breath. I expected it, but still. The familiar feeling, the bile in my throat, the heart thumping, the prickling at the back of my eyes. The room senses it, and in a moment there is silence, thirty pairs of eyes looking curiously from me, to their head teacher.

I stand taller.

"Mrs Gladstone," I say into the silence, "I believe I did tell you but perhaps I should reiterate, it is not Mrs Crayer, because I am not married. It's Miss."

And before she has quite managed to consider an answer I turn to the girls and address them very deliberately.

"Hi there. You can call me Alice."

Of course it goes very well after that. I have instantly scored points purely for being, for whatever reason, in enmity with their head teacher. Mrs Gladstone, I am unsurprised to learn, is somewhat unpopular.

Predictably, she finds an excuse to sneak in at the end, at least ten minutes early. But I am prepared for it, and so I make sure to spice things up a bit for her benefit. My audience, sharp eyed and with a social intelligence which is lost on adults, realise this and play along. We have had a good session, we have earned our playtime.

I talk about faking it and vibrators, multiple orgasms and flavoured condoms. They catch on with enthusiasm, obligingly putting their hands up to ask questions about dogging and cottaging, oral sex and bestiality. They relate a few entirely made up stories about the lurid exploits of their aunt or their cousin, or Jinny down the road. I know they are made up because some of the details are physically impossible but it doesn't matter. It satisfies our audience who, tight lipped and disapproving, jumps up at the bell and with visible relief ushers them all out for lunch.

"Thanks Gladys," I say brightly, and nip out with them.

When I get back to reception, yellow skirt is busy. She is dealing with a bearded, earnest man who says he has come to collect Katy Simmons because she is being sent home with a headache. I wait behind him, trying to calm my nerves, to wipe my hands unobtrusively on the back of my skirt, to try to pretend I am not about to do something I said I was never going to do. Something I should have done years ago. Something which for reasons I can no longer accept, I remain hopelessly frightened of.

"OK, she's waiting for you in the nurse's room. It's through the doors on the right, turn left down the corridor and it's the third door."

"OK...and do I have to sign for her, or..?"

"Sign here please, and here, the date, and your car registration and the time you arrived."

"Oh...uh...OK..."

My parents are lost causes. I knew that years ago. I don't mind. I don't regret it. They were never my parents in the way that you hope for a parent to be. I would have liked the parents Tabby had. But mine were just...different. They've gone. I've gone. And neither of us felt the loss much.

"Thank you, Sir. If I can just tear this slip off and you can use that as your badge."

"Thank you."

"You're welcome."

He leaves. She meets my eyes.

"Mrs...Miss Crayer. Can I help you? Are you wanting to sign out?"

"Err...actually I was wondering if you could help me..."

"Of course"

There was a little girl.

"It's a bit of a shot in the dark really. But I was wondering if you might have a record..."

"What kind of record are you thinking of?"

She had hazel hair and hazel eyes with little flecks of orange. She was pale and thin and willowy. She used to look at me with something in her face that I never saw in anyone else when they looked at me. When she smiled I felt it was my creation. When she nodded it meant the start of play. She framed a picture for me for my birthday. It was special because it was the first one I was teen. When she needed me I betrayed her.

"I was wondering about the alumni records...I was wondering if..."

There was one time, after the worst had happened, in the days when she and I no longer spoke. She retrieved my coat from some puddle.

"Yes?"

When she handed it back to me it was dry. She must have held it all lunchtime under the dryer in the toilets. I ignored it. The last thing I needed was for her to be saintly.

"My sister moved recently. I said I would just check for her while I was here, that you had the right records. Her name is Tabitha Crayer."

"Oh I see, and she has an alumni from this school?"

"You make it sound like a disease."

She laughs once, mirthlessly. I try again,

"She likes to keep in contact. She donates quite regularly to the Healthy Minds Fund."

She said that when she grew up and left, she would always keep working to make school experience better. That she would be an alumni and stay in touch and do everything she could to prevent other children from going through the pain that she did.

"The what fund, sorry?"

"Healthy Minds...I think. It was for providing counselling services on the school campus."

They set it up shortly after I left. I read about it in the paper. I half thought she might have had a hand in it. But I guess she was still only a child herself then. I was sure she must have given something to it at some point.

"Healthy Minds...oh they disbanded that a few years ago. It's the ADAVRA now."

She notes my blank expression, "Association for the Development of Altruistic Values and Reflective Action. They do workshops."

"Oh."

I hated her and oh how I have missed her. She gave me her address. She wrote to me. But Dave is so maddeningly obedient.

"Ah here we are...hold on just a minute...what was the name again?

"Tabitha Crayer"

"Tabitha..." She pauses for a moment to reprimand a young boy who has just skidded past the doorway at top speed, wearing his tie round his head like a bandana. Eventually, having bored him half stupid, she turns back to me.

"Sorry about that."

"It's all right."

She stares intently at her computer and thumbs the mouse a few times. I try not to crane my neck round the desk to see the screen.

"Now then, here we are – Tabitha Clarkeson *nee* Crayer. Is that the one?"

So she's married.

"Um. Yes. That's the one."

She's Mrs Clarkeson.

"OK. Yes she did give to the Healthy Minds Fund. Before it became ADAVRA. But only for a few years," she frowns at the records, "it sort of petered out."

She didn't keep it up. It was all talk. She forgot about it. She got distracted. She left the country and got on with her own life. My sister, my always perfect sister - is not only married – but actually human.

I am still taking this in when she picks up her pen and says, "OK so what's her correct address? I've got one in New Zealand. Is that right?"

"Err, yes, what's the full address you've got? Only she moved in New Zealand so I just want to check"

"One Charter Court?"

Heart thumping, I simply stand there and hope she will continue. I can't see the screen for the light and the angle of the computer and I can't make it obvious or she won't give it out. She sighs, impatient. "One Charter Court, Raleigh Street, Christchurch 8714, New Zealand. Is that right?"

Birds whoop in my ears.

I fight an overwhelming impulse to climb across the desk and kiss her. Every law on data protection mutters and grumbles and turns in its grave.

"That's right. Yes! That's right."

One Charter Court, Raleigh Street, Christchurch 8714, New Zealand.

I repeat it over and over in my head, memorising it for the first opportunity I can get to punch it into my phone.

But she is frowning, "Are you sure? Only that's the only address for New Zealand we have and you said she had moved."

I lied.

"No, that is the right one, she must have not given you the previous one."

"But –"

"Anyway, thank you. Better go. Thanks again. Bye."

I exit the building. I type it frantically, into my phone. I skip out of the school gates.

One Charter Court, Raleigh Street, Christchurch 8714, New Zealand.

Simple as that.

I drive home, swing into the carpark with a jubilance that is only just short of collision. The car park is quiet, the evening still and a little colder than it has been recently. I notice that they've started the landscaping work. There are some shrubs now, where there was once a patch of nettles, and a single white rose bush, sporting wicked looking thorns. I shiver a little and turn away.

There is a For Sale sign outside Patrick's flat.

I stare at it for a while, thinking of nothing. It seems a moment for profundity, for revelations and inspirations and emotional responses. I feel nothing except a dull sort of sadness. Inside the flat I can see Patrick, or a version of Patrick. He is a tired, hunched shape, blurred and bowed at the edges. As I watch, I see him stretch and stand. He seems to shrink as he does so. Then he turns and plods towards the kitchen, engulfed by the darker depths of the room.

I reach into my pocket and bunch my fist around the object inside it.

In the shadows of Patrick's flat I can just make out a number of ruined doors, divorced from their frames, leaning dark against the plaster. A jagged collection of spikes and splinters. A heap of spattered memories.

I walk to the drain in the centre of the carpark. Then I pull out my hand and open my fist. In my palm is a tiny, silver key.

I drop it, gently, into the grate.

People Who Helped Build This Novel

This book, which was approximately 70,000 years in the making (or so it felt), has been, very definitely, a group effort.

THANK YOU to the myriad of people who answered Facebook requests for advice, from whether it is possible to be locked into your own house, *(thank you Owen Kingston, Alex Guérandel, Emma Jones, Colin Wilson, Marieka Bogaerd, Rachel Raey, Emily Hale, Adrian Tellwright, and Lucy McMahon for your harrowing stories and practical advice)* to police road accident practice and whether the Force have budgets for tea *(thank you Helen Woodland, David White, Ian Rennie, Bodil Tse and, especially, Eleanor Mullan)* to website and self-publishing advice *(thank you Lisa Preston, Judith Kingston, Nicholas Gregoriades, Sarah Hall, Kara Tenant and Kim Cook)* and, finally *Peter Mendham, Rob Alexander, Nezia Morgan and Al Pike* for taking every possible opportunity to be supportive, amusing and generally good humoured.

THANK YOU to *Matt Hill*, who wrote me long messages from the other side of the world as we worked out together the plausibility of a storyline involving an academic missing a publishing deadline.

THANK YOU to Bubblecow (https://bubblecow.com/) who provided friendly, free advice on top of their paid services, and who's editing service made this book.

THANK YOU also to *Pat Oliver* for her free proof reading, and for attempting to teach me to distinguish between the spelling of 'lose' and 'loose'.

THANK YOU to Bookplanner.com who kept me on the path, to Bookdesigntemplates.com who provided me with a way to DIY an affordable book interior without selling a kidney, to *Amazon Createspace* (www.createspace.com) for opening the door to self publishing and making it cool, and, as I may have previously mentioned, to *Claire Rutter*, who is **my sister**, for her cover design.

THANK YOU very warmly to *Emma Rinaldi, Heather Roberts, Séverine Béquin, Ellen Tait Moore, Charlotte Cox, Nicole Devarenne, Hannah Williams, Lauren Dawson, and the entirety of both my and my husband's sides of the family* who have all at some point encouraged me, took time to read my work, (in some case the very earliest (and worst) drafts, and still made me feel as though I might, actually, have the right to call myself a writer.

THANK YOU to my wonderful husband, *Martin Hall-May*, who has endlessly supported me, endured my self-obsessed reading of extracts of the novel while he was trying to do something else and generally loved, cherished and put up with me.

ABOVE ALL, I owe the greatest debt to *Kate Pogson and Heather Dibb*. Without these two people, this novel would be gathering cyber dust in a long forgotten file, never to be opened and one day to be accidentally deleted. They patiently (even eagerly) read my novel in emailed installments and it was their enthusiasm, engagement, and endless encouragement which kept me writing, kept me positive, and kept me laughing.

THANK YOU

Katie

Katie Hall-May

About the Cover Designer

It is my small claim to fame that the cover design of this novel was designed and produced by Claire Rutter, and that Claire Rutter is *my sister*.

Somehow managing to fit this around a warm but hectic family life, a responsible job and the odd 'sisterly chat' over a drink with the author, Claire is a talented photographic illustrator. To create her pieces she first builds a miniature, shoe box sized 'set', which she tweaks, recreates, tears down, starts again and then – finally - photographs.

Each 'set' is painstakingly lit to reflect the appropriate mood, weather or time of day. This design has a deliberate 'hand-made' look, for a sense of fragility (an early draft of this novel was entitled *Paper Castles*).

Claire uses simple materials to construct her sets, (the 'night sky' on the front of this book happens to be the back of a dark woven armchair, speckled with glitter stars) and adjusts how 'real' they look to create her characteristic sense of another world that *could* be this one...but isn't quite.

You can email Claire at clairemrutter@yahoo.co.uk.

Did I mention that she is *my sister*?

Katie.

About the Author

Thank you for saying hello. My name is Katie Hall-May and, part time, I am a writer. *Memories of a Lost Thesaurus* is my moonlighting debut. Full time, I am a wife, corporate something or other, cat lover, and incurable optimist. I have also found time to become addicted to *Netflix* and dark chocolate stout.

I have been lucky enough to be a winner of the *WriteOnSite* competition and I was longlisted for the Bath Short Story Award in 2016. These are my other small claims to fame.

Since childhood, I have been scribbling stories, novels and plans for novels in increasingly illegible handwriting. Now, finally, I am publishing this one with that mixed sense of pride and embarrassment which seems to be common to any artist, whatever their craft.

If you would like to get in touch you can email me at katie.hallmay.authorcontact@gmail.com, visit my website at www.katiehallmay.co.uk or rate this book online via Amazon and leave me some feedback.

Best wishes, and whatever you're doing, good luck with it. I hope you enjoy reading this, and that it somehow lives up to the genius of its cover design.

Katie.

30192510R00217

Printed in Poland
by Amazon Fulfillment
Poland Sp. z o.o., Wrocław